More advance praise for

## THE ALCHEMIST'S DAUGHTER!

"Set during the twilight years of Henry VIII, with vibrant characters, a compelling plot, and accurate historical depictions, *The Alchemist's Daughter* brings the darkness and danger of Tudor London vividly to life as it weaves its suspenseful tale. This beautifully written addition to the medieval mystery genre is sure to delight all fans of the period."

—Sandra Worth, author of *Pale Rose of England*

"I absolutely loved *The Alchemist's Daughter*—the characters, the authentic feel of the period, and of course the richly drawn story."

—Dorothy Cannell, author of *Murder at Mullings*

D0052634

# The Alchemist's Daughter

## MARY LAWRENCE

KENSINGTON BOOKS
www.kensingtonbooks.com

KENSINGTON BOOKS are published by

Kensington Publishing Corp.
119 West 40th Street
New York, NY 10018

All Kensington titles, imprints, and distributed lines are available at
special quantity discounts for bulk purchases for sales promotion, pre-
miums, fund-raising, educational, or institutional use.

Special book excerpts or customized printings can also be created to fit
specific needs. For details, write or phone the office of the Kensington
Sales Manager: Kensington Publishing Corp., 119 West 40th Street,
New York, NY 10018. Attn. Sales Department. Phone: 1-800-221-2647.

Kensington and the K logo Reg. U.S. Pat. & TM Off.

eISBN-13: 978-1-61773-711-4
eISBN-10: 1-61773-711-9
First Kensington Electronic Edition: May 2015

ISBN-13: 978-1-61773-710-7
ISBN-10: 1-61773-710-0
First Kensington Trade Paperback Printing: May 2015

10 9 8 7 6 5 4 3 2 1

Printed in the United States of America

*In memory of my parents,*
*Mary E. Wilkins and Joseph C. Lawrence, Jr.*

For, behold, I will send serpents, cockatrices, among you, which will not be charmed, and they shall bite you.

—Jeremiah 8:17

# Chapter 1

*London, March 1543*

Imagine a time when the good king's ship the *Mary Rose* moors within sight of His Majesty's Whitehall residence, its four masts reaching skyward like trees sprouting on the river Thames. Her sails are furled, waiting for the sun and wind to call them open. But it is night, and plying the waters beneath the galleon floats a humble wherry steered by one not of the stuff of man but of something else.

His wherry skirts the hull of the king's mistress, and the ferryman looks up to admire her rows of cannon, the iron threatening even in silence. He chuckles at this king's indulgence—man does love his guns. A watchman stands guard near the gunwale, leaning hard on his longbow, having mastered the appearance of duty while sleeping standing up. He does not notice the odd spectacle floating just beneath him.

This suits the ferrier, for there is little fog this night, and he is not one to work without its cloak. He must soon make his way toward Romeland, where a merchant ship will dock, laden with sacks of grain and goods from a trip abroad.

The ferrier lifts his nose into the air, catching a scent beyond

London's usual fare. Her streets of stagnant puddles and ditch latrines—the stench of the Thames with its dumped offal from market—can't mask what this ferrier wants.

He touches his pole to the water and sails past a flotilla of moored wherries. No humans, not even those reeking of drink, would need a ride at this hour. So they sleep in their hulls beneath their woolen blankets, oblivious to their comrade floating past.

The steeple of St. Paul's peeps over the city wall as he nears the mouth of the Fleet, flanked by massive Bridewell—abandoned by Henry for his preferred palace to the west. Giving wide berth to the discharge of river, the ferrier relishes the silence of man's creation, London—its jumble of brick and mortar housing a warren of crowded, slumbering souls. He's seen more than one king, more than one merchant ship, more than one plague mark this town. He's plied these waters for . . . years? More like eons, he thinks.

A rat treads water beyond his skiff, and he descends quickly upon it, snatching it out of its watery grave only to give it a new one. He digs his long fingernails into the rodent's back and sharply smacks its head against the gunwale, then tosses it over his shoulder to land squarely atop a pile of others.

This night has not been fruitful. He's harvested less than half his usual take. But he has a chance to salvage what remains of the dark. A merchant ship is lumbering up the Thames, headed for Wool's Key. It is rife with rats. He can smell them.

Ahead, London Bridge spans the river, its twenty starlings taunting the fainthearted with its rapids, swirling and churning the drink into a raging torrent. Most passengers prefer to disembark and portage the hazard by foot. But he is untroubled. He's shot the bridge so many times before.

He points his skiff into the curling tongue of river without touching his pole to water. After all, he mostly commands his boat by thought. The sluice accepts him, and it is as if he has entered a dragon's mouth, the water gurgling and rushing about like saliva all around him. The rapid grabs hold of his vessel, spins it around. It scrapes the stone cavern of the bridge's underbelly, bucking and rocking. His head barely clears the massive supporting timbers. All the while, he never loses his nerve.

Then, as if the dragon has tasted him and is repulsed, he is spewed out the other side into the slowing current. He blinks up at the Queen Moon winking at him from behind a veil of gossamer clouds, and he blows her a kiss.

In the distance, the dim outline of the merchant vessel noses its way up the Thames, closer but still a long way off. On the opposite bank, the bear-baiting rings are quiet as the lights of Southwark flicker and fade in spent tallow. Its rogues, cutpurses, theaters, and bawdy houses are exhausted from a full night of vice. He is contemplating a sated belly when his attention is drawn to an argument on the mudflats, where two muckrakers are the only visible proof that the town is inhabited.

Poor muckrakers, he thinks. Such a demeaning existence, scrounging through the slime for scraps of leather, rope, maybe a lost buckle or piece of jewelry, anything with which to barter a meal or sell for coin.

Their voices carry across the water, and he slows to watch them shove and sling each other about. It won't be long before one of them stumbles and lands in the slop. He cannot make out their words, but he can see that one is a man and the other is a woman, for her skirt grows visibly weighted by the heavy muck.

Could it be a lover's spat? He watches with interest, distracted from his course down river. No, he senses little affection between these two. Their words grow louder, and he wonders why no one comes to investigate. But it *is* Southwark, home to London's most depraved and criminal, and this quarrel would not earn much notice.

The man grabs hold of something around the girl's neck and pulls so that she reaches up and cries out in pain. He flings her sideways, and she loses her footing, falling into the mud with a splat. The man laughs, and the girl curses. She struggles to her feet and outruns her aggressor in the viscid sucking muck. The ferryman moves on.

He directs his skiff toward the opposite shore, where quays

and pulleys line the waterfront. Bales of wool and barrels of molasses are lashed to the piers, waiting to be stored in warehouses or shipped to ports elsewhere. Beyond the wharves, massive walls encircle the Tower and its grounds, where queens and traitors have met the executioner's axe. He floats clear of the moored ships rocking gently in the current. He's careful to maintain his distance and watches as the *Cristofur* comes into sight.

Like an old woman weary from life, the ship creeps up the river, worn from her voyage at sea. A few men post the yardarms and prow, seeing that she sails true without causing injury to herself or others. Her hull creaks as if complaining about this final demand, but she hasn't much farther and then she can rest.

The piers are not manned. No one expects the *Cristofur* to arrive at such an unholy hour. No one will come to her aid by rowing tenders out to pull her into moor, so the captain orders the sails wrapped and the anchor dropped.

The shrill pipe of the boatswain pierces the quiet, and the iron weight speedily pulls a line of rope through the hawsehole. The anchor hits the water with a satisfying splash, then disappears beneath the surface on its journey to the river's bottom. He admires man's ability to maneuver these cumbersome beasts. It still fascinates him.

Soon this sleeping maiden of a city will stretch her toes and yawn. But there is still enough dark that he may only be seen as a hooded figure standing in his wherry. Just another ferryman waiting for business. No one can see his arms as thin as bones or his skin as gray and pale as the moon. The heap of dead rats is not obvious, but it is about to grow taller.

As the *Cristofur* settles, it is as if a signal has spread among the vermin that land is within sight. Rats escape from portholes and over the sides, leaping into the river to make for better spoils on shore. The water teems with them, their ratty noses protruding just above the waterline, smelling their way to a new home.

If anyone had noticed, they would have seen his eyes glow green like a cat's. He moved swift upon the hapless rodents.

Breakfast.

# CHAPTER 2

Jolyn Carmichael had one hour to live.

She clasped her new cloak at the neck as she trudged down the lanes of Southwark toward her friend's room of alchemy. The morning still held winter's chill, though they'd had several days of warmth and even sun the past couple of weeks. But spring seemed a long way off, as did Bianca's quarters. The air was laden with a consumptive damp. A pain gripped her side, and she stopped to let it pass before walking on.

The waves of nausea had grown in number over the past two weeks. At times they were so severe she couldn't stand straight. She had tried to determine the cause. Was it that time of month or the candied figs she'd eaten? It could have been the sherried chestnuts—she wasn't accustomed to the rich food he'd heaped on her. She wiped the end of her nose with a gloved finger and paused to admire her doeskin gloves, another gift.

Jolyn smiled at her good fortune. Just over a month ago, she'd left the mudflats to live at Barke House. Her previous life raking mud had been a hard one. She had never slept in the same place twice, nor had she known what it was like to eat more than one meal a day.

To what did she owe this good fortune? It began with a find. A ring poking up from the muck near Winchester House. Its gold caught the morning light and Jolyn's eye. She could have sold it, but she liked its weight in her hand, and the etching on its surface intrigued her. The next day and then every day after, she found something of value to sell at market that could assure her a decent meal. The ring had brought her luck. If necessary, she could sell it, but she was not keen to part with her find.

While selling scavenged jewelry near the bear-baiting venue, Jolyn met Mrs. Beldam of Barke House. The old matron fingered the odd pieces, biting them and holding them up to squint at their stones. Finally, she bought a small brooch with a garnet center. As she handed Jolyn the money, her gaze fell to the signet ring hanging around the young woman's neck.

"How lovely," she said, her gray eyes growing round. She reached to touch the piece of jewelry. "Where did ye get this?"

"I found it," said Jolyn.

"How much would ye take for it?" asked Beldam, turning it over.

"Oh, I will never sell it. It has brought me luck—something money cannot buy."

Mrs. Beldam drew back. "Indeed." Her eyes flicked up at Jolyn's, then returned to the ring. "No amount of money?"

"No amount of money."

Mrs. Beldam dragged her eyes from the necklace and tipped her chin. "Do ye live near?"

"In Southwark."

"Ye is a scavenger, then?"

Jolyn nodded.

"Can'ts be easy, that life," said Mrs. Beldam. "Ye have a place to lay your head at night?"

Sleeping in doorways and under bridges might be disgraceful to those who only knew soft pallets and pillows, but Jolyn was not embarrassed to admit her circumstance. To Jolyn, not much separated most from a similar fate. "I make do," she said.

Mrs. Beldam studied her. She patted her purse distractedly as she thought. Eventually she stirred from her contemplation. "Ye knows, I run a home for young womens, Barke House," she said. "I takes in girls who needs a help in life. I could use an errand girl. Ye might keep to your muckraking if ye so like it. But ye'd have a place to stays."

Jolyn perked to hear this. Here was a woman offering a step up in life. She would be cautious, though; wary that she could be taken advantage of and end worse off.

So Jolyn visited the home for women and left satisfied that Mrs. Beldam did have a charitable heart. Jolyn moved in. She never regretted her decision, and in fact, her life got even better because of it. She cheerfully fetched goods from market and delivered sealed letters to London addresses. Even though her hands grew raw from washing laundry and scrubbing floors, she was content. Compared to muckraking, this was a life of easy meals and shelter from the cold.

It didn't matter that Barke House was once a stew with a reputation as questionable as the king's taste in wives. All Jolyn cared about was that Mrs. Beldam had saved her from scraping out a meager existence in the mudflats. And for that kindness, she was eternally grateful.

Once the layers of river clay were scrubbed from her skin and hair, Jolyn emerged something of a swan. The coat of grime had preserved her skin and left it pale so that her blue eyes appeared a startling contrast. Beneath her coif was a head of daffodil-colored hair.

At Barke House she caught the notice of a rich merchant. A man who doted on her. Mrs. Beldam tried to discourage her from seeing him, but Jolyn believed soon she'd step into an even better life.

Another wave of nausea gripped Jolyn, and this time she couldn't control an urge to lose her stomach's contents behind a hedge off Bankside. No one stopped to ask if she needed help. She wiped her mouth discreetly on the inside of her cloak and hurried on. This current dyspepsia was probably caused by her new lifestyle, to which she was still unaccustomed. Like so many other obstacles in her life, Jolyn figured this, too, was only temporary and once she had gotten a remedy from Bianca, she'd be as good as new. What she didn't know was soon she'd be dead.

# CHAPTER · 3

No sign marked her door. Only the odor of a simmering concoction hinted at what lay on the other side. Passing pedestrians would scrunch up their noses and hurry on, being sure to detour her rent on their return. Sometimes even *she* couldn't bear the smells and she'd run out into the lane, gasping for air, preferring the stink of Southwark to those of her own making.

Bianca Goddard observed the lethargic drip of a distillation as it collected in a vesicle. A labyrinth of coiled copper spanned the length of a table. She studied the remnants of crushed herbs, mashed frog bones, and pulverized chalk; her blue eyes were tinged nearly purple with fatigue. An idea had roused her out of sleep, and she could not rest until she had begun to pursue it. She was nothing if not obsessed.

Wedges of apple and a hunk of cheese from Eastcheap market lay untouched on the plate while John licked his fingers from his portion. He eyed the browning fruit. "The fruit is going off, Bianca," he said. "You should take the time and eat." He looked at Bianca, annoyed she had ignored his offering. "Because if you aren't going to have it . . ." Then, rueful for wanting the food for himself, he said, "Can I at least steep you some tea?"

Bianca shrugged and, with eyes still fixed on her latest experiment, pointed toward a shelf lined with crockery. "It's next to the jars of herbs."

John retied the leather strip gathering his hair into a wheaten tail that reached between his shoulder blades. He crammed several wedges of fruit in his mouth, then wandered over to the shelves of Bianca's room of Medicinals and Physickes, as she preferred to call it. She was riled if anyone called it a room of alchemy. She'd been here for less than a year, having spent her childhood running errands for her father in his quest to discover the philosopher's stone. Eventually Bianca had come to reject her father's line of inquiry for one of her own. She combined the parts of alchemy she found useful with the knowledge of herbs she'd gleaned from her mother. To this combination she added a healthy dose of curiosity, and the result was a salve to tame the French pox. Its popularity afforded her this room off Gull Hole in the undesirable but, for her, affordable area of Southwark.

John squinted at the array of jars and cracked bowls, some labeled with torn bits of precious paper scribbled on in charcoal and stuck on with snail ooze. But the mucilage had dried and several labels had floated to the floor, though some had been rescued and hurriedly stuffed inside the jars. He found a container labeled "ceylon," but he couldn't be sure if it wasn't cayenne. Either way, they'd soon find out.

"So, what is this latest madness?" he asked, gesturing to Bianca's experiment. He set a pan of water to boil on top of a calcinating stove. The stove belched a steady plume of blue smoke, to which Bianca had provided an escape through a cracked window. Despite her effort, John's eyes still watered, and he thought he'd never get used to the smells and fumes that accompanied Bianca's dabbling.

Bianca brushed the hair from her eyes. The linen cap that usually hid her mussed locks hung on a hook by the door. She didn't wear the troublesome coif in the privacy of her rent, and John appreciated seeing her hair—as black as the knocker at Newgate—frame her pale face.

"I'm distilling," she said, running her hand along the expanse of coils. "I'm trying to separate this mash of barley and throatwort into a liquid." She pointed to the mixture boiling on a tripod, then swirled a flask at the end of a tube that was shaped like a pig's snout. "I'll combine its purified essence with my salves."

John stirred the leaves in his own experiment and watched them bleed brown into the water. "Seems like a mountain of effort for a pebble of worth." He stood back, then looked around the room for two mugs, or anything clean that could hold their drink.

"These will do," said Bianca, emptying the ground powders from a couple of bowls, then wiping the insides with a corner of her woolen kirtle. Her skirt was a record of ingredients and chemistries. Hopefully none were combustible—as they certainly were potent, both in staining and devouring the fabric. The smell alone was enough to stop a boar at twenty feet. But Bianca didn't seem to notice, much less care. She handed over the bowls.

"People depend on me for remedies to ease their boils and ague. I'm not so quick of hand as when I picked pockets." She spied a mouse beneath a pile of rush covering the floor and, with some effort, cornered it with her foot, then snatched it up by the tail. "Perhaps I'm more conspicuous than when I was twelve. I haven't a license to beg. How else am I to survive?" She carried the creature to the door and flung it into the alley.

John set the bowls on the table and found a thick cloth to handle the pan. "I can think of a way," he said, simply.

Bianca's ears pinked. Her affection for John rivaled her irritation. She knew he wanted to marry her or at least become a greater part of her life. Marriage, with all its demands—not least of which were children—would put an end to her chemistries. To Bianca, it was not a desirable offer. She could no more abandon her love of experimenting than move back home with her parents. So for now she avoided the subject and, instead, posed a matter for John to consider.

"John, first you must finish your apprenticeship with Boisvert. Then you face years as a journeyman in silversmithing. After that, you must set up shop somewhere, and you know Boisvert will not take kindly to competition. I expect you'll have to move."

"I could move here," offered John, handing Bianca her bowl of brew.

"John, this is not a home."

"But you live here."

Bianca set her tea down, exasperated. "I have no choice. I'll not move back with my parents. Besides, you could never bear living here. I'd rather not listen to you complain about the smell."

John couldn't argue. The smells did bother him. It would never do for them to live where she practiced her art. As for moving back with her parents, Bianca's father, Albern Goddard, was an alchemist with a dubious past. He'd been accused of plotting to poison the king in an attempt to subvert Henry's religious "Reformation." A devout Catholic, Goddard still ascribed to the authority of the pope even though it was dangerous to do so. Bianca had risked her own life to prove he had been wrongly accused, and for that peril, she had yet to forgive him.

Though, to be honest, Bianca owed much of her success and present circumstance to what she had learned from her father. From the time she had been able to fetch water without spilling it, she had assisted him in his "noble art." He was disciplined, if not a bit disorganized, and she followed his methods, having never witnessed a more orderly approach. And, like her father, she was devoted to her science. Sometimes excessively so. Especially to John's eyes.

Bianca took a sip and suddenly blew it out, spraying her new still. "Phaa! What *is* this?"

John leapt back, patting her spittle from his front. He stuck his finger in his bowl and tasted. "So it was pepper after all."

Bianca stalked to the door and threw it open. She cocked her arm to catapult the offensive liquid into the lane, where standing opposite, with her fist poised to knock, stood her friend Jolyn.

"Another fouled concoction?" she asked, eyeing the bowl in Bianca's hand.

"This one is of John's making." Bianca tossed the contents.

"John, I didn't know anything but metals amused you," said Jolyn, cautiously stepping into Bianca's room. One never knew what one might find there. Once, she'd nearly been trampled by a goat wishing to escape. "Boisvert would be disappointed if you switched allegiance and joined the brotherhood of puffers."

"I think he was trying to poison me," said Bianca, shutting the door. She hated to be compared with alchemists, but she ignored her friend's tease. Instead, she noted Jolyn's new cloak and doe-skin gloves. "What's this?" she said, touching her friend's garb. "I should quit my experiments and sweep floors at Barke House."

Jolyn smiled. "My wages consist of a roof over my head and board for my belly."

John dispensed of his pepper tea more discreetly. He set it by a stack of crockery and covered it with a plate. "More gifts from your suitor then?" he asked.

"Aye." Jolyn shrugged off her cloak and draped it on a chair, well away from Bianca's chemistries, then pulled off her gloves and set them by.

"For such gloves I can't say your hands have benefitted." John added another dung patty to the furnace to ward off the chill. "They look raw and red from the cold."

Jolyn stood next to the furnace, stretching her fingers over the heat. "It's not the cold. Mrs. Beldam has me sweep out the rush and scrub the floors with lye. But my hands look better than when I was picking through the flats." She examined her blisters, turning her fingers over. "Mrs. Beldam believes in spring cleaning. She doesn't want the neighbors thinkin' we's a clutch of clapperdudgeons."

"But you *are* a bunch of beggar-born," said John, poking the fire.

"I'll have you not speak poor of Barke House. It *used* to be a stew of ill repute, but not anymore. Women come to Barke House hoping to escape the streets and start a better life."

"It's hard to shake a spider out of its web." John leaned the poke against the furnace, observing Jolyn's cheeks beginning to flush. Her skin had been protected by river clay for so long that now, with it scrubbed, her complexion was usually as pale as a baby's bottom. "I'm simply saying, reputations are difficult to lose," he said.

"True, but we must put a good face forward, eh?" said Jolyn. She sat at a bench opposite Bianca and the contraption of copper. "Last week I spent the only warm day toting bed linens to the fields of Horsleydown to wash and spread dry. My hands have yet to recover from the cold and soap."

"Mrs. Beldam is getting her use of you," said Bianca.

"I earn my keep. But if Mrs. Beldam hadn't been so caring, I'd still be sloshing through sewage."

Bianca checked her mash and gave it a stir. "I don't know how she affords to run such a place. She must have a charitable heart—or a patron with a bigger one."

"Or a bigger purse," added John.

"The girls and I give her what we can. You don't run a place like Barke House hoping to grow wealthy."

Bianca agreed, then, settling on her stool, traced the course of a trickle of fluid and tightened a juncture in her apparatus. "So, what does Mrs. Beldam say of your suitor?"

"She doesn't like him. But if I should marry him, it is one less mouth for her to feed." Jolyn sniffed a bowl of rendered suet and rubbed a dab on her cracked hands. "One of the girls suggested that he probably reminds Mrs. Beldam of someone she once loved. The rumor is she was abandoned in her youth and had to raise a daughter alone."

"Is it true?"

Jolyn worked the oil into her skin. "She's never spoken of a daughter."

"So, when will you see him?" asked Bianca.

"Soon. His ship is in. He has matters to attend."

"He's a captain?" John pricked up his ears.

"John should join a crew," said Bianca. "All those years living in a barrel behind the Tern's Tempest and being seduced by sailors' wild stories of adventure and swag."

"He's not a captain," said Jolyn. "But his business involves ships. He does well by it. He brings me sweetmeats and oranges, stuffed figs . . . all manner of exotical foods." She pressed her hand to her stomach. "It doesn't always suit my constitution. I'm used to tavern scraps and ends from market."

"Perhaps you might save some for Bianca to try. She doesn't care for the fare I bring."

Jolyn studied her friend's neglected platter. "You're as thin as a sparrow. You should eat."

"I forget."

"To eat?" Jolyn looked over at John and shook her head. "John, remind her there is more to life than this . . ." She waved her hand at the display of coils. "This . . ."

Bianca watched her friend struggle to find the right words. "This room of Medicinals and Physickes?" she finished, lifting her brow.

Jolyn rolled her eyes. "It's frightening, Bianca, how absorbed you become in your chemistries."

Bianca shoved an apple wedge in her mouth. "There is nothing else I'd rather do. Discovering medicinals is more worthy than searching for the philosopher's stone."

"So your father's work is of no merit?" Jolyn thought anyone who worked indoors and was able to support himself must be cleverer than she.

"None I've seen." Bianca swallowed. "He has spent a lifetime trying to transmute gold from worthless metals and mole brains. He's nothing to show for it." She wiped her mouth with the back of her hand. "At least what I do benefits the sick and ailing, so it has some purpose."

"True. But some would argue that in aiding the shadier side of Southwark, you are in fact perpetuating it."

"If someone is in need, I help," said Bianca. "It is not for me to decide who merits aid."

"You sound like a nun," said Jolyn.

"I do a respectable business with the gentler side of London. Merchants and earls buy my balms, too. And Meddybemps takes my salves to Smithfield and Newmarket."

Jolyn pulled her eyelids back and rolled her eyes around in her best imitation of the storied streetseller. Meddybemps had a roving eye that could make a person seasick just talking to him.

Bianca couldn't resist reciting one of Meddybemps's rhymes—

"Hey biddle dunny,
I diddled me honey,
        And fiddled my pizzle did she.
Now I'm sorry to say
That we shouldn't have played.
        Instead of one heir I've got three."

She bit into the wedge of cheese while her friends snickered.

But Jolyn's smile faded, and with a wince, she gripped her side. "Do you have a tonic to settle my stomach? I ate at the Dim Dragon Inn last night."

"Was Burke cooking? His food kills more men than the footpads in the alleys around it. I nearly lost my liver from eating his meat pie," John said.

"I have some peptic carminative on the shelf. It stimulates the bile and soothes stomach flux." Bianca fussed over her fire and mash, letting John search through the bottles. "Mind that you don't grab anything with 'Capsicum' on the label."

"What's Capsicum?" asked Jolyn.

"Pepper."

John's head bobbed up and down as he squinted at the bottles, some labeled with Bianca's precarious system of identification and some unmarked. He repeatedly pulled out jars, scowling as he tried to decipher what they were.

"I should stop patronizing the Dim Dragon. Too many muckrakers frequent the place." Jolyn's hand went to her neck, and she fingered her scarf. "I don't fancy rubbing shoulders with them anymore." She watched Bianca stir her mash. "A mudlark

from Falcon Way saw me and accused me of stealing from him."
She sniffed and shook her head. "He thought I'd cave from embarrassment."

John found a jar that read "peptic" something and set it before
Bianca. "Is this what you wanted?"

Bianca ran the jar under her nose, then dumped the contents
into a pan. "Aye. Can you set this to boil with a measure of water
from that bucket?" She ticked her chin in the pail's direction.

John dipped a ladle into the bucket and added it to the pan.
"So, what did you steal?"

"I didn't steal anything!" Jolyn shrugged. "He's a cozen to
trouble me." She studied her nails. "I know a few rooks who'll
settle a score as a favor."

"You've made some enemies," said John, setting the brew on
the furnace to boil. He gathered his hat and scarf from a rafter
over the furnace.

"How can one avoid it?" asked Jolyn. "Everyone makes enemies."

"Just temper your treatment of them," advised John. "The alleys are dark at night."

Bianca stirred the brew for Jolyn and found an empty flask to
pour it in. "Jolyn knows the risks better than anyone."

The mixture bubbled and burped. Bianca fetched a square of
linen and stretched it over the mouth of the flask, concentrating
as she poured the hot tincture. A dribble of liquid scalded her
finger, but she endured the pain and finished pouring. "This
should soothe your flux. Have you felt this way before?"

"Not oft, but I have to say, the past week the pain has been
worse. Sometimes I cannot stand for the cramping."

John wrapped his scarf around his neck and plopped his cap on
his head. "I've stalled long enough. Boisvert will wonder where
I've got." He ducked a row of drying herbs dangling from a beam,
sidled between two worktables, one piled with rue and strangely
shaped roots that Bianca had started to mince, and the other
table littered with retorts and crucibles filched from her father's
alchemy room.

Bianca squeezed the last bit of liquid from the cloth and swirled the flask. "Let this cool, then drink it down."

"You should see him out," said Jolyn, accepting the remedy and ticking her head toward John fumbling with the latch at the door. Bianca hesitated. Sometimes her friend could be so distracted. "He cares for you so," she urged.

Jolyn stretched her legs out on the bench as Bianca's expression softened. She began to rub her sore legs. "Perhaps I've got the Black Death," she said, calling after Bianca, who was now heading for the door. "I've got the aches all over my body."

Bianca spoke over her shoulder. "Let's hope that it is not the plague but the damp and cold that you feel."

John bid good-bye to Jolyn, then pulled Bianca into the lane. But Jolyn knew what they were about. She whistled and whooped loud enough for them to hear her teasing and laughed when John slammed the door.

Jolyn rubbed her upset stomach and eyed the hunk of cheese. She didn't have much of an appetite, but it might settle her stomach. She snatched the wedge off the plate and munched happily while studying the copper tubes of her friend's strange contraption. She admired Bianca for forging a life of her own. For being clever enough to have figured out a way to make money. Jolyn had always been envious of the fact that Bianca had a home—an actual place to sleep with a roof over her head. She didn't blame Bianca for avoiding her father. Still, at least she *had* a father. Jolyn rubbed under her rib. And Bianca had a mother. *She* had neither. She sniffed the brew steaming before her. A hint of mint, maybe cinnamon, something else . . . Jolyn lifted it to her lips, blowing into the flask. She tried a sip and found it soothing.

"You haven't spoken of your mother in a while," said Jolyn, as Bianca closed the door.

The sheepish look on Bianca's face fell away, replaced by a pang of guilt. Jolyn had lost both her parents, giving her little choice but to delve into the world of muckraking. Scavenging was marginally better than begging, though there were those who'd argue otherwise.

"She fares well," said Bianca, "I suppose." She slid onto the bench opposite Jolyn and rested her chin in her hand. "I haven't visited in a while." The truth was, Bianca wanted to be on her own, and returning home, even for a visit, was fraught with feelings of guilt at leaving her mother alone with her father. But her mother had her own interests, herbal remedies being one of them, and the two coexisted under the same roof if only to eat and sleep. "Father came close to hanging, but it seems his brush with death has not humbled him."

"Your father misuses everyone for his advantage."

Bianca did not disagree. She rubbed her eyes, gritty and sore beneath the lids. She really could use more sleep.

Jolyn handed the flask back to Bianca. The brew settled in her stomach, and the two continued to talk about John and Barke House. Jolyn's faith in her friend's talent was unshakable—even when, after a few minutes, a sharp pain stabbed her gut, causing her to double over.

Bianca looked up in alarm. "Jolyn?"

"Most likely it is the warm liquid on an empty stomach. Nothing more." She straightened and rubbed her side, turning her head toward a guttering candle.

But Bianca thought Jolyn's nonchalance was forced. She watched Jolyn through the copper coils. Only a crescent of blue iris showed around Jolyn's enlarged pupils. A thin line of perspiration glistened on her upper lip and forehead.

Jolyn mopped her brow with the hem of her skirt, drawing herself up as if nothing was wrong. "Well, it has passed," she said. She leaned on her fist and grinned.

Jolyn talked about her suitor, and after a few minutes, Bianca relaxed because it did seem she was showing no further sign of discomfort. Perhaps Bianca had been overly concerned. She turned her attention to some shelving where a stack of glassware hid a pair of tongs.

"So are you going to marry this man?" asked Bianca over her shoulder. She reached over the flasks into the back of the shelf, upsetting a glass vesicle with her elbow and making it fall. It shattered on the floor, but a louder crash came from where Jolyn sat. Bianca spun around.

Jolyn had fallen off the bench, taking half the distillation tubing with her. The copper made a terrible clatter; crockery smashed, scattering shards of glass and pottery on the table and floor. Liquids streamed from the table onto the bench. But more disconcerting to Bianca than losing her latest experiment was seeing Jolyn writhing on the floor.

Bianca rushed to her side, lifting Jolyn's head into her lap. But it was as if her friend had flown to another place and time. Jolyn's eyes stared up at her, vacant and unseeing.

"Speak to me!" Bianca slapped her cheeks, hoping to jar Jolyn back. Instead, Jolyn's arms swung up in an abrupt spasm. Bianca just missed being hit. She grabbed hold of Jolyn's wrists to pin them against the floor, but her friend's strength was greater. Unable to control her friend's convulsions, Bianca sat back, helplessly watching Jolyn thrash. Jolyn's head wrenched at an unnatural angle, her jaw tipped up and clenched tight as a vise.

Perspiration soaked Jolyn's flushed skin, and her hair stuck to her forehead as if she had been caught in a storm.

Bianca threw herself across Jolyn's chest, leaning in with all her weight, hoping to control her bucking. Eventually the thrashing ceased and the convulsions subsided. Bianca sat back and laid her hand against Jolyn's neck. Her friend's pulse grew thready and began to fade.

Had her remedy caused her to convulse? The thought was too awful, and she immediately dismissed her misgivings as she scanned the room for something, an antidote, anything she could give Jolyn to save her. Spying a flask of rancid goat milk, she leapt to her feet and grabbed it off a shelf. The smell made her gag, but she knelt beside Jolyn and forced the liquid down her friend's throat.

"Jolyn, drink, swallow. I will not let you go. I am here. Please. Look at me. Swallow . . ."

Jolyn began to retch. She turned her head and vomited into the rush, drawing her knees toward her chin. Relief washed over

Bianca in hopes that her friend could purge whatever was causing her suffering.

But with Jolyn's last heave, her body grew still. What little strength remained . . . vanished, and Bianca felt the full weight of Jolyn's head settle in her lap. She peered down at her friend and saw her mouth part. A trickle of purple-tinged blood coursed from her lips.

Bianca screamed. She shook Jolyn and slapped her face. When finally her anguished cries faded to whimpers, she laid Jolyn out on the floor and stared into her friend's wide, unblinking eyes. Eyes that saw nothing but Bianca's failure to save her.

# CHAPTER 4

Banes Perkins stuck his finger into the wax of a burning candle. He withdrew it, letting the wax cool, then peeled the cast off his fingertip and admired it. He had made a modest pile of impressions when he heard Mrs. Beldam's shrill voice carry down the stairs. He ignored her, knowing she'd lose patience and eventually seek him out anyway. Banes had time to melt the casts over the flame before she saw him wasting their precious wax candles.

"Banes! *Banes!*" she called, tromping down the stairs. She arrived in the doorway to see him blow out the candle and shove it away. She eyed him suspiciously. "Banes, a rat has got in. Ye needs to take care of it straightaway." She stood like a sentry, ready to bark at him if he didn't move fast enough.

Banes pushed himself from the board with his one good hand. He had a talent for dispensing with vermin—he'd had plenty of practice at Barke House. The residence stood within sight of the Thames and Morgan's Lane stream—effectively an open sewer. The rats treated Barke House with the same disregard shown by their neighbors. Neither took Mrs. Beldam's attempt to redeem its sullied reputation seriously.

Before Banes got two steps, Mrs. Beldam blocked his exit.

"I'll need you to go for purgative, but take care of the rat before one of the girls gets bit."

Banes skirted her scabbard-gray eyes, avoiding their astute stare. She had a way of demeaning him even when he'd done nothing wrong.

"Aye, m'um," he mumbled, squeezing past her squared shoulders.

He grabbed a cloth he'd reserved for just such occasions and climbed the stairs to the second floor. A few of the women were away for the day, trying to earn what they could by working in taverns or picking pockets at the theater or bear-baiting venues. Not all shillings earned were honestly made, but the aim at Barke House was to at least try. The women's ultimate goal was achieving a more virtuous life, but it was nearly impossible to do. It required a certain amount of cunning to survive, and wiliness was not akin to godliness.

Banes sidestepped a pile of laundered clothing waiting to be put away. He moved with stealth, not wishing to alert the rat or women of his arrival. Perhaps he might glimpse Pandy or, he hoped, Jolyn in a state of partial undress.

He clutched his rat cloth with his right hand, and with the fingers of his left (for he had no thumb) lightly touched the wall to balance as he crept up the stairs. The risers usually groaned with a shift of weight, but he knew where to place his foot on every stair. He was practiced at keeping silent and unnoticed.

He reached the landing and stood for a moment to inhale the scent of lavender and crushed rose petals wafting from the women's rooms. The smell was thought to repel mice and centipedes, but as both retreated into the wall cracks ahead of him, Banes thought perhaps the ladies should rethink this idea.

Jolyn's room was nearest, and he noted with disappointment that she was not in. He moved forward, hoping to peer undetected into Kara's room, when suddenly Pandy burst into the hall, screaming hysterically and swatting a rat with a broom.

"Banes, get him!" she shrieked. Pandy ran behind the homely lad and pushed him forward.

The rat ran toward them, but when Pandy screamed, it turned and scuttled down the hall in the opposite direction.

"Kill it! Kill it!" Pandy's shouts were answered with another scream, this time from Kara's room, where the rat had ducked.

Banes straightened, relishing the attention. Mostly he was ignored at Barke House. He heard their titters and saw the distaste in their eyes. One cannot help being born with a shortened arm and missing thumb. Did they think he chose this?

He stepped forward, readying his cloth, and peered into Kara's room. The rat had trapped itself in a corner and was desperately scratching at the wall as Kara sat on a window ledge with her knees pulled up to her chin. "Banes, hurry!"

Banes took in the room, a rare opportunity for him. He saw a petticoat draped across a chair, stockings drying from a nail on a beam. A brush lay on a table with lustrous bronze hair caught in its bristles. The smell of lavender, the smell of a woman . . .

"Banes!"

Banes startled, feeling his face color. He held the cloth open, advancing on the unwanted guest. Kara swept up her dangling kirtle and sat on it for fear the rat would dig its claws into the wool and climb. She spewed a stream of foul language at the rodent, and if Banes didn't soon dispense with the creature, it would be directed at him.

Banes clicked his tongue at the rat. The creature glanced at the curious-looking human but returned to its frantic scratching instead of running. Banes crouched, steadied his rag, and fixed his inscrutable black eyes on his prey.

Kara fell silent, entranced by the way Banes approached the rat. He was certainly practiced, but the lad's eerie manner was oddly mesmerizing. The rat seemed to be listening to his strange clucking. It stopped scratching and quieted as if waiting for him—almost as if it trusted him.

Banes lunged. He grabbed the rat out of the corner and, with the four fingers of his left hand, threw the cloth over its head. Its legs kicked and its torso squirmed as Banes tightened his hold around its neck. After a minute, its legs went slack. Its ringed tail fell limp. He had squeezed the life out of it.

Kara noticed the young man, to his credit, did not take pleasure in his task. He was composed in his office, dispensing the rat with cool efficiency. For Banes, it was a matter of routine at Barke House. If she had seen a gleam in his eye or a hint of a smile on his lips, she'd have trusted him less and noticed him more. Instead, once Banes had strangled the rodent and left her room, she'd give little more thought to the lad.

And that was how Banes preferred it.

With the dead rat held at arm's length, Banes passed Pandy, who shrank back, then followed him down the stairs. "That's the second one in a day," she said. "'Ow they gettin' in?"

Banes did not answer. He did not know. But he *had* noticed the increase. He opened the door and glupped across the muddy lane toward the field stream as Pandy watched from the stoop. He glanced once over his shoulder, assuring himself of an audience, then hurled the rat downstream in the direction of the Thames.

By the time he returned, Pandy was in conversation with Mrs. Beldam in the kitchen.

"We've already gone through it," said Mrs. Beldam, peering into a jar on an upper shelf. The statuesque woman looked even more forbidding when standing on a footstool. Everyone else seemed to shrink by comparison.

Pandy stood next to the board, gazing up at her. "Like I's sayin'. It's rainin' rats. One climbed the vine outside and was starin' in at me with its beady eyes, it was. I had to scare it off with the end of a broom. Was likely to have me for dinner, it was." Pandy settled at the table.

Mrs. Beldam looked through another couple of jars before stepping down from her boost. "Well, it is that time of year. Spring brings 'em out. They're mad to nest a brood." She frowned at the sight of Banes. "Did ye take care of it?"

"Aye, m'um." Banes sat at the board next to Pandy, who

scooched away. He leaned his chin on his good hand and watched the two of them.

"I'd like to know how they be getting in," said Mrs. Beldam. She settled her fists on either hip and gazed around the room as if considering it from the point of view of a rat. Her sharp nose and calculating stare did little to dissuade Banes from thinking her akin to one.

"I bet it got in when Jolyn came home," said Pandy, scratching her neck. "Probably lurked outside the door. It was still mostly dark, then."

"Where is Jolyn?" asked Mrs. Beldam. It was midmorning, and she hadn't seen the fair-haired beauty since yesterday.

"I don't knows. Not my job to watch 'at one." Pandy stuffed a loose strand of hair back under her coif. The young woman was blessed with a creamy complexion rivaling Jolyn's, but the latter had vivid blue eyes that drew a man's notice faster than a dog on a crumb. Pandy's own eyes were a nondescript hazel and mirrored her cunning. "I do know it was the wee hours in the mornin'. I heard her stumblin' about on the stairs."

"She didn't have breakfast and then she is gone again so soon?" said Mrs. Beldam, furrowing her thin brow.

"I say she thinks she's above us now that she's taken up with Wynders." Pandy toyed with a wood spoon as her eyes slid sideways to catch Banes's reaction. She was not above planting seeds of mischief.

Mrs. Beldam glanced at Banes, whose shoulders, at the mention of Jolyn and her suitor, sagged. "Well, as long as she is here, she's no better than the rest of ye," she said, disparaging the girl in her campaign to make him believe that Jolyn was not worth losing his heart over. "She must earn her keep like everyone else. Until Wynders drops on one knee, I put little faith in all his supposed mollycoddling."

Mrs. Beldam knew the boy was captivated by the rescued gamine, and she did not approve. He'd be a fool to think that girl would ever consider him more than a grotesque cuffin, one to be shunned and jeered for his devil-cursed deformity. She wished she could make him see his lunacy. Make him set his affection upon someone more his kind.

"It's not supposed," said Pandy. "She keeps prancing in with new boots and gloves."

"You're jealous," sang a voice. Kara leaned against the doorjamb with her arms folded, listening to every word. She stepped into the kitchen and fetched a drink. "The minute Wynders saw Jolyn, he was done with you."

"Well, he *never* looked at you."

"Perhaps because I never looked at *him*."

Banes reveled in the girls' sniping. It was one benefit to living at Barke House. The entertainment was worth more than a ticket to a dogfight.

"We've more important matters." Mrs. Beldam drew herself to her full height and fixed them with a stolid glare. "The two of youse need to be on about your day and stop dallyin' about and givin' me fits. We haven't enough to feed the rat traps, and now they's ready to take up lodgin' here." She riffled through the coins in her purse with a crooked finger. "I've barely enough for necessities today." She cinched it closed and let it dangle from the rope attaching it to her waist. The cord was frayed and grungy, but she never replaced it or even removed the purse from her body. "Get on now," she said to Kara and Pandy. "I've had me fill of ye."

The two women sauntered from the kitchen and sullenly headed up the stairs. Banes anticipated a gusty bout of name-calling before they finally made it out the door that morning. When he turned back to the table, Mrs. Beldam was watching him.

"We 'aven't enough for the rat poison and purgative both." She placed a shilling on the table in front of him. "For now, fetch the purgative. We'll deal with the rats later."

# CHAPTER 5

Bianca sat in a daze as two men peered down at her friend's corpse. She'd run to Boisvert's and roused John from the silversmith's shop, much to the Frenchman's irritation, but seeing her distraught and with eyes nearly swollen shut from crying, he relented. He sent them on their way, foisting a bottle of wine on them, which for him was a tonic for all matters both good and bad.

John sent her home while he sought out the watch and constable from Southwark, who now stood over Jolyn, taking turns scratching their heads and making obvious comments.

"Well, I would say she's not with the livin', that's for definites," said the watch. "Should I fetch the coroner, sir?"

Constable Patch looked up after a moment. His costume appeared shabby and worn, befitting an official not of London but of the more battered Southwark, across the river. A poniard hung from his waist, Bianca thought for show, for the man did not seem to possess the wit to use it. "Aye, this time of day 'e's most likely at the Turn Bull. Look there first."

The watch scurried out the door, eager to tell the coroner and anyone else the news about a young woman's death.

The constable crooked his head to look at Jolyn from another angle. "And she just dropped—dead as dung?"

Bianca flinched at the comparison. She hated public officials. She found them less useful than a hangnail and would not have bothered if John hadn't insisted. "They'll hang you straight up if word gets out a girl died in your rent," he had told her. "You can't conceal her body or that she died here, Bianca. How would you get her out with no one noticing? And then what would you do with her body once you got her out?"

She had caved to John's appeal, but this shivery ass did little to convince Bianca that this had been a good decision.

"So's ye say she groused of stomach complaints? Feelin' squeamish and a bit noxious?"

Bianca did her best to answer the man with an even temper. "Aye, she mentioned she had eaten of rich foods she had not been used to. And she said she was *nauseous*."

"Rich foods," repeated Patch, pulling his goatee. "What sorts of rich foods?"

"She mentioned sweetmeats, stuffed figs, exotical fare."

"Exotical fare," echoed Patch. He continued to tug at his spotty facial hair. "And how might she 'ave come by that, do ye suppose?"

"She had a suitor, sir. He brought her treats from abroad."

"Treats from abroad." Constable Patch considered this. "So 'e's a sea captain?"

"Nay, he is not." Bianca had little faith that this public official could make any more sense of Jolyn's death than she. "He might have been an owner of a ship, or perhaps he worked shoreside. I do not know."

"And did this suitor possess a name?"

Bianca looked to John. "I don't believe she mentioned it. Or, if she did, I don't recall."

John shrugged and shook his head. "I don't remember her saying."

Patch turned his sights on the young silversmith and studied him before speaking. "Ye don't remember?"

Bianca watched Patch continue to work his chin hair and thought the man would soon have nothing left to pull.

"Perhaps ye don't remember because ye don't want to say?"

John clamped shut his mouth, stifling the urge to protest. To a man such as Patch, arguing could be construed as evidence of conniving or, even worse, guilt.

"Sir, she did not say." Bianca had no qualms setting the man straight.

Patch now turned his stare on Bianca. His eyes drifted to the elaborate copper contraption that loomed behind her. "And what is it ye do here?" Patch's gaze traveled the length of the room, taking in shelves lined with jars and crockery. A pear-shaped pot with a neck like that of a swan sat neglected in a corner. Bunches of herbs hung from beams, the smells mingling with more unpleasant ones. Not the usual stuff of a young woman. A red cat perched on a joist, its eyes staring back at him, mirrored yellow.

But as Bianca started to explain, a knock came at the door, and into her room of Medicinals and Physickes stepped a man most like a roast beef, dressed in a brown doublet and small ruff choking what would be his neck. With a lift of his chin, he appraised his surroundings.

"Coroner," said Patch, offering the man a slight bow.

"Patch," acknowledged the man in a stentorian voice, but he paid no more attention to the constable than he would a gnat. He tolerated the sniveling fool because he had to. No one else in the ward was willing to take on the role of constable of this godforsaken precinct for so little pay and so little respect. He despised coming to Southwark; nothing good ever came of it.

"Coroner, we was jus' disgusting what 'appened here," said Patch, drawing himself erect to equal the man's height. This task Patch could achieve, but girth was a challenge and one not worth striving for.

The coroner arched a brow at Patch and took a breath to correct the man's verbiage, then thought better of it. "Indeed," he answered. He looked about and, one eye closed, registered an unpleasant smell. He lifted the pomander hanging around his neck and inhaled. "And where is the body?"

Patch led the coroner to where Jolyn's body lay. Bianca had not moved her, mostly because she did not have the strength, but partly because she had left in a panic to find John. She now stared at her friend. Disbelief and sadness churned her insides.

The coroner regarded Jolyn before speaking. He looked up and found Bianca, his face revealing nothing. "Perhaps you could tell me exactly what happened?" He directed his question to Bianca but trained his eyes on Jolyn.

"Sir, I was working when my friend came to visit."

"And the name of the deceased?"

"Jolyn Carmichael."

"What is it you do here?"

"This is my room of Medicinals and Physickes. I create salves, balms, and ointments for the ailing."

"And these items," he said, gesturing to the distillation equipment and furnace, "are required of your . . . vocation?"

"Aye, sir."

"Why aren't you in a nunnery?" he asked. "Or married?"

"I prefer this."

The coroner glanced at John, then looked around at the dank, smelly nest that was Bianca's room. He lifted an eyebrow.

With effort, he crouched beside the body and put his fingers to her neck. Not finding a pulse, he pushed her scarf away, revealing bruising and a purplish ring about her neck. "Curious." He leaned in for a closer look. "It appears she has suffered some bruising. Perhaps from a cord." He lifted his pomander to his nose and closed his eyes, breathing deep.

Bianca thought back to Jolyn sitting at her bench. Was Jolyn wearing her necklace? Bianca had grown so accustomed to seeing the jewelry hanging from her neck that it no longer drew her notice. She hadn't seen any bruising, nor did Jolyn complain of soreness, but Jolyn's scarf had been wrapped about her neck, Bianca had thought for warmth. Had she wanted to conceal her wounds, or protect them? Bianca came around the table and knelt beside her friend. The abrasions and discoloration ran on either side of Jolyn's neck, but Jolyn's necklace was gone.

"She used to wear a necklace, but I don't see it."

The coroner did not answer and continued his examination, lifting each hand, noting their redness and blisters. He peered into Jolyn's unblinking eyes, then touched the corner of her mouth and studied the blood on his fingers, rubbing it between them. "The blood has a purple tinge." After a moment he stood and removed a square of linen from a pocket, taking care to thoroughly wipe his fingers. "The appearance is that of poisoning."

Bianca had considered as much, but to hear him say it still came as a shock. She had dismissed the notion, refusing to believe Jolyn was a victim of ill intentions, preferring instead that her friend had died from a natural cause. The words sounded with such authority that she dreaded where this might lead, and from the look on his face, so did John.

Patch wasn't so dim that he, too, couldn't see where this logic was going and immediately spoke up. "So's this vacation of yours . . . did the deceased come to you for one of your balms?"

Bianca stood to fix the constable with a hard stare. "No, she did not."

"Well, why 'id she come here? What for?"

"Jolyn is my friend," said Bianca. "She came to visit."

"We've been friends with Jolyn for a while," said John. "She's been doing well as late, and she wanted to talk about her suitor."

Patch squinted at John. "I says we need to find this *suitor*," he said, drawing out the word to give it emphasis. "So was there any jealousy between ye's? She had a suitor, after all."

"Of course not," answered Bianca. "I was glad for her."

"Did she 'ave somethin' maybe ye wanted?" Patch ticked his head toward Jolyn. "Like maybe that necklace?"

Bianca grew indignant. "She was my friend. I don't care a spot about jewelry. Search my room if you want."

Patch considered, but continued to question her. "Well, maybe it was made of gold. Maybe ye could have poisoned her, then took the necklace, needin' the gold for your . . . alchemy."

Bianca was riled. The unwitting constable had no idea the dragons he unleashed insinuating she would poison her friend and referring to her work as alchemy.

"Sir," said Bianca, seething, "what I do is *not* alchemy. I would thank you not to refer to it as such."

Unperturbed, Patch pressed on. "Aws, wasn't ye father an alchemist? Albern Goddard? Why, I remember that he was accused of tryin' to poison the king." His mouth twitched. "Maybe it's just what ye do. Maybe it's just what ye know."

"That was a false charge, sir. My father has been absolved of that crime."

"Constable Patch," said John, "Bianca only makes salves and tinctures to help the sick. The unfortunate business of her father has no bearing on Jolyn. Bianca has severed ties with him. It is a completely separate matter."

"A separate matter, but worth bearing in mind," added Patch, looking to the coroner for agreement.

The coroner snorted, enjoying the drama that was playing out between Patch and this alchemist's daughter. He studied Bianca a moment before speaking. "It is probably of no import," he said. "However, did you give Jolyn anything to drink or eat?"

Bianca hesitated. Should she admit she had concocted a drink to soothe Jolyn's flux? A sinking feeling settled in her gut. She knew where this question was leading. Ultimately, the onus would be on her to prove her innocence.

She would have to discover why Jolyn had died. She didn't trust that these two men could (or would) figure it out. Constable Patch looked ready to lock her away, and the coroner seemed as though he'd lose interest as soon as he walked out the door. She opted to lie, if only to give herself more time. "No, I did not," she said.

The coroner glanced at John, but John was practiced in deceit and knew when to keep his own counsel. He liked to think Bianca had learned her guile from him.

"So did your friend seem well?" asked the coroner.

"Generally, sir, she did. I thought she looked happier every time she visited. She no longer had to scrounge through the mud-flats to survive." She took a breath to speak of Jolyn's complaints when the coroner interrupted.

"Did she voice any distress—physical or otherwise?"

"She complained of an unsettled stomach," said Bianca, relieved she could tell him that Jolyn had not been perfectly healthy when she arrived. "She blamed it on the exotical foods her suitor had given her."

The coroner studied her with steady eyes. "And would you say she had enemies?"

John broke in, unable to stand by any longer and watch the coroner interrogate Bianca. "Jolyn mentioned a muckraker at the Dim Dragon Inn. He confronted her about stealing something from him."

"Do you know who this muckraker might be?"

"She did not say."

"She did not say . . . much," he noted. His gaze shifted from John to Bianca. "Has she any family?"

"None I know of," she said.

"Tell him where Jolyn lived," said Patch, eagerly.

Bianca glared at Patch, knowing full well his intent, but she answered simply, as if it should be of no import, "Jolyn lived at the Barke House."

Patch cast a knowing glimpse at the public official, a smug smile on his face.

"She was employed there as an errand girl," Bianca told the coroner. She turned to address Constable Patch. "Nothing more."

The coroner studied John, the smell of Bianca's room nettling his nose. He again lifted his pomander and inhaled, as if it might transport him to more pleasant surroundings—smelling of orange and clove, with a tankard of mulled cider in one hand and a woman's buttocks in the other. Alas, he opened his eyes and found himself back in this den of crockery with a dead girl at his feet. He turned to the constable. "Patch, let the madam at Barke House know she has one less tenant," he said. "If she should ask, burial will be at Cross Bones."

"Cross Bones!" exclaimed Bianca. "But that land is unconsecrated." The insult was too much. Neither she nor her friend observed the king's religion, but she resented that Jolyn would be condemned for all time. "She may have lived at Barke House, but she was not a woman of disrepute. If she's buried at Cross Bones, she'll be labeled for eternity."

The coroner remained unmoved. "If this suitor, as you say, exists, then I'm sure he will desire otherwise. In which case, he will have to see me to arrange burial elsewhere." He read Bianca's long face. "My dear, it is admirable that you should wish better for your . . . friend." He inhaled his pomander, then dropped it. "But it is of my opinion that where she is buried should be your least concern."

# CHAPTER 6

His belly full, the ferrier tossed the skeletal remains of his breakfast into the Thames, his catlike tongue licking his chin and
nose, savoring the last delectable taste of rat on his skin. He had
had an easy time of it. The *Cristofur* had afforded him an abundant supply of vermin eager to escape her moldering hold and
swim for better spoils on land. It did not take much effort for him
to capture the hapless creatures. As he floated within sight of the
moored vessel, happily sated, he was privy to a curious sight, the
likes of which he had never seen.

Before the day's first light, a lonely seaman appeared at the
starboard side. As he picked the rat gristle from his teeth, the ferrier saw the seaman raise a lantern, then signal toward shore. All
London appeared dark and unaware, content in the slumbering
peace of its citizenry. But then a singular light appeared shoreside—a light from an upper window of a warehouse that blinked
once, then twice, then was extinguished.

The Rat Man lifted a brow and watched with interest.

Soon, the prow of a long skiff nosed its way silently toward the

*Cristofur.* It drew alongside her hull, floating in tandem with the merchant vessel.

The Rat Man turned his wherry for a better look.

A hatch creaked open from the starboard side. After a minute, a shrouded object, resembling the shape and length of a body, was lowered by rope onto the skiff. Perhaps this would not cause much notice to a casual observer, but when the object was followed by another, and then another of similar shape and size, the Rat Man could not bring himself to leave, nor could he drag his eyes from the sight.

By comparison, the heap of shrouded bodies in the skiff was higher than the pile of rats in his. The man put oar to water and, with effort, began to row the teetering skiff. He headed back toward shore, the gunwales dangerously near water level. Apparently, the voyage had not been an easy one for the crew, and the ferrier now looked upon the exodus of vermin with renewed interest.

Something was amiss.

# CHAPTER 7

Banes stood outside Bianca's room of Medicinals and Physickes, waiting for her to answer his knock. She was taking longer than usual, and he wondered if perhaps she wasn't in. He was about to peer through the cracked window when the door swung open, and out poked a head with wheaten locks to ask him his business.

"I just came from the Barke House. The missus sent me."

The young man looked harshly upon him, then slammed the door.

Banes thought this unusual, not to mention rude. He was considering what to do next when the decision was made for him. The door opened warily, only this time, a head of black hair appeared. Bianca looked at him.

"Oh, Banes," she said. "Come in." She glanced up and down the street before ushering him through the door. "Something horrible has happened." She took him by his good hand and pulled him into the rent, closing the door and securing it.

Even though the day was overcast, it took a minute for his eyes to adjust to the dim light of the interior. The room was filled with the usual array of strange crockery and odors. Nothing seemed out of place—the room was always a mess. Banes followed Bianca past a furnace where several pots sat, their sides and bottoms scorched from boiling, but his eyes were drawn to a table where a row of candles glowed.

At first he couldn't be sure that what he saw wasn't a joke. Jolyn lay on the board, surrounded by lit tapers, as if she were sleeping or maybe the centerpiece of some queer alchemy ritual. Who could tell with Bianca? He'd seen his share of the bizarre in his year of fetching potions for Barke House. Once, he had been just steps away from her door when he heard a loud explosion. Out stumbled Bianca, her face smudged with smoke, her hair blown back from the percussion. But today, as he drew near the table, he could see that Jolyn's color was ashen, almost gray. And even with the three of them peering over her, she remained completely still.

"Banes," said Bianca, "Constable Patch is on his way to Barke House to tell Mrs. Beldam."

Banes stared at Bianca, then back at Jolyn. He'd seen the girl just hours before. She'd come down the stairs before the rest of the house was awake and had eaten an end of stale bread. He'd watched from the peephole in his room next to the kitchen. "I don't understand."

The blond man touched his arm. "She's dead, Banes."

Banes blinked in disbelief. How could it have happened? Jolyn was healthier than he was.

"She came by to visit, and we were talking," Bianca said. "All of a sudden, she bent over double as if a sharp pain pierced her stomach. She collapsed in convulsions." Bianca took a breath, fighting to control her emotions. "I couldn't help her." She shook her head. "There was nothing I could do."

Banes had never seen Jolyn at such close quarters. He'd spied her through his various peepholes he'd worked in the wood with a pick, cracks he'd enlarged, knots he'd pushed out. But these holes afforded him only glimpses. Bits of bared flesh, like pieces of a puzzle left for him to fit together in his head. Now he ran his eyes up the length of her, unfettered. True, she was fully clothed, but he could see the curves of her breasts and the slight mound of belly below them. He would never know what her skin would have felt like against his. But then, neither would anyone else.

"They want to bury her at Cross Bones," said the strapping young man. Banes wheeled to look on this person. Who *was* he? The question must have been etched on his face, for Bianca stepped over to the shiny-haired rascal and took his arm.

"Banes, this is John." She leaned her head against his shoulder.

There was an intimate familiarity between the two of them, and Banes took an immediate dislike to the fellow.

He turned back to Jolyn and gazed upon her sculpted profile. She *was* lovely. He would miss spying on her. She had been the object of his fantasies ever since she'd moved to Barke House. But he wasn't surprised they would bury her at the infamous graveyard. A young unmarried girl . . . and living at Barke House? It was easier for a constable to assume her lot in life than to ask. Besides, what difference did it make where her body was buried? As far as Banes could tell, everyone was going to hell anyway, if Southwark wasn't hell already.

But he could see the mention of Cross Bones upset Bianca. Was she fearful of a similar fate? When death dances, everyone wonders when his own life shall end. Banes, however, kept his tongue. He looked from Bianca to John and caught John staring at his deformed arm. He moved it self-consciously behind his back.

"It's wrong," said Bianca.

"It's inevitable," said John. "We don't have the money to do otherwise. The best we can do is ready her for burial."

Bianca gazed down at her friend. "The coroner believes she was poisoned," she murmured. She looked up. "Banes, do you know anything?"

Banes shifted his weight. Jolyn's suitor, Wynders, worked at Wool's Key. He had money, or the pretense of it. The rogue was always heaping gifts on Jolyn—new boots, cloaks, trinkets. Pandy had suffered from his fickle handling and nursed a seething contempt for Jolyn that boiled over in accusations that Jolyn had "stolen" him. But Banes wondered what, if any of this, he should tell.

"No." Banes shrugged, avoiding her steady gaze.

"What about that suitor?" asked Bianca. "Do you know his name?"

Banes felt no obligation to protect the philanderer. "Wynders," he said. "I thought him shifty." He relished adding spice to the stew.

"Shifty?" repeated Bianca. "How do you mean?"

Banes had an instinctive loathing of the man. "He'd come round and pay Jolyn all kinds of attention, then disappear. No one would ever see him or know anything much about what he did."

"Do you think he intended to marry Jolyn? You must have heard the women talk."

"Men come round, but they never marry anyone from Barke House." Banes scratched his foreshortened arm, forgetting his self-consciousness until he glanced at John. "It's happened before."

"I'm sure," said John.

Banes noted the rogue's lean build and broad chest and wondered if he was an apprentice in a trade requiring some brute strength. A ripple of dislike rolled down his spine. He thought through the possibilities. Blacksmith? No . . . they had the smell of iron about them. Farrier? No . . . his fingernails would be black with stable filth . . . Wherryman? He hadn't caught a whiff of the Thames about him. . . .

"They think I killed her." Bianca plopped down on the bench.

"They must have a reason for believing that." Banes's intention was not to goad her but to learn why Bianca would be accused.

"A death in someone's presence does not a guilty man make. It is my ill fortune that she should die here, in front of me, with no witnesses. My word means nothing. A constable and a coroner want someone to hang. I seem the likely culprit—why should they bother an ounce of effort to find the real cause of Jolyn's death?"

Banes knew the constables and coroners were as lawless and lazy as the citizens they were supposed to protect. He could think of no official who wasn't tarnished in some way, be it by bribes, laziness, or indifference. It was a rare person in London who possessed any kind of sense of justice, and certainly no one in Southwark was a model of morality. Still, Banes felt sorry that Bianca should find herself so grievously wronged. Not that he could do much about it. Someone had to swing. It might as well be her.

Bianca stared absently at the smashed beakers and heap of copper coils. She dropped her hand to the flask that held the tonic she'd made to soothe Jolyn's flux.

"Are you sure you gave me the right jar?" she asked John, holding up the empty vesicle at eye level.

"I gave you what you wanted," he said. "Peptic . . ." His face colored from confusion. "I don't remember the names you give these foolish concoctions."

"These 'foolish concoctions,' as you call them, are made of ingredients. Herbs, tinctures, and powders ground from seeds and ores. They are important to me and to the people whom I help. I'll thank you not to speak ill of it."

"I'm not speaking ill."

"I think that you are."

"I think you are blaming me, Bianca."

Banes cheered to hear them quarrel. A visit to Bianca's room of Medicinals and Physickes was proving more entertaining than the bickering women at Barke House.

"I am not blaming you. Just show me what you gave me to put in Jolyn's tonic."

"It was your responsibility to make sure it was the right . . . ingredient," said John, being careful not to make the same mistake twice.

"I was distracted. Just show me the jar."

"I don't know where it is. It probably got smashed when the apparatus fell."

Bianca started to search through the shards of glass. She moved copper tubes and set alembics aside to right overturned crockery in the hope of finding the missing jar.

Banes was riveted. He forgot the purpose of his visit until Bianca reminded him.

"You never told me why you came, Banes."

The question felt like a dunk in cold water. He was sorry to have the attention turn to him. "I am to fetch purgative," he said, remembering the shilling in his pocket and digging it out.

Bianca's brows furrowed.

Banes hoped to avoid another long discourse about why she hated to dispense the concoction, but Bianca never sold the powerful powder without having something to say about it.

"I don't know who is more to blame," she said, "women or men." She sniffed with annoyance. "Such cleansings are harsh. If men had to endure such purging, I'm sure there'd be less need of them." She retrieved one of the candles next to Jolyn's body, then situated a stool that would let her reach into the recess of a high shelf.

John watched the stool wobbling and offered to find the jar for her.

"I can manage," she said, shortly.

Banes and John exchanged looks as Bianca fumbled around, clinking bottles and jars until she found what she wanted. She brought the candle close to the label, squinting at her nearly illegible writing.

John's temper flared. "Well, I suppose you can manage well enough without me then." He didn't wait for an answer but turned on his heel and stalked toward the door.

Untroubled, Bianca stepped down from her stool. With a final glance over his shoulder, John flung open the door. He slammed it behind him, rattling a human skull off a shelf and sending it crashing to the floor.

Banes's eyes grew wide. He admired her composure. Either she was truly engrossed in her work and didn't care what this John did, or she was a good actor.

"Here you are," she said, handing him a stoppered jar. "I don't need to tell you how to use this. Mrs. Beldam knows."

# Chapter 8

Bianca saw Banes to the door and, once she had closed it behind him, slumped against it. She stared across the room at her friend lying motionless on the board, surrounded by candles. How could this have happened? She loved Jolyn like a sister. She would have done anything for her. The grief she had tried to contain now overwhelmed her, and she unleashed its fury, sobbing uncontrollably as she sank to the floor. What if the tonic she had given Jolyn had killed her? Could she have unknowingly poisoned her own friend? She could barely think on it. She cried inconsolably, feeling her loss. Never again would she hear Jolyn's laughter or share her deepest thoughts. Her misery consumed her—and she let it. Eventually, her stuttering sobs slowed and her breathing calmed. She drew herself up and angrily dashed away her tears, determining to find the cause of Jolyn's sudden demise.

Constable Patch and the coroner believed she was responsible, and it wouldn't be long before Patch dragged her away to gaol and an uncertain fate. She cringed, imagining her head displayed on a pike overlooking London Bridge, greeting townsfolk and visitors with its silent, grim warning: *Caveat, quisquis hic ambulat.* Mind, ye who tread here.

She would prove her innocence. She held little hope that the coroner or Constable Patch would consider other suspects or possibilities, not when they could point a finger at her and be done with it. Only she had a vested interest in discovering the truth.

The thought of being accused of killing Jolyn or anyone dismayed her. Her sole intention, her reason behind all this experimentation, all this obsession with tinctures, was to help people. To willfully and meditatively harm someone was inconceivable. Though once, she *had* been forced to stab a man. And she had had hate in her heart when she did it—but that was long ago, and the memory she quickly suppressed.

Proving her innocence would not be easy. But the second, more difficult part must be her first focus. If Jolyn *was* poisoned, *who* poisoned her? And with what?

Bianca crossed the room and stood over her friend's body. She thought of what John had said once when they had come upon the corpse of a man in Denby Alley one morning. The man had suffered the mortal slash of metal between his ribs and had died where he lay. His doublet was sodden with blood. They had crouched beside him to check for a pulse; then, not finding one, Bianca had asked the body, "How did you meet such a fate?"

John, accustomed to fortune's fickle hand, had answered, "Bianca, the dead don't speak." He rifled through the man's pockets and filched a pence and an ivory toothpick. "And for that we can be glad," he said, setting the pick between his teeth in a saucy gesture.

But if there was one thing Bianca had learned in her years of observing the sick and dying, it was that the dead *do* speak.

It wasn't so long ago that she spent her mornings collecting herbs along the bank of the Thames on the way to her father's room of alchemy. She had often witnessed some poor wretch struggle in the throes of disease. She'd watch him at a respectful distance and study how he met his final breath. Was he thin with disease? Did he clutch his chest or sides? Did he gasp for breath or writhe in pain? Once he had died, she'd kneel over the body and note the coloration of the skin, whether he exhibited buboes or a rash, whether his eyes had dulled and yellowed. All this and more, she committed to memory.

So with this catalog of symptoms and maladies in mind, she concocted her salves and balms for the awful afflictions that plagued the citizens of London and Southwark.

But Bianca was not interested in being a piss prophet or in balancing humours. Prescribing remedies with no basis in anything but imagination did not interest her. She'd seen plenty of that with her mother.

Although her mother was knowledgeable in herbal remedies from the old country, she was often unsuccessful with concoctions she made from plants gathered nearby. Her mother would dispense old-world wisdom that rendered no relief for the patient, except for the loss of a few eggs or a hen in barter. Her mother's most unorthodox advice was to rub one's gums with a rusty nail for a toothache, then drive it into the ground outside of St. Paul's for continued relief.

Nor did Bianca believe her father's pursuit of the philosopher's stone, or the "elixir of life," would amount to anything more than years wasted in convoluted alchemical methodology and subservience to the vagaries of metal. As far as she could tell, his search had gotten him nowhere.

What she did believe was that plants had their own healing powers. Plants could yield a world of effects, some subtle, some not, and Bianca was consumed with learning their silent language.

She leaned over Jolyn and opened an eyelid. The pupil was dilated, a possible indication of poisoning. But Bianca had often seen pupils as large as the iris in the recently dead.

She then pried open Jolyn's mouth. Taking a candle from a holder, she leaned close to look for redness or sores on her tongue and palate. She looked for signs of swelling. Finding neither, she lowered herself on the bench and jammed a fist under her chin in thought. The tonic she had given Jolyn was a simple infusion of ginger, fennel leaves, and meadowsweet—a soothing carminative for restless stomachs. If a poison had been in the brew, it would have burned her mouth and inflamed the skin.

Instead, the tea had set in motion a fatal reaction. Jolyn had responded violently. Thinking she must help purge Jolyn of the drink, Bianca had poured rancid goat milk down her friend's throat. But why had she assumed Jolyn needed an emetic? Bianca thought back to her friend's complaint of an upset stomach. She had eaten food that had not agreed with her. Was it something her suitor had given her? Something she had eaten at the Dim Dragon Inn? Whatever it was, it had lain in wait. Something had required the tea to cause the reaction that led to death.

Bianca pushed the dwindling tallow back into its holder, then massaged her temples. Her head throbbed from fatigue, and she fought the urge to lay her head on her arm. Precious time would be lost in slumber, and she didn't know how long she had before Constable Patch showed his sniveling self and dragged her away.

Then, buried in the rush, Bianca spied the jar John had fetched for Jolyn's remedy. The label had been lost, but the contents still smelled of the familiar mix. Bianca inhaled, scrutinizing the scent of each ingredient, noting exact proportions of each. She knew these smells by heart and could detect when one ingredient overwhelmed another. With incorrect proportions, the medicinal could have the wrong effect and thereby be rendered useless.

The mixture smelled as it should. Bianca shook the contents. Enough remained so she would be able to test it. At least she would know if her brew had been to blame.

She found a clean bowl and, just to be sure nothing would skew her results, wiped the inside clean with the hem of her kirtle. Embers still glowed in her furnace, and she threw several dung patties on the fire and gave it a few pokes. As she stared at the sparking glow, Bianca tried to remember the smell of the mixture before she gave it to Jolyn. But the sequence of preparing and pouring the tea had been second nature, and she couldn't recall the smell or whether she had noticed anything wrong. She could barely even remember preparing the brew. With Jolyn and John talking and laughing, she had been distracted. Bianca thought back to the moment and her confidence faltered. She might have made a fatal mistake not checking the brew before handing it over.

Bianca pondered her error and went to the alley for a bucket of water. Fog had settled, and the air was thick with the smell of earth and moss. The cistern's slimy lid slipped from her grasp as she lifted it off to dip her bucket, and she longed for the warmth of late-spring days. They'd been in a cool, dank damp for weeks.

Just as she shut the alley door, an insistent knocking came at the front. Dreading the return of Constable Patch, she slowed near the front window and peeked through its smoke-grimed pane. Relieved to see a woman at the door, Bianca readily opened it.

"Ye must be Bianca." The woman leveled her eyes on her.

Before Bianca could utter a word, the woman pushed past and, once inside, stopped and scanned the room. Her face was void of expression. Bianca wondered if this was someone referred to her by Meddybemps, or perhaps someone who had learned of her remedies through word on the street. Bianca was in no mood to cater to a customer and was about to ask the woman her business when the woman drew in an audible, sharp breath. Her eyes had found Jolyn.

She immediately crossed the room to Jolyn. After a moment of peering down at her in silence, she drew a hand to her heart, then lightly touched Jolyn's forehead. Bianca waited for the woman to speak. Eventually, she did.

"What 'appened?" she asked.

Bianca was not about to explain anything to someone who just showed up, uninvited and unknown. She minced no words of her own. "Who are you, and why are you here?"

"Ah, forgive me," she said. "It's a bit o' a shock. I'm Mrs. Beldam. Of Barke House." Her eyes flicked over Bianca's face, then settled back on Jolyn's. "Constable Patch told me what 'appened. I came as soon as I coulds. Poor, dear girl . . ."

So this was the matron of Barke House. Bianca had sold her

concoctions but had never met her. She wasn't as she had imagined. Somehow she expected the woman to resemble a bulldog rather than the statuesque housemother who stood before her. Bianca took a breath and began to explain Jolyn's visit. She left out the part about Jolyn's stomach complaints, preferring instead to tell Mrs. Beldam that Jolyn had suddenly been gripped with convulsions that she had been helpless to stop. She saw no need to have yet another person think her complicit.

"Maybe demons was battlin' for her soul," Mrs. Beldam said, in earnest.

That demons had anything to do with mysterious behavior was an explanation that Bianca believed convenient for those too lazy to think otherwise. Granted, Bianca had witnessed plenty of strange behavior that probably could be attributed to demons. However, Jolyn was not weak in spirit and Bianca didn't believe a demon would suddenly decide to use Jolyn for a battlefield. Still, it might be best to be sure. "Had Jolyn suffered convulsions before?"

Mrs. Beldam did not answer. Instead, she asked a question of her own. "'As the Coroner pronounced a cause of death?"

"It is not proven." Bianca snuffed out a sputtering candle and hesitated. She looked up to find Mrs. Beldam studying her. "The coroner believes she was poisoned."

Astonished, Mrs. Beldam sucked in her breath and stared at Bianca. "But ye 'ave ye doubts," she said, watching the young woman's face.

"I'm not saying she wasn't poisoned. I just have to eliminate other possibilities."

Mrs. Beldam gazed around the room, her eyes settling on the pear-shaped retorts that looked like birds with long beaks made of clay. The skeletal remains of mice sat in a bowl on a table in front of her. She scrunched her nose at the peculiar mishmash of sharp and musty odors. "I've sent Banes to fetch me purgatives and rat poisons from ye."

"Aye. He left not long ago."

If the accoutrements of Bianca's profession puzzled Mrs. Beldam, she didn't let on. She refocused her gaze on Jolyn's body. "Seems I might recall her havin' one of them fits before."

"Do you remember when?"

Mrs. Beldam shook her head. "I can't say for sures."

"A week ago, longer?"

Mrs. Beldam frowned. "Maybes a week ago or so," she mumbled, staring down at Jolyn.

"Did anyone else see it?"

After some consideration she spoke. "I don't thinks anyone else was around." Mrs. Beldam's eyes wandered beyond Jolyn to the table and shelves.

"What did you do when it happened?"

"Wells, nothin'. I was in the kitchen, and I heards the thumpin' and carryin' on from her room. Then it stopped. I didn't think nothin's of it really."

"But weren't you concerned?"

Mrs. Beldam looked pointedly at Bianca. "It's a home full of women. If I ran after every sound I heard in Barke House, I'd never rest." She shook her head again and returned her gaze to Jolyn. "She 'as a good person. A right carin' young girl. Sad she ended this ways. Sos young."

"The burial is at Cross Bones tomorrow," said Bianca.

Mrs. Beldam tsked. "Shame that is. Shame the reputation that goes with bein' buried there. Shouldn't be like that. Some of the best girls I know beens put to rest there."

"Does her suitor know?" asked Bianca.

"No, naws," said Mrs. Beldam. "'Aven't seen him in some whiles." She smirked.

"Jolyn told me she expected him any day."

Mrs. Beldam didn't answer, but then shook her head dismissively.

"You don't think much of him?"

"Men come round. They find a willing love, promise the moon. Come and goes as they please. Never amounts to much. Shame this 'un fell for that. Thought she was wiser than that."

The fire in the furnace crackled, and Bianca was reminded of her task from before Mrs. Beldam arrived. She dipped a bowl into the bucket of water and set about readying the steam bath, fiddling with the damper. "I understand her suitor's name is Wynders," she said, making conversation as she worked. When Mrs. Beldam didn't respond, Bianca looked over her shoulder. The woman was stooping over Jolyn, inches from the girl's face.

"Is something wrong?" Bianca asked.

Mrs. Beldam straightened, and her eyes jumped. "Na, no," she said, shrugging.

Bianca thought her odd but turned back to the steam bath, setting a flask of water in the middle to boil.

"Well, I needs to return to Barke House," said Mrs. Beldam. She started for the door, then stopped a few feet before it. "You'll be at Cross Bones tomorrow?"

"Aye."

Mrs. Beldam flashed a quick smile. Her eyes ran around Bianca's room as if taking it all in one last time. With a final nod she saw herself out the door.

# CHAPTER 9

Like a predator to prey, the Rat Man knew where to go for the easiest pickings. He was a student of habit, even if it had only been one night of plenty.

The Rat Man steadied his wherry near the *Cristofur* for a second night, keeping her within his sights, and licked his lips with anticipation. Perhaps more delectable vermin would be released when the holds were opened to off-load goods. Fog had settled in, muting the few lamps that still glowed on shore.

The first day in port had not gone well for the owner of the *Cristofur* and her crew. When the customs authority rowed out to her mooring, he noticed only a few mates manned the decks. Perhaps the owner had purposely employed a small crew to save money on payroll. Maybe the captain had had to deal with insubordination at sea. But perhaps something else had thinned the ranks. Sickness? Disease? The customs authority cursed the doctor who usually accompanied him; he had been unable to find the piss sniffer in his usual haunts and had not cared to spend the energy or time to hunt him down. So the added burden of fishing out disease would fall on his already stooped shoulders.

Permission to board was granted, and the customs authority grimaced as he climbed the tenuous rope ladder to the deck. He was getting too old for this job, and his joints protested every time he had to scale the primitive devices, but until he married a rich widow, he was doomed to his life of drudgery.

The captain was eager to off-load the goods and that was typical, but his skittish manner and darting eyes roused the customs officer's suspicions. The captain was not one for small talk and shoved the manifest at him before he'd even set foot on deck. He offered nothing in the way of greetings or cordialities.

The customs authority studied the manifest, noted the port of trade and that ivory and silk filled the hold. He eyed the captain and looked over his shoulder at the sparsely manned vessel. "The *Cristofur* has been to Africa. Have you engaged in human trade?" asked the weary clerk.

"Nay. It's damned hard keeping a crew fed, much less fifty extra gullets." The captain excused himself to piss in the Thames. He returned with a sly, despondent smirk. "How much longer do you expect this to take? I have goods to be rid of and a crew to pay."

The authority studied the listing and dates scrawled thereon, and while he scrutinized and calculated, he glimpsed a rat scurry by in broad daylight, disappearing into the dark recess of the hold. His stomach rolled in distaste. Checking the cargo with the manifest would not be pleasant.

As he gripped the lantern he had appropriated from the first mate, he left the captain above deck and followed the officer down a flimsy set of stairs into the hold. The brush of something against his calf as he stood still letting his eyes adjust to the dark was just an appetizer.

The bolts of silks and textiles were stacked high, cramming every available cranny. He got a rough number of how high and deep and set about calculating the store, then jotted down his findings. The officer moved him to another section of the hold, separate from the other. Here, he swung the lantern over his head, illuminating several rows of ivory tusks. He checked the manifest for the reported number and found it at three hundred and fifty. Poor beasts from whence they came, but the king would be glad to collect the tax and even gladder to buy the baubles and carvings from royal artisans once they had been worked into pieces of art. He estimated the tax on the entire haul, and when he looked up finally from his arithmetic, the first officer led him hurriedly past a closed door and toward the waiting stairs to above.

But the customs authority was a seasoned emissary and knew when something didn't seem right. "What is behind that door?" he asked, stopping in front of it.

"Sleeping quarters for the men." The first mate wavered, then added, "Some are still sleeping off a rough voyage before off-loading."

The authority made a move to open the door, but the officer slid his body in between. "I wouldn't disturb a sleeping crew if I was you."

"Sir, I might as well disturb them now and save them the irri-tation of coming above deck. I have no medic, and I will have to check them myself before you are allowed to dock."

Perspiration sprang from the temples of the first mate, and the customs officer noticed.

"Is there something you rather I not see?"

The officer grumbled and seemed at a loss for words.

"Stand aside," announced the customs officer. He pushed past the mate and shouldered open the door.

True, it had been a sleeping berth. Hammocks swung from posts, and unlit lamps dangled from beams. But the vile smell of putrefaction and decay struck him as heavily as if he had been bludgeoned with a mast. In horror, he slammed the door, but not before he had seen several decomposing bodies being gnawed apart by rats.

He fled for the stairs and escaped to the upper deck, gasping and heaving, bending over the gunwale to lose the contents of his stomach. "Sir," he said, turning back to face the captain and wiping his mouth on his sleeve, "this ship is hereby quarantined until further notice." He gulped in fresh air before speaking. "Remove the *Cristofur* to the yellow buoy forthwith and await my directive."

Uninterested in the captain's reply, he stuffed the manifest into his doublet and nearly ran to the rope ladder suspended over his skiff. He flung his leg over the side and descended the unsteady contraption as quickly as his overweight, arthritic body would allow. He had gotten halfway down before he saw what was waiting for him in his rowboat below. Choking down what was left of his undigested meat pie, he drew his anlace and speared seven rats eagerly waiting for a ride to shore.

After disposing their furry bodies into the Thames, he hollered to the ship's captain, "Do not presume to off-load or dock anytime soon. You must await orders from the king's ministry or else feel the effect of the king's guard, sir." With that, he hastily sat himself in the middle of his skiff and rowed like hell for shore.

But all this was unknown to the ferrier.

He merely saw that the *Cristofur* had changed her mooring from the night before. The yellow buoy bobbed nearby, appearing from out of the fog, and he duly noted its portent.

Two hundred years ago, the Black Death had raged across the king's isle, claiming half the population. The symptoms of the disease were always the same. What began as a small lump swelled to the size of an apple and turned as red. Maybe a man noticed one near his groin when he loosened his trousers to relieve himself. Perhaps he would notice an egg-sized tumor on his lover's neck when he bent to kiss her there. The swelling was disconcerting, but what followed was even more so.

Inevitably the bubo would darken to a deep bruised purple, then black. It spawned. Other buboes sprang from once smooth skin. Joints ached until it became difficult to fetch water or even eat. Fever and delirium took the victim beyond his conscious world. If a leech was attached to rid the patient of his ill humour, the exuded blood would be black and vile in smell. One can't bleed a man dry, can one? Nothing could be done for the victim except to make the sign of the cross and get away posthaste.

Since that dark time the scourge had wreaked havoc but did not devastate the populace as it once had. But like a demon, its evil intent was well known and feared by all. Rarely spoken of except in hushed tones and never completely forgotten, it patiently hunted its prey like a cat watching a mouse hole. And so it lay in wait.

The Rat Man cruised the circumference of the *Cristofur*, scanning for an errant rodent treading water for shore. He gave chase to one determined creature that had managed to dodge the ferryman's first attempt by diving under the hull of his boat but was assuredly snatched up when it surfaced for air on the other side. It took the Rat Man two whacks to dispense with what usually only took one.

The windfall he'd experienced earlier was not to be his fortune tonight. Well, no matter, this one was fat enough for two. He ripped off its head with his pointed teeth and spat it into the water, then sucked long on its marrow. But as he savored the creature's vital blood, he discovered this one had a disagreeable aftertaste. It was tainted.

He tossed the carcass into the water and watched it disappear below the fog-kissed surface of the Thames. *"Nos omnes perimus, sed non sine pugna,"* he muttered under his breath. We all die, but not without a fight.

# CHAPTER 10

Beneath a dreary sky, a contingent of Jolyn's acquaintances gathered at the cemetery to see her body laid to rest. Or, as in this case, unrest. That so many had collected to see her interred should have given pause to the sexton. Perhaps he should have sought a holy person to spout a couple of "ashes to ashes and dust to dusts" just to be sure he wouldn't get any grief for his unenviable task. Instead, he continued his digging at the single women's cemetery, grumbling his displeasure with an audience while flinging shovelfuls of Thames river bottom over his shoulder.

Out of sight of the nearest parish church, the lumpy land of Cross Bones was within sight of the Clink, a prison harboring those who had offended the king's religion. That it should be overwrought with skeletons was testament to London's preference to dispose of the dispossessed within the confines of its shady sister, Southwark. This had been going on for hundreds of years, but the current coterie of onlookers did not know, much less care, what had gone on before they took their first gulp of British air.

Mrs. Beldam was present along with Pandy and Kara, Jolyn's

most familiar housemates. Banes stood to their side and a little behind, content to be ignored, and studied their figures at leisure.

Bianca stood opposite the women of Barke House. She had abandoned testing the contents of the tea when a parishioner arrived to take the corpse. Bianca had pleaded with him to let her cleanse her friend's body and anoint it with hyssop and cistus oils for burial. She had filled Jolyn's mouth with dried lavender and rosemary to drive away bad vapors and then found a rough woven cloth to wrap her. That night, Bianca had not slept well. Her mind could not rest. She kept hearing the accusations and pondering the symptoms of Jolyn's last moments.

Bianca found it difficult to watch the sexton finish his digging. Each scrape of the shovel seemed louder than the one before. A group of muckrakers arrived at the gate, laughing and joking, their voices intruding on the solemnity of the graveyard. They ambled across the grounds toward the small gathering, lowering their voices when faced with the indignant stares of those already waiting. Bianca had never met any of them, but could put names to faces just by their appearances, which Jolyn had been expert in describing.

There was Becket, a toothless codger, bony and reeking of the mud and stray pigs he pleasured in. Then there was Smythe, lanky and lithe, a "diver" working in tandem with Mackney, who was too old and pudgy to wiggle through windows anymore. The two ingratiated themselves with the watch in the borough so long as they gave him a share of their pickings. A few other muckrakers or desperate sorts milled about, shifty-eyed and restless, though intent to bid Jolyn farewell. But there was one who stood apart from the others. He caught Bianca's eye because he was the beneficiary of Mrs. Beldam's evil one. Bianca didn't know who he could be; he fit no character that Jolyn had described.

He moved away from the gathering and withdrew a small flask to take a swig. Bianca moved to observe him better and continued to survey the contingent of rascals and lowlifes. She was surprised when John appeared at the cemetery gate and crossed the grounds, finding her in the gathering, then averting his eyes as if he were there for a casual stroll. He came and stood next to her. Neither said a word. They each shifted their weight from one leg to the other and cast sidelong glances.

At last the sexton stabbed his shovel in the pile of dirt next to the grave. He leaned out of the pit and started to tug Jolyn's shroud toward its edge.

"Shouldn't someone say something?" said John.

Bianca agreed but was unable to think what would be worthy of her dear friend. Finally, as the sexton pulled Jolyn's body into the grave with a grunt and thud, she spoke out.

"'For the living know that they shall die: but the dead know not any thing, neither have they any more a reward; for the memory of them is forgotten. Also their love, and their hatred, and their envy, is now perished; neither have they any more a portion for ever in any thing that is done under the sun.'" She wasn't sure if she had remembered the verses correctly, but she thought them appropriate and fitting.

The onlookers "hear, heared" their assents as if she had offered them another round of drinks. The women of Barke House stared fixedly across at her as if trying to figure out what manner of nonsense she had just spouted.

"May God have mercy on her soul," finished Bianca. She stared down at her friend as the sextant threw a shovelful of dirt on her shroud. Unable to watch him roll other bodies on top, Bianca stepped back and observed the characters around her.

"Sees, he never gave a piss for her, else he would have been here. 'E should have seen to it she didn't end up in a community grave of wanton women. Jus' proves to ye, he didn't really care." Pandy pulled her shawl up over her exposed shoulders, for her bodice exposed more skin than was sensible given the chill in the air.

"Aws, shuts your flap," said Kara. "Just because he didn't show don't mean nothin's. He may still be away."

"Oh, I bet he knows," said Pandy. "Anyways, we'll soon see what his true feelings are."

"Enough of you twos," said Mrs. Beldam. "Ye thinks this is about you?" She shot them a harsh look, then settled her eyes back on the lone rascal standing apart from the others. He was solid and blocky in build, filthy with dried clay on his face and clothes. Perhaps a muckraker, he had the appearance of one.

Bianca watched as Mrs. Beldam hastily crossed herself and pushed past the two girls. She pursued the young man, who had turned and sauntered off.

"I'm sorry about last night," said John, offering to bridge the silent gulf that had grown between him and Bianca.

Bianca shrugged. "No matter," she mumbled. She was more concerned with watching Mrs. Beldam. The matron caught the young man's arm, but they were enough out of earshot that Bianca could not hear what was being said. Pandy and Kara still quarreled, and if she was to hear what concerned the owner of Barke House, she would have to abandon John and his efforts to make amends. Without another word to John, she drifted away and ranged closer.

"I'm trying to apologize," said John, following after her. "You can at least acknowledge I'm here, couldn't you?" His voice rose in frustration, and Bianca shushed him harshly. She turned back to try to hear what the pair were saying.

John followed her gaze to a young rogue, rugged and coarse in looks but possessing a certain allure for women who liked dangerous men. Not exactly the kind of fellow who'd typically attract Bianca's eye, he thought, but then, he could never be sure.

"I get the feeling you don't care if I was here or not. You would be just as happy if I left you alone!"

Bianca focused on Mrs. Beldam and tried to read her lips. The rogue shook his head in response.

"I'm talking to you," John insisted.

"John, can't you keep quiet just this once?" Bianca hissed. She was trying to appear nonchalant, but it didn't matter to Mrs. Beldam and the young man. Mrs. Beldam looked to be harshly questioning him about something to which he claimed ignorance.

"If it's silence you want from me, I'll give you plenty!" John stalked off, brushing past the conspicuous pair, who looked up, saw Bianca watching them, then broke away from each other.

Bianca sighed in exasperation. John had a flair for the dramatic, probably learned from years observing the clientele at the Tern's Tempest. Drink and turmoil made terrible bedfellows, but it was the norm for a young man who'd known no family but the characters who frequented the seedy boozing ken. Bianca watched him march out of the cemetery. He didn't even glance back at her. She'd smooth over his wounded feelings and set them right, but first, she had more pressing matters.

Bianca's aggravation was replaced by something even more dismal, and it came in the form of Constable Patch strolling through the gate. Bianca fell in behind Pandy and Kara, hoping she could slip by without his notice. But apparently the constable had arrived with the sole intent of finding her.

"Bianca Goddard. I've been looking for ye." Constable Patch stepped in front of her, practically twitching with delight at having caught her trying to sneak out. "I see ye have successfully made your friend to rest." Patch nodded at the sexton leaning against a heap of dirt and swigging from a flask.

Bianca kept her silence, knowing her mockery could end in worse than what she already feared.

"The coroner has ruled Jolyn Carmichael's death a poisoning, and since the deceased expired in your presence, ye is the likely culprit. I must, with the power vested in me by the just and honorable citizens of Southwark," said Patch, playing to the gawping onlookers, "and by the power of His Majesty, King Henry of the Eighth, noble and wise liege of our gentle isle, prolific maker of wives and taker of lives, religious reformer and papal scourge, arrest ye for the murder of the most regrettable death of Jolyn Carmichael."

"How does a person dying in the presence of another make one guilty?" argued Bianca. "Poisons can take days, even weeks to kill. Jolyn was with me when the poison finally overcame her, but I did not poison her."

If there was a benefit to living in Southwark, it was that its residents knew criminal malfeasance when they saw it and weren't timid to voice their dissent. Before Patch could even reach for his scraggly beard, an unruly mob was shouting and barking displeasure.

Mackney, well schooled in the vagaries of enforcement officers, spoke movingly of a brother wrongly accused of purse snatching, for which his hand was lopped off. Unable to work, he took to begging outside of St. Paul's and was later thrown in the Fleet Prison for not having a license to beg. There he perished from starvation, a slow, painful death, unable to fight for the paltry scraps of food they tossed in his cell.

This further incensed the crowd, and they grew increasingly contentious, to the point of Patch fearing for his own person. His ill-timed public condemnation was his own undoing. Who would have thought a cemetery would be fertile ground for a riot?

The indignant constable scrambled up a mound of fresh graves and began to shout over the pack of raucous grievers. He hoped bluster and the power of public office might save him, but eventually he cowed to their jeering, though not without a concession of his own. "I will honor your wishes to conduct an investigation into the murder of Jolyn Carmichael. If I am unable to find the murderer, then I will arrest Bianca Goddard and charge her with the crime . . . since, after all, she *is* the most likely offender," he couldn't help but add. This last aside caused more grumbling, and a clod of dirt was thrown, just missing his head, but at least Bianca was saved from the Clink's putrid accommodations, if only for one night.

Bianca had hoped to avoid the squirrely Patch long enough to find Jolyn's murderer and cause of death, whether it be natural or otherwise. She had precious little time.

# CHAPTER 11

Robert Wynders stared at the sign outside Chudderly Shipping before taking a breath and heaving open the door. The shipping company had been founded by his wife's grandfather during Henry VII's reign when the king amassed a fortune in illicitly traded alum. Philip Chudderly had made enough money fattening the king's coffers that he was afforded some latitude and had continued to profit his company in commodities benefiting the king and other nobility.

Robert Wynders had not been born of this trade but came to Chudderly Shipping by way of his late father's employment there. His father had a special acumen for keeping the books. Not only was he expert in reducing the taxes owed the king's Exchequer of Receipt, but he also smoothed the way for any additional deals that could weight the pockets of both parties.

Philip Chudderly held the Wynderses in such high regard that when his granddaughter came of age, there proved no more propitious endeavor than to join the two families in wedlock. Twenty years ago, Robert Wynders had the looks and charm for such a position and he held much promise. Now he possessed neither. The same could be said of his wife. The bloom was off the rose, and she'd lost those petals within their first year of marriage.

Wynders climbed the long flight of stairs to the second level, where the Chudderly offices looked out over the river Thames. Only the most moneyed businesses had such an address on London Bridge. Yet their only advantage, thought Wynders as he labored up the stairs, was their privies emptied directly into the water below.

He reached the landing and paused to catch his breath before entering to speak with Sarah's father. He so hoped his wife had busied herself elsewhere this morning. Couldn't she visit the dressmaker's or run the help ragged like other women of her position?

With a resigned sigh, Wynders opened the varnished oak door and stepped into the office.

He sought to have a private word with Thomas, apart from the employed minions who kept the shipping company running smoothly. However, not only was the office charged with a feeling of alarm, but when he stepped into the room, the collective agitation focused on him. The accountant looked up from his ledger, his ink-stained fingers frozen round his pen in midair. A merchant whose cargo had just arrived in port glared at him, and a messenger tipped his cap to Mr. Chudderly and quickly sidled past Wynders and out the door.

Thomas Chudderly stiffened at the sight of him. He hurriedly ushered the merchant out, appeasing him with promises he could not keep. When he'd closed the door and had listened to the man's final footfall on the stairs, he turned and faced his son-in-law. "Robert," he said, "what is this matter of our ship?"

"Sir, I've spoken to the customs authority—"

"So have I," said Thomas. "The *Cristofur* has been moved to quarantine."

"A matter of protocol, sir."

"Protocol is an inspection. A requisite quarantine might happen; however, the *Cristofur* has been moved there indefinitely. I've no information for how long."

"Sir, it is not unprecedented for a ship's crew to take ill during a journey."

"Do not speak to me as if I know nothing." Thomas Chudderly's eyes bored through Wynders so that he felt the wall behind him must be smoking.

"Sir, if I may explain—"

"Oh, you will explain," said his father-in-law. "Of that you may be certain." Thomas Chudderly motioned Wynders to his office, then glared round at the wide-eyed vassals of his employ, who dived back into their respective tasks. Chudderly pulled the door firmly closed.

Robert Wynders did not sit because his wife had the only other chair. Sarah had her eyebrow cocked and a haughty look on her face. She did not greet him. Her fingernails garnered more concern than his entrance.

Thomas Chudderly walked round his table and sat. He rested his hands on the armrests and waited.

"Apparently the ship took on unexpected stowaways," said Wynders evenly.

Chudderly gave a little snort. "Apparently."

"We have had dealings with the port of Genoa before. The area is heavily populated, and the clime stays relatively warm year round. Any pestilence or bad air will fester in such conditions. But it is company policy to have our captains inspect the ships before they depart."

"It is our policy, yes. But explain how it did not prevent our current predicament."

"I can question the captain."

"Questioning after the fact does not rid us of the problem now."

"I understand, sir. However, I may impress upon the captain that we are not pleased and that his dismissal may be imminent."

"Imminent?" Thomas Chudderly slapped his hand on the desk. "It is certain."

Wynders nodded.

"It is your responsibility to oversee these matters. Why was no skiff dispatched?"

"Per protocol, a skiff was sent on her arrival." Wynders cleared his throat. "It is just that . . ." He glanced at Sarah. "We were caught off guard. It was nearly morning when the ship arrived."

Thomas Chudderly's nostrils flared. "This has not been the first time our ships have sat in port while products rot in their holds. Not only have I tradesmen and workers ready to off-load, but I have the king's exchequer watching. Movement of goods during quarantine warrants steep penalties, as you well know." Thomas Chudderly rose to his feet. Rather than berate his son-in-law in front of his daughter, like he wanted, like Robert deserved, Chudderly stalked to the window and glared out at the Thames.

It was not the first time Wynders had suffered his father-in-law's scorn in front of Sarah. By now, he should have been more resilient. By now, he should have had ample time to prove his worth to the company. But it wasn't for lack of trying that he was unable to please Thomas. Wynders simply lacked the brilliance of his father, and it plagued him like a disease. Thomas always found fault with Wynders's method—be it trivial or imagined.

Wynders dared not interject. Instead, he gazed at the family crest hanging on the carved walnut wall in front of him. It wasn't so much a family crest as a conceit commissioned by Sarah's grandfather. To the uninformed, it appeared the family was descended from nobility. But Wynders knew otherwise.

The crest was a shield edged in gilt and painted in bold scarlet and black, divided into thirds. One third of the crest held three tridents, symbolizing each generation of Chudderly. Though, thought Wynders as he glanced at his barren wife, the heir to the shipping magnate had not been produced.

Opposite the tridents was a cockatrice, a beast with the body of a dragon and the head of a rooster. Such a hideous creature for a family crest, though he could not think of a more appropriate mascot to represent the likes of the Chudderlys.

"How shall you proceed?" asked Thomas, startling Wynders from his thoughts.

For the first time since he'd walked in, Sarah stopped admiring her cuticles and looked up.

"I shall take care of the problem, sir. I shall speak to the customs authority and dispatch the . . . er . . . stowaways."

"And how shall you dispatch them?" asked Sarah.

Wynders flinched at the sound of his wife's voice. He would have preferred her to continue studying her fingernails rather than remind him of her presence. Without looking at her, he explained that he would procure a measure of rat poison for the *Cristofur.*

"But what of the sailors' bodies?" she persisted.

Did she think she was capable of running Chudderly Shipping herself? Wynders blamed her father for indulging her in this notion. She had the wiles of a spoiled child and the competitiveness of a noticeably absent male sibling.

"I shall have them removed and given proper burial."

Thomas Chudderly continued to stare out the window. "Expensive, considering it should not have happened." He was silent a moment, then added, "You shall incur the cost since it is a result of your negligence."

Wynders knew it would not serve him to argue. Quarrelling in front of his wife would only make for a more miserable existence at home.

Sarah's expression conveyed what she did not say. Yet again her husband had proved a disappointment. It was of no consequence to her that Robert's wages would be docked. Her father took care that she had everything she needed and wanted. So why hadn't she divorced him? Divorce was something the king did. Besides, Robert did serve a purpose. She could heap a lifetime of petulance upon his shoulders, and he would let her. On the occasions that they appeared in public, he presented as a caring husband and competent provider—even as an asset to the family business. It was a code of conduct to which Robert subscribed, and as long as he did not publically humiliate her or Chudderly Shipping, she saw no reason to change any of it

Wynders resented paying the burial expenses for a bunch of dead sailors. But he had expected as much. Shouldn't sickness and disease be an implicit cost of doing business? After all, the shipping trade was fraught with liability. Storms capsized ships, ships ran aground, crews mutinied. If Sarah weren't presiding over their meeting, he would have pointed this out to his father-in-law. But she *was* there, and so he remained composed and respectful—though inside, he could scarce tolerate the humiliation.

"If that is all, sir, I have much to take care of," he said.

Thomas Chudderly dismissed him, and just as Wynders's hand gripped the door, Sarah called him back.

Wynders yielded to her appeal. "Sarah?" He swaddled her name with as much temperance and feigned accord as he could muster. He even met her eyes.

"Bear in mind that the Chudderly reputation and good name must be preserved. Do not embarrass us."

# CHAPTER 12

Bianca shook the remnants of Jolyn's concoction clinging to the sides of the jar. She knew she must brew the leftover tea and test it, but in truth, she feared the results. What if she *had* poisoned Jolyn? How would she prove it was an accident? The constable was certain of her guilt and as immovable as the Tower of London.

Bianca set the jar on the table and recalled the people who had attended Jolyn's burial. She remembered one face in particular. Jolyn had mentioned that a muckraker had accused her of stealing and that he had hoped to shame her into returning whatever he believed she had stolen. Bianca didn't know the fellow whom Mrs. Beldam had confronted at Cross Bones, but their exchange had been heated. If he was that muckraker, she didn't expect him to be forthcoming, especially if he had any business with Jolyn, but she would gauge for herself if he was hiding anything.

With his face still fresh in her mind, Bianca grabbed her coif and plopped it on her head as she headed for the door. Just as she lifted the latch, a hand held the handle on the opposite side.

"Bianca, my dainty dove. Where might you be to?"

"Meddybemps," said Bianca, surprised and more than a little annoyed. "I haven't got time. What do you want?"

The streetseller removed his cap, ignoring her desire to leave. "I've done an able way of selling your salves, my pet. I have your monies, and I've come for more liniments." He stepped inside her room of Medicinals and Physickes and immediately sneezed. "I prefer the chicken feathers of Cheapside to whatever it is you diddle with here. I won't be longer than you can stand me."

He loped over to the large table and pushed aside crockery to clear a space. "What say you to this?" Making sure she was watching, he dumped the contents of a purse onto the board and whisked away the leather bag with a flourish. His itinerant eye rolled with satisfaction.

Bianca had never seen so many coins fall from his purse. She came and stood over the table, her eyes wide. She would have money for new ingredients, food, and rent for another month, maybe more. Her mind ran with possibilities; then a sudden grim reality set in. What good was money if she was hanging from a noose?

"It's . . ." Bianca stepped back.

"Breathtaking?" finished Meddybemps. He saw her dark mood and sought to cheer her. His features full of animation and drama, he began to patter—

> Of ten and seven years you've seen,
> Of thick and thin but mostly lean,
>> Is there still a better fate
>> Than standing at good fortune's gate?
> A gate of gilded, fine-wrought gold,
> Of hopes and dreams as yet untold,
>> Seductively she lures you there
>> To cockle you and leave you bare.
> No promises or vows to trust,
> Your good intents have turned to dust,
>> And still you love and pine for more,
>> Poor fool distraught at fortune's door.

Hey nonny nonny, a dunstical fool I be,
When given thrice a chance to go,
I'll stay on bended knee.


Meddybemps danced a jig, his lanky frame and elbows jutting and thin legs bending like a nattily dressed skeleton.

She smiled, though she tried not to. After she tired of his performance, she announced gravely, "I've been accused of poisoning Jolyn."

Meddybemps straightened, and his face grew serious. "So I've heard."

"What? Is it common knowledge?"

"No. At least not yet. I saw John and he told me."

Bianca grumbled, and her pale complexion grew even more ashen. "What did he say?" Then, she quickly added, "Don't answer that," and looked away. "Constable Patch would have dragged me off if it hadn't been for the muckrakers attending the burial."

"Constable Patch is a yammering lob. He has been after me to show him my license to vend. Such utter cack. No one cares but him." Meddybemps wiped his eyes with the palm of his hand. He was used to foul smells, but sometimes Bianca's room rivaled the worst London had to offer.

"Well, he and the tax collector." Bianca smirked.

Meddybemps picked up a bowl and dipped a finger in and tasted. He grimaced, then set it down. "In all the years we've been friends, I've never seen a murderous streak about you. Patch is misguided, if not a little daft."

"If I don't prove my innocence and find out how she died, then I'll be thrown in the cage, then hanged."

"Nah, I won't let that happen to you."

"I doubt you could stop it."

Meddybemps's eye rolled into the back of his head as if an answer lurked behind his brain. "I know plenty of stews that would be willing to hide you for a few days. Patch hates to deal with some of the more randy ones." He snickered. "His genitories are fodder for ardent mocking." Meddybemps's eye quivered with amusement.

"I'll take my chances." Bianca wasn't keen on spending time in such a place.

Meddybemps shook out his cap and returned it to his nearly bald scalp. "Much as I rue saying it, I suppose you could leave these parts."

Bianca had only been as far as Spitalfields to the north and Horsleydown to the south. While her sense of adventure and taste for the exotic perpetually called her, a fear of robbers and other highwaymen outside the limits of London prevented her from venturing far. She'd heard tales of counterfeit cranks, rufflers, and other lowlifes preying on unsuspecting travelers. Surviving a trek on the roads beyond took a good deal of wiliness and knowledge of deceptive sorts if you hoped to arrive unscathed at your destination. While she'd had plenty of education on the streets of London, the surrounding countryside was a different matter. "Where would I go? Where *could* I go?"

"My plum, don't worry yourself over such matters. I'm sure you'll find a way out of this." Meddybemps flashed a broad smile. "If all fails, you have a young man who'd see to your safety."

John. They had parted on bad terms, and Bianca knew she shouldn't have ignored, then disparaged him. She hoped he understood her preoccupation and would eventually forgive her—if she lived long enough. "I'm not so sure he'd help me."

"Don't spout such rot! Why you put him off is still a mystery to me. Love should not be taken for granted." Meddybemps grabbed a flask and waved it at her. "It isn't something you can easily concoct, like your potions."

Bianca had known John since she was twelve and cutting purses at Cheapside. She'd been caught snatching an old woman's purse, and if John hadn't distracted the ward by kicking him in the shin, she could have had a finger lopped off. As the ward gripped his painful leg, John had grabbed Bianca's arm, and the two of them ran past crates of squawking chickens and carts heaped with turnips. They ran through the streets and back alleys until they reached safety in a soggy graveyard. At the time, she had feigned indifference, but if he hadn't rescued her, she would have ended in a bad way. She knew that, and while it wasn't her nature to heap thanks and kisses on him, eventually his persistence and cunning had won her admiration. And as they grew older, she had to admit, he had won her heart.

Meddybemps had given his sermon about her inability to trust too many times for her to suffer through yet another. But she *did* trust John. What she wasn't so sure of—what she couldn't trust—was love. Love was fickle.

King Henry was no doubt already courting his sixth wife. If love had been so enduring, would he have divorced two and beheaded another couple? Not that she took cues from their swollen sovereign. She just needed to be sure. But even more than that, a commitment to John would mean giving up her chemistries. If she couldn't pursue her passion, she knew she would grow resentful and sullen. Chemistries fascinated her and kept her cheered. Even John couldn't engage her mind the way experimentation could. Until she felt otherwise, she knew she had to pursue this first.

She looked at Meddybemps waving the flask of liquid and assuming a pose of authority. Meddybemps had a reputation that stretched from the brothels in London to the ones in Southwark. He'd even seduced her mother. She thought of this, and her resentment surfaced. "Who are you to lecture me in love?"

Meddybemps frowned and set down the flask. "I admit constancy is not my best trait, but I do have some years of wisdom. I have avoided marriage's anchor of responsibility by loving whom I please and committing to no one. Am I happier? I have no one to nurse me when I ail and no meal to greet me at the end of the day, no one to share my bed on cold nights. But the only mouth I have to feed is my own. It is like your measure scales." He picked the rusty balance off the table and tapped one side to send it tottering. "Which is better? You must consider what is more valuable to you. John is on one side, and your obsession with medicinals is on the other. Only you can weigh which is more important." He set the scale down on the table. "Maybe you can find a balance. But only you can measure what you need."

Bianca headed for the door. "Before I can think on such matters, I need to make sure that I'll be around to even try. If I don't find out who killed Jolyn and why, then I will hang at Newgate and you can spend all the time you want shaking your head and telling me how I've wasted my life. Unfortunately, though, I won't be around to hear."

Meddybemps was used to Bianca's occasional outbursts. He let her rail and kick until she had spent her anger. She was learning what it was to be a woman, and he was glad to see it. "Well, can I at least collect some more salves and balms to fill my cart?"

Bianca petulantly threw open the door. "Take what you want."

She took a step and bounced off a figure standing there, much like a wall and about as solid. She stumbled back and looked at the man blocking her exit.

"Is this the room of Medicinals and Physickes?" he asked, peering down his nose.

Bianca stared up at him. She couldn't be sure this man wasn't some sort of king's minion or guard. He was dressed in finery, wearing a doublet of maroon velvet decorated in gold braid, the collar reaching halfway up his neck and trimmed with a modest ruff. An épée swung at his side, hung from leather crossing his chest. She gulped but did not respond.

"Are you Bianca?"

Bianca glanced over her shoulder at Meddybemps, who ticked his head reassuringly. She faced the man. "I am."

He removed a pheasant-plumed hat and entered Bianca's room with a proprietary air.

From behind, Bianca peeked out at Meddybemps and mouthed a silent "Who is this?" to which Meddybemps shrugged and made a face.

The man gazed around the room. "You sell rat poisons?"

Bianca followed him back inside and closed the door. "I do."

"I'm in need of a fair quantity."

Relieved that the man was a customer and not someone enlisted by Constable Patch to haul her away, she asked, "What would you call 'fair'?"

He fixed his gaze on Meddybemps, sizing up the scraggly streetseller and deciding the knave peculiar but not a threat. Still looking at Meddybemps, he turned his head toward Bianca. "I need enough to rid a ship of vermin."

Bianca received the request for rat poison regularly. She did not think it particularly unusual, and if she could hurry up and take care of him, she could get to the Dim Dragon Inn before any more time elapsed. She'd never met the man before, and usually when a new customer arrived, she was curious enough to ask how he'd found her. But all she could think of was getting to the Dim Dragon Inn. She ignored Meddybemps's ogling and emptied the rat poison into a pouch and cinched it closed.

The man accepted the poison and instructions with a polite tip of his head and paid her generously. Without further offering or questions from Bianca, the man left as briskly as he had come.

Meddybemps raised his brows as the door closed. "You should have asked his business."

"I doubt he would have answered." Bianca stuffed the coins into her purse and jammed it deep into a pocket on her skirt. She then helped herself to several coins Meddybemps had brought and stashed the rest in a jar on a shelf. She had enough for a pottle pot and pie in case she had to spend any amount of time waiting for the muckraker to turn up at the tavern.

Before she could collect her scarf, Meddybemps was out the door.

She hollered after him as he shoved his cart into an alcove next to her rent. "Don't you want to stock your cart with more medi-cines?"

Meddybemps shook his head, waving her off. "Later, my dove."

If she wasn't going to find out about this puffed-up prillywig, then he would.

# CHAPTER 13

If Meddybemps admitted the truth, it wasn't so much curiosity about the man as it was about stealing his purse. He knew money when he saw it. And though this nattily dressed stranger was probably a few years his junior and twice as brawny, Meddybemps had years of sneakiness and knavery under his belt. Not to mention a razor-sharp stiletto.

He had hurried after the pompous prig and glimpsed him turning a corner onto Maze Lane. He took chase, scampering up the muddy road as fast as his bony legs could take him. Peeking around the corner, he watched the man stride confidently up the lane, ignoring the queans camped on stoops of houses of ill repute. Such willpower was impressive.

Meddybemps followed, lingering with the ladies long enough to leer at the pickings, then remembered the goal was coin first and pleasure second. He galloped to catch up with the man as he swept down the lane, looking as purposeful and focused as Meddybemps would never be.

A tavern door flew open and a brawl spilled onto the street, bringing with it the requisite clientele to taunt and place bets. All the better to get lost in the ruckus and remain inconspicuous, but Meddybemps bristled at the thought that someone might spy his prey and get there before him.

Again the man skirted the distraction. He turned a corner, and the streetseller thought he might be heading for London Bridge, but oddly, the man turned in the opposite direction. Well, perhaps the blowfart didn't know his way in Southwark—which was to Meddybemps's advantage.

He trailed his quarry at a fair distance, wondering where he might go. The man had no choice but to stay his course as the street wove along the Thames. There were no intersecting lanes except a narrow alley farther down toward Morgan's Lane. Meddybemps anticipated his route and cut back and across to the alley's dreary entrance. Eventually the man would pass at its intersection—the perfect spot to nab his prey. Meddybemps crabbed down the shadowy wall and waited.

Meddybemps tilted his ear and strained to hear the sound of sucking mud that would warn of his victim's arrival. Then, he would jump from the alley and thrust the knife into the man's liver. He hoped no one would see. He knew these undertakings were better left for the cover of night, but when the opportunity presents itself, mused Meddybemps, take it.

Still, his caution niggled him, and he peeked into the lane to see who was around. A doddering old woman inched up the street, probably too blind to see, and a pig rooted through a festering pile of kitchen scraps. Neither posed much of a worry. Farther down he saw his intended prey. Meddybemps drew his knife for the ready.

It wasn't so long ago that Meddybemps had helped Bianca save her father from an untimely death. The old puffer had been accused of trying to poison the king. A man had died, and Bianca swore the blame was wrongly placed, but she never said who the culprit was. Meddybemps had helped her slip into the Tower to find her father and prove his innocence. Meddybemps shook his head. Poor girl. Now *she* was accused of murder. What was it with that family?

At least the mother didn't have any murderous tendencies—so far as he could tell. She was a lovely creature, that one. Dark hair like Bianca's, but with cleavage a man could drown in. Meddybemps talked down the bulge in his pants. Shame the father didn't hang. Damn shame.

Still, Meddybemps adored Bianca. She was as a daughter to him. Smart, cunning, a bit of the thief about her, but she had a kind heart. Too much so for her own good, and he'd told her as much. But who was he to tell her anything? She had a wit about her. She'd figure it out.

Meddybemps felt the damp seep through his thin jerkin. Was he leaning against a wet wall? Aggravated, he stepped away and pulled the scratchy fabric from his body. Soon he could be warming himself by a fire in a tavern. Meddybemps sniffed with irritation. Where *was* that prillywig?

Another minute passed, and Meddybemps thought about a bowl of beef stew and ale he'd soon buy. Not ale, no, he'd not chance his hard-gotten money on that unpredictable swill. He didn't trust anyone in Southwark to give him a decent pottle pot. He'd get sack. And he'd go to the better part of London to buy it.

Meddybemps fumed with impatience. He peered out into the lane even though he knew if the man saw him, the element of surprise would be gone.

But his villainy was not meant to be.

Meddybemps caught sight of the man just as he disappeared through a door. The streetseller cursed his bad luck. He wasn't about to wait in a dank alley until God knew when. He might as well retrieve his cart and head back to market. An honest coin was better for his riddled soul than one got dishonestly, though at this point, neither heaven nor hell would want his soul.

He started back up Bermondsey Street, pausing in front of the establishment to spit in its general direction. He scrutinized the just closed door and tutted at what he discovered. Perhaps this might be of interest to Bianca. The man had gone into Barke House.

# CHAPTER 14

Banes woke to the sound of voices coming from the entry of Barke House. He pulled the rag out of a peephole and watched as Wynders and Pandy spoke.

Apparently the ship's agent had not been told of Jolyn's death, and so Banes grew curious to see how the philanderer took the news. He eagerly anticipated his response, though he did feel slightly sorry that the man had to hear it from Pandy and not someone else.

Pandy was light of character and had harbored a profound dislike for Jolyn. Banes could only imagine how the news would feel coming from someone so cold, and with a vested interest in retribution.

But Wynders did not respond as Banes had expected. He did not crumble from learning that he would never see his young love again. Instead, the man accepted the news in silence and immediately asked for Mrs. Beldam. Didn't he believe Pandy? Perhaps he needed to hear it from a more reliable source.

Banes sniffed. These merchant types were a cold breed indeed.

Banes pressed his ear against the thin plaster wall. He couldn't hear their muffled exchange, so he pressed his eye against the hole and saw the callous dastard push her away. Pandy fell against a wall and cursed after him as he strode from the room.

As Pandy dissolved into tears, Banes stuffed the rag back into the peephole and ran to another. This one had a view of the kitchen, albeit an obstructed one since the missus had rearranged the board and storage bins. Still, he could see well enough and no one knew the better.

Mrs. Beldam was at the table sipping ale when Wynders arrived.

"Is it true?"

Mrs. Beldam carefully set down her cup as if it were made of parchment. "If you is referring to Jolyn, it is."

Wynders, as cold as January, didn't even ask when she died. Or how. Banes took a step back and tutted. How sad. And to think Jolyn had been so enamored of the man. The girl had deserved better. Banes returned to the hole, but was annoyed that Wynders had shifted so that his back was to him and he was unable to see his face.

"Well," said Wynders. And in a low voice he said something that Banes could barely hear.

Banes blinked, unable to decipher the mumbled words.

Mrs. Beldam did not immediately answer. She stirred her ale with a finger, as if hoping to rouse the words from its bottom, but she did not reply.

"Then, I am done here." Wynders puffed out his barrel chest.

Banes saw Mrs. Beldam's ruddy complexion turn an exceptional shade of plum. He took some satisfaction seeing the missus so deflated, but he was stymied by Wynders's indifference. He pressed his hand against the wall to steady himself and stared intently for some sort of clue—a facial tic, a whispered grievance, anything that might help him understand.

Nothing. The man returned his feathered cap to his head, and Banes thought he resembled a rooster with a strangely sprouted plume. Gentlemen's fashions were so peculiar. A man should try to resemble a nobler creature, not some bird with overloud lungs.

"Good day," said Wynders, turning to leave.

He had not taken two steps when Mrs. Beldam called him back. She tapped a finger on her cup. "This is not the end of it," she said, regaining her characteristic menace. "Don't assume that I won't find another way." Her eyes did what a rapier could have done. They cut him swift and clean.

Mrs. Beldam continued to tap her finger on the rim of her cup long after he strode from the room. What Banes would give to know what terrible thoughts festered in her head. But the sound of Pandy's voice carried from the entry, and he stuffed his rag back in the kitchen peephole and ran for the entry one.

"I knows something youse might want, Wynders," she taunted. She sallied up to him. "I tooks care of it," said Pandy. "I dids. There's no reason for you to looks elsewheres." She tilted her chin in a saucy gesture. "I knows who the missus hired."

Banes's toes curled in anticipation. He dared not blink.

# CHAPTER 15

As far as seedy boozing kens were concerned, the Dim Dragon Inn was a typical tavern serving watered down ale and dubious meat pies. In Southwark such establishments were frequented by all manner of shady characters lacking the funds or inclination to journey across the bridge to more reputable kens.

Bianca pulled open the door to the ken and ducked inside. She was met with a chorus of whistles and stares, which she had expected, but the reception didn't make it any less disconcerting. Usually only wenches and wagtails dared enter where drunken denizens sat in rows swilling their sour wine and tankards of ale.

Bianca squinted through the haze of smoke hanging in the air as thick as porridge. She didn't see the muckraker who had quarreled with Mrs. Beldam, but a hearth near the kitchen was her best hope for staking a spot with the door in sight. Most men avoided the fire, wary they'd keel over from the heat or choke from the putrid smoke of burning dung. Bianca took advantage of the open bench and welcomed the chance to warm her bones.

She picked past the men, some leering, some already bored and preferring the view of their pottle pots to her. She deftly avoided wandering hands groping for a buttock as she sidled through and was nearly to her chosen post when a casualty of too much drink stood in front of her, listing like a ship in a storm. He gazed down and grinned a tartar-toothed smile.

They were face to grubby face. Neither could pass unless they both turned sideways or one leapt on a table to get by. Bianca wasn't about to dance down a table, nor was she going to turn her back on the sot as she tried to squeeze past. The man enjoyed the predicament and waited for her to move.

A few interested customers perked at the chance to see what this lass was made of. A rumble of taunts and advice encouraged his next move. But the lout didn't need counsel to help him decide. He needed to get to the alley to make water and didn't have time to ponder his opportunity. With a vulgar smirk he spread his palm over Bianca's breast and squeezed.

This pleased the clientele, and the place erupted into insults and howls that drowned out the sound of chatter and farting that usually held reign. Bianca was not about to be made a fool. She reached down and grabbed the man's bollocks—mindful no codpiece protected him—and returned the gesture.

This got the appropriate response. The lout yelped and doubled over, covering his tender todger, and clamored past Bianca as fast as he could. The other customers whooped, and Bianca, now redeemed and unchallenged, got her spot by the hearth.

A tavern maid wended over to the young wench and lifted her chin approvingly. "A pot o' ale for your trouble?" she asked.

"Aye, that." Bianca pulled out a coin. "What kind of board tonight for this?"

The woman placed her hand on a hip. "We've got cabbage stew that'll warm you right well. Made this morn."

Bianca thought a boiled stew couldn't do as much harm as kidney pie, so she ordered that and a pint. She most often drank a tea of mint or fennel and didn't care much for ale, but she didn't trust the place to boil its water, which she had found improved the taste.

The heat from the fire warmed Bianca's back, and she settled in to study faces. She was careful not to stare too long at anyone in particular. It would not do to invite trouble or unwanted attention. She thought all this might have gone better if John had accompanied her, but she couldn't dwell on that. She only hoped that her luck was good enough to find the muckraker and ask him some questions.

The tavern maid returned from the kitchen and, after knocking into a few patrons with her loose-swinging hips, set the bowl and a hunk of bread and mug of ale on the table. Bianca was glad to have something to do while waiting and watching.

A few patrons looked vaguely familiar, and she was glad to see Mackney waddle through the door with Smythe, his lanky diver. The portly curber adjusted his grungy ruff as he looked around for a place to sit and didn't notice Bianca in front of the hearth. He lumbered through the tightly packed benches, inadvertently bumping some patrons who took issue and weren't shy to tell him. Finally, he and Smythe reached a vacant space. Bianca finished her stew and made her way over.

"Do I know you?" he asked, looking up. His mouth was disconcertingly small compared to his ample cheeks.

Bianca slid onto the bench opposite. "I was at Cross Bones for Jolyn Carmichael's burial."

The tavern wench set leather tankards of ale in front of the pair of crooks. Mackney studied Bianca, as if trying to place her. "Of course," he said, realizing who she was. He lifted the ale to his lips and took a drink. "Constable Patch had some interest in you."

"Aye," Bianca acknowledged, keeping her voice low. "Do you come here often?"

"Enough to know better." Mackney wiped his mouth on a sleeve and belched.

"I'm looking for someone who may have had some dealings with Jolyn. Someone who accused her of stealing."

Smythe had not learned the finer art of concealing all he knew. He shot a furtive look at his partner.

Mackney said, "No one pays mind to that accusation. Not

around here anyways. But I happened to overhear something about that, aye." He looked at his fingernails and dug out a sliver of dirt. "It was Henley you was meaning. Didn't take it to mean much, though. Muckrakers—" He leaned in and spoke in a husky whisper. "They's always bellyachin' that one of thems got their goods and such. Don't means nothin' really."

"Do you know if Henley comes here much?"

"Practically lives here," said Mackney, leaning back. He looked over one shoulder and then the other. "Not around at the moments." He chewed a nail at the end of a sausage-sized finger.

"Can you tell me what happened?"

Mackney took another swig. He shook his head. "Alls I saw was them goin' at it here and Henley callin' her a thief. He was makin' a fuss, and Jolyn fairly well ignored him."

"What did he accuse her of stealing?"

"'Twas a ring from what I understood."

Bianca sat back in thought. Several weeks before, Jolyn had showed her a ring she'd found. It was a lucky find, and Bianca was glad for her. If Jolyn had sold it for gold, she could have eaten for a few months. They didn't discuss it much, but Jolyn had said she thought the ring brought her luck. She got work at Barke House, and finally, things were turning for the better.

Bianca tried to remember the last time she'd seen it. It wasn't on Jolyn's body. Maybe the muckraker had gotten it back. Maybe Henley was connected with Jolyn's death.

Mackney waved the tavern wench over to order kidney pie.

"You want 'nother ale, lass?" she asked.

Bianca declined, feeling the press of her bladder from all she'd had before. She didn't want to miss Henley, but she had no choice. She snaked her way out the door, again shrugging off offers to go upstairs, and found an alley to water the mud. Rearranging her kirtle, she thought she might pay a visit to Barke House. She pondered who else might have connections with Jolyn and realized that, though they had been friends, it was impossible to know everyone with whom she'd had dealings.

Bianca trudged back and heaved open the door to the Dim Dragon Inn to resume her watch by the hearth. If Henley practically lived at the alehouse, then surely he would make his appearance before long. She dropped herself onto the bench in front of the fire and sat in the cheap, smelly smoke.

Once the hoots had quieted and the clientele grew bored taunting her for a second time, Bianca relaxed enough to almost feel as if she fit in. Every time the door opened, she, along with the other patrons, turned a curious eye to see who entered. Eventually she was rewarded for her patience. In walked the fellow she'd seen at Cross Bones. When Mackney gave her a knowing nod, she knew it was him.

Blocky enough to command respect, the young thug stood at the entrance and scanned the collection of ruffians and lowlifes. Seeing no available space, he made some. He strolled to a table and took hold of a drunk winking off in his grog. Henley pulled him onto the floor so fast the man hardly yelped at his mistreatment and napped contented where he lay.

This roused the patrons, but after a minute they settled back to their bragging and tankards of ale. Bianca watched as he ordered a drink.

The bridge of his nose was noticeably flattened, probably from more than a few brawls. Rancorous eyes peered out from beneath brows thick as bear hide. He sneered at his tablemates and swilled his ale, finishing it off without setting it down once. But her time was at a premium, and Bianca knew she couldn't spend another minute studying him. She stood and made her way over.

Henley watched her approach.

She touched the arm of the patron sitting opposite, and he made room for the pretty lass even though she smelled like dung.

Bianca settled in, locking eyes with him. "You knew Jolyn Carmichael?" she asked.

Henley broke their stare and glanced around. "Where's the tavern maid?"

"Dealin' on the other side," said the man next to Bianca.

"I saw you at Cross Bones," said Bianca. "You were talking to Mrs. Beldam of Barke House."

Henley abandoned flagging down the tavern wench for another ale. He took one from his neighbor and drank it down, setting down the tankard with a thunk.

Bianca's eyes roamed his face and lingered on his mud-caked jerkin. He was a muckraker, but he was learning the ways of a criminal. She could see it in his manner. Most muckrakers, while cunning, were doomed to their livelihood unless they could find a way out. There was no glory in digging through the sewage of London, but it was a way to avoid starving in irons or getting shivved by hooligans when deals ran amok. He had the bulk for a miscreant, and he was learning the churlish manner that went with it.

"She had something you wanted." She watched his face for signs of deceit. "I don't believe you are as uninformed as you try to appear," she said. "I know you and Jolyn got into an argument."

Henley returned the stare but said nothing.

"Oh, aye, miss," said the neighbor whose drink Henley had stolen. "Henley here got into it right thick nights before lasts."

If looks could kill, Henley's would have drawn and quartered the man.

"Did you argue over a ring?"

Henley's gaze lifted to the tavern wench, and he waved his tankard above his head. "'Nother here," he shouted.

"Whose ring was it?"

"It belonged to me." His tone was impertinent.

Bianca found him as cooperative as a millstone in mud. Not only was he tight-lipped, he was lying. "How do you know Mrs. Beldam?"

The rogue leaned back and searched for someone farther down the bench. He mumbled something unintelligible. But their discussion had piqued the table's curiosity.

"Well, Henley. Answer the lassie's question," said one of the patrons.

Henley turned an angry face on Bianca. "Is nothin' to ye. Ye best make yeself small instead of stakin' out public venues where the constable is sure to nab ye. I saw 'e took a certain interest in you."

"A misguided interest. But I'll not leave until you answer my question. What business do you have with Mrs. Beldam?"

The entire table stopped talking and stared at Henley expectantly.

Henley's eyes jumped from face to face. His attempt to ignore her wasn't working. "Mrs. Beldam had me pawn some jewelry. That is all."

"If that is all, why take so long to say it?"

Henley's jaw tightened as he continued to glare at her. The tavern wench returned with his ale and set it down in front of him, but his eyes remained on Bianca.

"Next time you choose to lie, pick someone daft." Bianca stood. She grabbed his ale and downed the entire pint, then slammed the empty pottle on the table in front of him and left.

Bianca stood on the street outside of the Dim Dragon Inn, stewing over Henley's belligerence. The skate was lying, she was certain. She would wait until Henley left the inn, then follow him.

She stood outside the entrance and felt a damp chill seep into her bones. The swill they called ale did little to warm her, and it only made her regret being impulsive. But Henley had infuriated her. Now she felt the ill effects of her action as well as a creeping cold. She stared up the lane in the direction of the Thames and thought about heading home. As she blew into her hands to warm them, the man who'd bought rat poison turned onto the lane. His pheasant plume bobbed in cadence with his stride, and he was coming her way. Perhaps this might prove interesting. When he was within a few steps of the entrance, he acknowledged her before pulling open the door.

The inn's popularity was proving greater than she could have imagined. Bianca bided her time until another customer arrived, then followed him in, hanging in the shadow of the door, where she could watch unnoticed.

It wasn't long before she spied Henley deep in conversation with the man in the plumed hat.

# CHAPTER 16

Once she heard the door close behind Robert Wynders, Jane Beldam lifted the cup of ale to her lips and downed the remains without stopping. She turned the cup upside down on the table and laid her hand on its bottom.

Her efforts to perpetuate the lie had reached an impasse. Without more drastic measures, she and the women of Barke House were destined to return to their more sordid occupations in order to survive. Doing so would pique the interest of the exchequer, constable, and other lowlifes, something Mrs. Beldam had hoped to avoid.

She rested her cheek on her fist and stared vacantly at the shelving opposite. The flour and grain stores were dwindling, along with the rat poison and everything else. While she preferred her newfound respectability, it didn't mean she couldn't "flip the coin" if she had to. The girls depended on her for refuge and advice, and if they had to step up their filching and other endeavors, they would. But she hoped it wouldn't come to that. Barke House wasn't so desirable that the girls couldn't go elsewhere if she became too demanding. Then she'd be left with nothing.

With her youth and beauty faded, Jane Beldam relied on wits and cunning instead. No convents would accept the likes of her, nor would any man marry an old whore. She'd never find work again, anywhere—her reputation ensured that. But she had always managed to remain one step ahead of the authorities and avoid the Clink—she'd never live through such dour environs at her age.

Mrs. Beldam was deep in contemplation when Pandy strolled into the kitchen.

"Why ye let that eel-skinned bombast in this house mystifies me," said the girl, observing Mrs. Beldam's long face. "He never fails to leave misery in his wake." Pandy dropped onto the bench opposite her.

"I believe ye loved him once," said Mrs. Beldam.

Pandy had hoped Wynders's affections for Jolyn had been buried along with the beautiful muckraker. His cool reaction to news of Jolyn's death had left Pandy hopeful, but then his equally cool reaction to Pandy had left her bitter. "And I was a fool. There is no need for him to come 'bouts anymores."

"Ye may gets your wish," said Mrs. Beldam. Pandy's indifference didn't fool the veteran callet. She still wanted Wynders, and Mrs. Beldam knew it.

Pandy was of little use, having failed to complete even Mrs. Beldam's most simple requests. Upon arrival, Mrs. Beldam required new girls to turn over their coins and trinkets as a good faith contribution in running Barke House. If one refused or hid anything of value, then Pandy was to "remove" it and promptly deliver said item to Mrs. Beldam. More than once Pandy had claimed failure when all the while she had kept an item for herself. But Mrs. Beldam had a keen eye, and nothing escaped her notice—not even the malevolent glint in Pandy's eye.

"Methinks ye'd better to leave off the man," said Mrs. Beldam. "He'll come up against what he deserves. Ye'll see." Then

Mrs. Beldam, feeling she might not have sufficiently impressed the girl, added, "Besides, if it is a husband ye want, there are better men to choose. Robert Wynders is as married to Chudderly Shipping as he is to his wife."

Pandy's lips pinched, and she looked away.

"Now get on with it," admonished Mrs. Beldam. "No need dwellin' on the past." She stood up and got Pandy a cup of ale. "Ye need to not let yeself get parched. Ye need time to heal what all ye been throughs."

Pandy dutifully drank down the quaff and stood. She lifted her chin, but failed to hide the tears welling in her eyes.

"Go on now. Ye be all right," said Mrs. Beldam, and she watched Pandy straighten and march from the room.

Mrs. Beldam had never approved of Pandy's affair with Wynders. She knew it would end badly for the girl, especially once Jolyn arrived at Barke House. She had been at a loss to discourage either girl from involving herself with the man. She couldn't understand why anyone would want the arrogant whoremonger. But, she thought with regret, they had not been the only women to fall prey to his charms.

# CHAPTER 17

It was hard enough pouring a bucket full of molten metal over delicate molds, but to do it while a meddlesome Frenchman lectured him on matters of love was too much for the young Anglais to endure. John tried to concentrate as he tipped the scalding silver, then hauled on the chain to move it to a new mold. He didn't fancy burning himself.

"So this matter of the Bianca," mused Boisvert, watching from a safe distance, "she is still not sure of you?" The master silversmith chuckled. "These *jeunes filles*, they are splendid creatures, *n'est-ce pas?*" He adjusted his codpiece with a faraway look in his eye. "Well, so your lovemaking skills must be *négligent*."

"That is not the issue," sputtered John. His patience with the round-bellied foreigner was wearing thin. True, the man had rescued him from living in a barrel outside a boozing ken, but he, too, had had a part in Boisvert being able to conduct his business with some modicum of peace. It wasn't easy for a Frenchman to navigate the social customs of the Anglais, even if he was a master in his craft and widely sought for his casts of plates and even coins. "She is accused of murdering her best friend. Instead of asking for help, she is pushing me away." John worked the chain, easing the iron bucket back into the orange coals of the foundry.

"That is enough for today," said Boisvert, putting up his hand. He wandered to the rear of the forge and returned with a bottle of wine.

John dampered the chimney, but he still had the casts to recover, and so he carefully moved a mold with heavy tongs over a trough of water. He tried to push the aggravation out of his mind, but Bianca was like a splinter—under his skin and irritating.

Boisvert, refusing to let the matter go, poured himself a glass of wine and pulled up a chair to watch his young apprentice. He had no qualms assuming all men of English descent were boors in the bedroom.

"John," said Boisvert, swirling the glass of wine under his nose, "if it isn't your love skill, then why the Bianca doesn't run away with you?"

John dropped the mold of coins into the trough, sending a cloud of steam hissing into the air. The mold fell apart with a satisfactory crack, and the coins clinked to the bottom. John fought the urge to grab Boisvert by the collar and dunk his French face into the water. "I told you. She has been accused of murder."

Boisvert sipped his wine and considered this. "Perhaps this Bianca is not the one for you. Maybe you should find a lovely *fille* more amenable."

"I don't want another *fille*. I want Bianca."

Boisvert's eyebrows skipped in appreciation, and he chuckled softly. "My poor boy. This is not the first time the Bianca has found trouble. It wasn't so long ago that she was running about in the Tower *Blanc*, trying to rescue her father from a charge of treason." Boisvert undid the last button of his doublet, releasing his belly from the constricting fashion. "I would say, you must be careful the company you keep."

John retrieved a long-handled ladle to scoop the coins from the bottom of the trough. He fished about for the silver and deposited it with a loud clank in a metal pail. "It isn't as if she goes about seeking this sort of trouble," he said. "She just seems to have come across some unexpected twists of fortune."

"You call it 'twists of fortune.' I call it a plague of *mis*fortune. And it is best to avoid that sort. Bianca is misery."

"She is not misery."

Boisvert polished off his glass of wine. "Suit yourself," he said knowingly. "You would be much happier without the Bianca."

John deposited the last coins into the pail, then hung the ladle back on its hook on the brick wall. He thought about Bianca this morning, in the vaporous gloam of Cross Bones graveyard. Her eyes keenly brilliant in the gray murk. She had been preoccupied; perhaps he had been too quick to anger. All he wanted was for her to acknowledge him. Show a hint that she cared. He dropped onto a stool and stared at the forge. Perhaps he should offer his help. Then, just as quick, his anger flared and he thought to hell with it. Her eyes had been on some other fellow. She had hardly said two words, much less cared that he had come to apologize for his snit. If she needed or wanted his help, she'd seek him. He would wait. He would wait for her to show that she wanted him.

"Are you going to let in whatever is pounding at the door, or are you going to sit in a stupor for the rest of the day?" Boisvert crammed the cork back into his bottle, sorry for the interruption. A good bottle of wine should never wait to be finished.

"Ah, just who I was hopin' to find," said Constable Patch when John opened the door. He stepped inside, nodding to Boisvert, then turned back to address John. "I was hoping ye might know where your friend is."

"Whom do you mean?"

The corner of Patch's mouth slid up in a half grin. "Your friend Bianca, of course."

"She is not my friend."

Patch tilted his head and glanced at Boisvert and winked. "Well then . . . acquaintance?"

"I haven't seen her since the cemetery. We aren't speaking."

"Not speaking," repeated Patch. He studied John with surprise. "Why might that be?"

John ignored the question. He might be upset with Bianca, but he wasn't prepared to make it easy for Patch to find her. He stared innocuously at Patch until the constable blinked.

"I have something of import to tell her."

"And that is . . ."

"It is between her and me."

"Like I said, I haven't seen her. She certainly hasn't sought me out." John turned his back on him and went to finish his work.

Patch glanced at Boisvert and then gazed around the brick-lined forge. The place was pleasantly warm and dry. He appreciated the brief reprieve from the dreary weather outside. A bucket of silver coins sat near a trough of water. He wondered if the coiner ever clipped the king's currency for a little extra in his pocket. He sized up the little Frenchman sitting like a toad in his comfortable chair. It wouldn't take much to wield his authority over the silly snail-eater. But the question would have to wait for another day. He had a murderess to nab.

Patch studied John. The poor idiot was bitten hard by love, or probably lust, he mused. Look at him so determined to stay honorable and protect this girl. He'd not learned the better part of valor was to save his own skin first. Patch rested his hand on the hilt of his poniard as he casually crossed the room. The girl was playing a tiresome game of cat and mouse, running here, hiding there, avoiding arrest. If this boy was helping her in any way, he needed to stop it.

Patch stepped up to the lad, who was organizing tools on the back wall. "If ye should be party to hiding her, it wouldn't take much to clap irons on ye." Patch raised his head. "Why so gallant? I've got a murderess to remove from the streets, and I do not take kindly to those who interfere."

"Why are you so certain that it was Bianca? She may have knowledge of poisons, but that doesn't make her a murderer. I wager you haven't considered anyone else."

"I welcome suggestions." Patch's eyes narrowed while he considered John carefully.

"Why are you so certain she died of poison? She could have died of natural cause."

"What natural cause would turn her blood purple?" Constable Patch sensed a slight desperation in the boy's voice. "The coroner determined only a poison could have killed her."

The wine in Boisvert's belly began to curdle as he watched these two. If he could get the shambling official out of his forge, then he'd cuff some sense into the lad later. Rising from his chair, he tugged his doublet down over his gut and wandered to the pail of coins to inspect them. He picked one up and polished it against the velvet of his sleeve. "*Gendarme*, it is obvious the Bianca girl is not here," he said. "Nor has John seen her. *Monsieur*, if that is all, we have other matters to attend."

At first, Patch took insult at the Frenchman's curt dismissal. Then he saw the shiny coin in Boisvert's hand. Yes, that would go a long way in buying them the peace they desired. Besides, he had yet to be paid by the royal treasury for his duties this month. But the little propriety he possessed did not allow him to ask for the coin outright. No, he could not do that. His eyes flicked back and forth from the coin to the silversmith's face. This Frenchman knew how to play the game.

Patch strolled leisurely toward the door, patting his pocket. He turned and gave the two a final nod before exiting. His honor might be slightly tarnished, but the coin in his purse was decidedly not.

# CHAPTER 18

Bianca slogged up the lane away from the Dim Dragon Inn, passing a group of revelers leaving the bull-baiting at Paris Gardens. Bianca had been to see the sport once with John, and that was enough for her to leave off the bloody pastime. She had watched a dog relentlessly taunt the poor beast into charging. Over and over the dog crept close, keeping a vigilant eye on the creature, gauging its chance to dart forward and seize the bull's nose—the most tender and vulnerable spot. The bull turned and turned, always facing its foe, exhausting itself as the dog sprang away just as it charged.

When she learned the handlers cinched the bull's bollocks in iron cramps, then stabbed its back with knives to provoke it before leading it into the ring, she wanted to leave. But John wanted his full money's worth and would not budge. So Bianca started shouting, cheering for the bull to gore its handler instead of the dog. The crowd turned on her and started yelling that maybe *she* should be gored next. When she looked at John, he merely shook his head and shrugged.

"Why don't you say something?" she had demanded.

"Because this is what they paid to see."

"This is cruel. Don't you see it?"

"If you don't like it, you can leave."

Furious, Bianca stood, rousing the crowd behind her to shout at her to sit.

Bianca left in disgust, uncertain if she was more upset about the bull-baiting or with John. Animals had no say in what they were forced to endure. They only knew loyalty to their masters, no matter how poorly they were treated.

Though Bianca was troubled by the brutality, that did not make her soft of heart. She'd seen plenty of criminals hanged in the gibbets at Aldersgate, their bodies blackened and skeletal thin from beatings and starvation. She'd witnessed public executions, and even stolen into the Tower grounds to see Queen Catherine beheaded. To her reckoning, though, most people were responsible in some way for their predicaments. No doubt the innocent were persecuted more often than the guilty, and while she was sorry for this injustice, she saw it as typical and the unfortunate occurrence that went with this king's reign. And while she worried of becoming a victim herself, she believed that her fate was still in her hands. It was up to her to find who poisoned Jolyn, and so save her own neck.

She wondered what business the ship's agent had with Henley. Perhaps the muckraker had seen the man had money and seized the chance to cheat him. To sell him something? No, it appeared the man had sought Henley, not the other way around. The two would not have dealings with each other unless it was for a reason. It could not be an accident that the two had been deep in conversation.

What could a muckraker and a ship's agent possibly have in common? Was the agent Wynders? Could he be Jolyn's love? He seemed officious and full of himself, not the sort Jolyn would have had much patience with or interest in. Bianca dismissed the idea as fast as she skirted a cutpurse sizing her up from ahead.

Though the days were lengthening and should have afforded some warmth, the air was chill. The smoke from cheap fires hung low over the lane, merging with the moist air from the Thames. The thick stew was as unpleasant to walk in as it was to inhale. Bianca squelched through the mud, wishing for a pair of pattens to lift her above the muck and keep her feet dry. Her ankle-length boots were worn through at the toe, and she hated sitting in the alley behind her room, washing her feet in cistern water nearly as cold as ice.

She was thinking of what to do next, whom to question, when just ahead she saw the red cap of Meddybemps as he pushed his cart of wares toward London Bridge. She hurried to catch him.

"My dainty dove," said Meddybemps, stopping to watch her galumph through the mud toward him, "I dropped by, but you weren't in." He maneuvered his cart to the side, allowing a man balancing a yoke of water buckets to pass.

"You'll have to wait if you want more salves. I've other things to take care of."

"Like saving your neck?" said Meddybemps, scratching an armpit.

"I've just seen Henley, a muckraker who accused Jolyn of stealing from him."

"I don't know him." Meddybemps's eye quivered. "But that is no matter," he said, brightening. He leaned in as if about to impart a wondrous gift. "I know something outrageously interesting. That overbearing cock who wanted rat poison for his ship? I followed him."

"I'm not surprised."

"Bianca, I know you prefer not to dangle at Aldersgate, so do not assume my reasons are always for personal gain."

"I've never thought otherwise."

Meddybemps could not be sure if she'd just insulted him, but he continued on in good cheer. "I thought there was something knavish about the man, and I intended to find out more."

Bianca wrapped her scarf another turn around her neck. This talk of hanging made her anxious.

"So I followed him, and where do you think he went?" Meddybemps didn't expect Bianca to answer and paused for effect, as if imagining a brass fanfare playing out. "He visited Barke House."

Bianca's eyebrows lifted. "Do you know why?"

Meddybemps grinned knowingly. "Why do most men go to Barke House?"

"It's not like it used to be," said Bianca. "It may have been disreputable once, but Jolyn assured me Mrs. Beldam had only the most honorable of intentions now. She was helping women start anew."

"My dear girl, how you survive in Southwark amazes me."

"Not everyone is out for themselves."

"Of course they are!" Then, hoping to shake some sense into his young charge, he said, "Don't assume everyone has noble intentions. The only person more gullible than Jolyn . . . is you."

Bianca colored to a shade darker than his cap. "Did you follow him inside?"

"Nay," said Meddybemps, taking up the arms of his pushcart and leaning into it. The display of talismans and trinkets swung wildly as a wheel rolled through a deep rut. "I didn't want to leave my cart unattended for so long. I am not so foolish. The streets crawl with criminals." A particularly full-bodied woman strode past, and Meddybemps's eye whirled in appreciation.

"I should visit Barke House and find out what business he had. Find out if he is the man Jolyn loved. Maybe they could tell me where to find him."

"If I was you, I'd stay at Boisvert's until I figured out how Jolyn died. Or until Constable Patch lost interest."

"He won't lose interest. He has nothing better to do but hang me for a crime I didn't commit."

"Exactly why I believe you should seek John for protection." Meddybemps hoped his young friend would take his advice—at least for now. But he knew Bianca would likely do the opposite of anything he advised. She merely shrugged and began to wander off in the direction of Barke House, distracted and obviously brooding over her predicament. She had shut herself off from anyone offering help or opinions. Resignedly, Meddybemps took up his pushcart and headed to market.

Barke House appeared no different from any other boarding hall or stew on Bermondsey Street. A mix of residences and squalid stews, the street was not so well traveled as it was just another lane running north and south. But for those wanting to avoid the rank sights and smells of the stream along Morgan's Lane, it was a preferable thoroughfare. And for those wanting a discreet romp, the relatively quiet lane afforded a man the semblance of privacy. A man could sneak down Bermondsey Street and slip into the arms of a waiting trollop as easily as he could slip into the arms of his coat.

Green moss clung to the wooden front door and shingles of Barke House. The shutters were closed, two akilter from broken hinges and woefully unable to keep out the cold. Bianca rapped at the spongy door, the sound of her knock muffled by the rotten wood.

After a moment, she put manners aside and pushed open the door. She entered a vestibule where an unlit candle sat on a small table. A slit of light from the interior leaked under a second door. She found it unlocked and peered into the quiet residence. She was about to call out when a girl, busy tying the laces of her bodice, startled to see Bianca.

"I didn't hears anyone come in. What do ye want?" she asked, regaining her composure.

Bianca recognized her from Cross Bones. She and another girl had accompanied Banes and Mrs. Beldam at Jolyn's burial. She fit Jolyn's description of Pandy. Wide-set eyes on a face as round and flat as a platter. Her figure, though, was decidedly unlike a platter as the laces in her bodice required a double knot to perform their duty.

"I'm looking for Mrs. Beldam."

"She's not here." The girl stepped within a foot of Bianca and looked her up and down.

"Do you know where I might find her?"

"Not my day to watch her."

"I saw you at Jolyn's burial. You must be Pandy?"

The corner of the girl's eye twitched. "I mights be." She seemed to be measuring if there was anything to gain by admitting it.

"I'm Bianca Goddard." Seeing the blank expression on the girl's face, Bianca added, "I've been accused of poisoning Jolyn." She hated to introduce herself as a suspect in a murder, but with these types she hoped the news might put her in good stead.

"Sorry that," said Pandy with such indifference it was as if she'd just pronounced that water was indeed wet.

Bianca staunched her irritation, though it was hard for her not to match the girl's insolence with some of her own. "Do you know if Mrs. Beldam is interested in a muckraker named Henley?"

"Why would ye think she's interested?"

"I saw her speaking with him at the cemetery. It seems odd she'd be speaking to a muckraker."

"Wells, maybe he knew Jolyn and was expressing his condolences."

Bianca's level stare let Pandy know she knew this was not so. She wondered how best to approach this girl, as she was getting nowhere. "I'd heard Jolyn had a tiff with a muckraker."

Pandy placed a hand on her hip. "Don't knows nothin' 'bout it."

And then Bianca took a chance. She didn't know how Pandy would respond. If what Mackney had told her was true, Pandy would be her measure. "I heard Henley wanted a ring Jolyn had found."

Pandy shrugged. "That don't surprise me. Fat and gold it was. She never took it off. Some rot 'bout it bringin' her luck and all." She smirked. "Didn't work so well—did it?"

"Why do you think he wanted it?"

"I don't knows. Nor do I cares. Like I said, it was fat and gold. Probably worth more than a month's pickings."

"Have you ever seen him come around here?"

Pandy lifted an eyebrow. "I's seen my share of men comin' and goin'. But nay. Can't say I have."

As Pandy started past, Bianca lobbed one last question: "Has Jolyn's suitor been by today?"

Raw fury replaced the girl's insolent expression. Pandy flung open the vestibule door and yanked a woolen shawl off a hook. Not bothering to drape it around her shoulders, or answer Bianca's question, she stomped out the door and flung it shut.

"Touchy subject, that," said Banes, appearing from a room off the entry. He held a candle in his good hand and clutched a rag against his chest with the other. "Would you mind holding this?" He handed Bianca the candle. "In answer to your question—aye, Wynders was here." Banes swabbed out the runny tallow from a wall sconce and pushed the fresh candle in the holder. It had grown dark and Banes lit the candle, but not before nearly setting his sleeve on fire from an ember he retrieved from a smoldering hearth.

"Did Mrs. Beldam tell him about Jolyn?"

"Pandy told him."

"He must have suffered a shock."

Banes shrugged. "Captains are as cold as the waters they sail."

"He's a sea captain?"

"Does it matter? He deals with ships and such. They are a breed apart."

"What did he say when he found out?"

Banes lowered his voice to a whisper and furtively glanced over his shoulder. "He came in puffed as a rooster, and after Pandy waylaid him made straight for the kitchen."

"Did he speak with Mrs. Beldam?" Bianca kept her voice low, thinking there must be good cause to do so.

Banes tucked the cloth under the armpit of his bad arm. "They spoke," he said; then, in a louder, more distinct voice, he added, "I was not privy to their conversation. I was busy tending my chores."

Bianca pondered what he had just said, and Banes took advantage of her distracted gaze to study her. It didn't look like she ate much. Her long, bony fingers clutched the dangling end of her scarf. She was as thin as frost. He wondered if this was an indication of her struggle to survive or if she preferred dabbling in potions to eating.

"Does he come here often?"

"It is not my business."

"Did Wynders visit Barke House before Jolyn took up residence?"

"Aye," mumbled Banes. He flushed from Bianca having caught him staring at her bubbies.

"Did Wynders come here for the . . ." Bianca thought how best to say it without embarrassing either of them. She knew Mrs. Beldam had tried to redeem Barke House's reputation. And, after all, Banes did live there and suffered its scandalous reputation along with the rest of the occupants. "Did he come here for the . . ."

Banes's eyes narrowed, daring her to say it.

". . . entertainment?" finished Bianca, putting it diplomatically. Now it was her turn to flush.

"Always." Banes knew that was not entirely true. Wynders did come for women, but his presence over the years had been long-lived. Most men patronized Barke House for a while, then disappeared. He didn't know if this loyalty to Barke House was built from a trust between Wynders and Mrs. Beldam or whether the man just preferred the pickings here. But Banes's allegiance was first to Barke House. It was his home, and he instinctively knew to protect it. Besides, he enjoyed seeing Bianca squirm.

Bianca looked around at her surroundings, more to hide her embarrassment than to sate her curiosity. The interior was sparsely furnished with a bench along one wall and a crooked cupboard on the other. No tapestries warmed the cracked walls or kept out drafts. Trampled rush covered the floors, already in need of replacement, as the itch on her calves from fleas could attest. A smoldering hearth wheezed smoke into the room with every downdraft. But what Bianca noticed more than anything else was the quiet. The place was oddly silent for a house of women. She had just thought this when she heard a chair scrape the floor.

Bianca looked in the direction of the noise. "I'd like to speak with Mrs. Beldam."

Banes cleared his throat. "She won't be back for a while," he announced.

Bianca looked past him toward the dim kitchen. She could make out the outline of storage bins. "Perhaps I could wait for her."

"She's likely out for a while. Can I tell her you called?" Banes showed her toward the vestibule door, steering her in its direction. He opened it and blocked her passage back into the house.

Bianca stopped and looked over his shoulder toward the kitchen. She had grown weary of Barke House's contentious residents. "Tell her I'd like to speak with her," she said, loudly.

"Certainly." Banes's cool stare gave nothing away. "I shall be sure to tell her."

# CHAPTER 19

Perhaps she should have marched into the kitchen. The matron must have been there, listening to every word. Bianca kicked a stone in frustration. Barke House was rife with deceit. Banes was obviously protecting Mrs. Beldam.

She plunged her hands deep in her pockets and turned the corner of Bermondsey. It was getting late in the day, but if she hurried, she might find Meddybemps still selling his wares at market. She thought vaguely of stopping to see John at Boisvert's but decided to think on that a bit more before deciding.

Beyond the rents and the river Thames, the White Tower and its fortress walls loomed in the distance, squatting on London's eastern border, leering over its pitiable subjects. She would not like to end there. More likely Patch would throw her in Newgate for a public hanging later at Tyburn Hill. Her stomach knotted to think on it. With the sun dropping beyond the horizon, another day had passed and she was no closer to finding Jolyn's murderer.

On London Bridge, she peered up at the tar-dipped heads of criminals skewered on iron pikes. They decorated the rim of the tower gate, and though she knew better than to look on their final grimaces, she couldn't deny herself the thought of how she might look among them. A shudder coursed down her spine, and she forced herself on with her head down, determined to stare at the cobblestones instead.

For all its gory trimmings, London Bridge was a handsome structure, the only bridge spanning the river and joining London with its wanton sister to the south. Covered and lined with the residences of successful merchants and tradesmen, it was the cheaper way to get to London, which could cost nearly a sixpence by raft. Those without fare could cross its length for free, but risk the price of a cutpurse lurking in the shadows, forcing pedestrians to part with what little they had or had wished to save on fare. But no matter to Bianca, she moved swiftly down its center, and having spent a few years as a thief herself, she knew their tricks and habits and was confident she could avoid them.

Bianca emerged at the other end into a twilight that afforded only slightly more light than there had been on the bridge. No doubt Eastcheap had thinned, and if she was lucky, she might find Meddybemps still crooning for a final penny before heading to a boozing ken. She avoided picking through the heaps of refuse choking the narrow alleys and stayed to the main thoroughfares, preferring to dodge carts and dogs instead.

She passed her old neighborhood, where her parents lived, and felt a pang of regret. She hadn't visited her mother in several months. Bianca still held a grudge against her father for nearly getting the two of them hanged, but more so for his treatment of her mother. She'd urged her to leave and come live with her in her meager rent in Southwark, but her mother had refused.

"He's a changed man since all that business," her mother had said. But Bianca doubted this. Her father had involved himself with dissidents, some associated with the king's court. These were men who sought to turn back time to before the king's Reformation and marriage to Anne Boleyn. They resented the king proclaiming himself Supreme Head of the Church of England. That was a privilege reserved for the pope. They had been staunch supporters of Catherine of Aragon and believed King Henry was a heretic to have divorced her. The dissolution of the monasteries had further incensed Bianca's father, as he saw it as a way to suppress the citizenry and increase their taxes.

Bianca understood these grievances and did not necessarily disagree with them. She'd seen the increased numbers of starving and destitute on the streets of London, the result of fewer religious houses that worked with the sick and poor.

In the end, her familial duty and concern for her mother's safety had prompted her to act. She scrambled to see her father absolved of the most egregious crime of trying to poison the king. They had both escaped, but just barely, and while she hoped her father had abandoned his subversive machinations, she could never be certain.

Try as she might, she could not convince her mother to leave him. Her mother had accepted her adopted country's treatment of women. Perhaps she saw it as an improvement compared to the old country from which she came. Bianca had witnessed her father's brutality toward her mother, his scathing criticisms, his self-indulgent pursuit of alchemy to the exclusion of feeding and providing for his family. But her mother accepted this and sold her herbals and old-world remedies to feed and provide for Bianca in spite of him. It grieved Bianca that her father did not give her mother the respect and love she deserved. It deeply troubled her every time she visited.

So she visited less and less often. And it certainly would not do for her mother to learn that *she* had been accused of murder. She could not bear to see her mother's face when she learned that unwelcome news. Bianca braced herself and trudged on. Perhaps when this was over and done, she would make amends, but she could not waste precious time now.

The butcher stalls of Eastcheap had cleared for the day, so if she hurried, she might make it to Cheapside before it grew too dark. A few residents had set a lamp to glow at their window to aid pedestrians still foolish enough to be out. But the guttering candles against horn panes did little more than waste that family's resources. Still, Bianca hoped to find her poetic streetseller.

Eventually she turned up Bread Street, the smell of yeast and rising dough momentarily masking the putrid smell of a decomposing rat. Passing Bow Church, Bianca emerged at Cheapside and helped herself to a drink of water at the standard conduit. Her nerves and brisk pace had left her mouth as dry as an August day. She looked up the street, then down it.

A few sellers carried cages of poultry back to their shops, abandoning their stalls for the night and leaving them to beggars, who slept on top or below, depending on the weather. Chopped chicken feet and plucked feathers littered the ground while dogs vied for rotting fruits dotting the mud. She saw no sign of Meddybemps and so turned toward Newgate Market.

She passed Eleanor's Cross and glanced at the towering token of love King Edward Longshanks had erected in honor of his dead wife. How lucky to be so remembered and loved. The only thing she'd be remembered by was a pile of peculiar crockery and a smelly rent.

A full moon rose and illuminated the road ahead, revealing two figures talking outside a residence. She slowed as she neared. One was dressed in the startling attire of a physician dressed for contagion. In profile, a mammoth beak shaped like that of a grackle and stuffed with rosemary and rue was strapped against a linen hood that covered his face so that he looked ready to play a monstrous bird at a theater in Southwark. Slits had been cut for his eyes, and he wore thick leather gloves and a robe that swept the ground. The other man had finished securing the door with an iron chain and padlock and dipped a reed brush into a pail of red. Bianca could hear the moans and pleas from within as the laborer painted a cross, the sign of quarantine, across the door.

She pulled her scarf over her ears, trying to muffle their cries. The inmates would be locked inside for forty days, and she wondered if it was the beginning of widespread sickness. She hoped not. There were always small outbreaks; hardly a year passed without the air rife with rumors of the Great Death. She well re-called a year of her childhood when corpses, piled neck high, lit-tered the kennels of streets, and ignorant of consequence, she had danced behind the death carts without a care, spurred by the ex-citement the carts attracted. Why she never fell ill from the plague was a mystery to her. She didn't believe in luck and suspected something else, though what that something might be, she did not know.

She shook her head as if dislodging those thoughts and looked ahead to the market at Newgate. The few remaining sellers hag-gled among themselves, their clientele having left long before. In the middle stood Meddybemps. His long-winded stories and desire to deal had delayed him yet again.

"Nay, I'd not enter a game of dice with the likes of you, Bran-ford, nor with any other of you cozen cheats. I am not so studied at the art of counterfeit die, and I'd hazard a guess you spend your nights slurring the roll to perfection. I haven't the notion to learn or perfect it, no matter how clever you've scored the die."

A willowy man threw back his head and roared with laughter. "Meddybemps, you old hound, my die is foolproof—even an ass like you could profit with not much practice."

"I'll save my earnings for sack and a little yank." Meddybemps winked and was met with a round of guffaws. "'Tis a profit more to me liking."

Disappointed he'd not convinced the wizened streetseller of a career change, Branford slapped him on the back with good cheer. "Ah, Meddy, my good man, not even the grave will stop your dealin'. Why, even the devil dreads the day you die. He'll have no peace with you around."

"No peace and no pence."

By then, Bianca stood within sight of her friend and caught his notice.

"Bianca, my turtle. What brings you about? The market is done, and another few minutes you'd have had to search the Turncoat Tavern to find me."

The men eyed Bianca, then, sensing she was of serious intent, dispersed with their carts but continued shouting insults at one another.

"Meddy, I've been to Barke House. I was hoping to speak to Mrs. Beldam, but Banes and one of the girls, named Pandy, said she wasn't in. I believe they're lying."

Meddybemps took a swig from a wine flask he had lashed across his chest. He offered the stained wineskin to Bianca.

"It'll make me sleepy. I can't."

"Some sleep might benefit you."

"Answers would serve me better." Bianca fell into step with Meddybemps as he pushed his cart forward. "I want you to try to find out about Mrs. Beldam and Barke House."

"And how am I to separate truth from hearsay?"

"Meddybemps, no one smells a lie better than you. Wheedle your way in or around. Go there if you must. But find out what you can."

Meddybemps stopped long enough to scratch under his cap. "Methinks you should make yourself small until a more notable murder distracts this Constable Patch. I've seen it happen before, and that donkey isn't so well paid to pursue anything longer than a month. He hasn't the teeth to care about a lowly muck-raker."

"He seems to have teeth to see me swing."

"That shall pass."

"And what if it doesn't? I can't take the chance that he'll forget." Bianca kicked a rock and sighed.

"My turnip, there are so many misdeeds in Southwark in any given week, the parish needs twenty constables—not one."

"Are you going to help me or not?"

Meddybemps stopped and faced her. He hated seeing Bianca in such a dismal predicament. He owed his good health to the young chemiste. She'd developed a salve that had cured him of the French pox. For such a strange pair, the two depended on each other. A certain amount of his wealth and fame came from selling her salves and balms. What would he do if she wasn't around to supply him with her cures? For that matter, what would *she* do without him to sell them? He couldn't imagine Bianca pushing a cart to market and having the patience or temperament to survive. Each of them would suffer immeasurably if they were to part.

"I'll see what I can learn of the taciturn Beldam and her Barketh Houseth," he said. If he couldn't tease her into a smile, at least he could try to lighten the mood.

The cart creaked down Cheapside, and as they approached the quarantined house, Bianca saw that the physician and painter had both departed, leaving behind the condemning mark of a red cross. Meddybemps followed her gaze.

"I don't fancy seeing that," he said.

"They were painting it just now."

Meddybemps leaned his weight into his cart and picked up his pace. "Perhaps you need to work on a remedy for the Black Death."

Bianca did not answer one way or the other. She'd always kept it in mind when working on her tinctures and medicinals. Her palliative for the French pox was one of the strongest balms she'd concocted. She had taken liquid silver, a known restorative used in alchemy, and combined it with a mix of herbals in a waxy base. If it didn't cure the buboes of the French pox, it did calm them enough to give some measure of relief. But the salve did not work on the buboes of the Black Death, and of late she'd had no reason to devote undue time and effort toward the feared plague. For some reason it had been kept in check, and whatever caused the ravage was not at issue. But the cross on the door could be a sign of things to come.

They hurried past the marked building, and Meddybemps eagerly put the matter out of mind and chided Bianca for not staying with John. "You could easily stay there tonight instead of venturing back to Southwark. It would give you a chance to make amends."

"Why should I make amends to him? *I'm* the one being accused of murder. He hasn't done anything to help me."

"Have you asked?"

Bianca made out the shape of an apple and reared back, kicking it free of a rut and sending it careening down the lane. "No," she protested, "but he should have offered."

"And he should be able to read your mind," added Meddybemps.

"He should have offered."

Meddybemps glanced sidelong at his young friend. How she could be so intuitive with medicinals and herbs and yet so dense when it came to people was baffling. He squelched the urge to further lecture her. She had a palpable aversion to that, and it was the one sure way to send her off, mad as a wasp. What she needed now was understanding and sympathy and someone who'd help. What was one day of lost sales? Meddybemps adjusted his codpiece. No carnal revelry—that's what.

"I'll find out what I can about Barke House, but you must promise me you won't forsake John. The poor lout loves you so. Of that I'm sure."

Bianca scowled moodily. The two of them turned south in silence, heading toward London Bridge. They were nearing Meddybemps's favorite tavern. His eye rolled in anticipation of a filling meal of kidney pie and the attentions of a certain randy maid who served it.

"You must heed my advice and not venture back across the river tonight," said Meddybemps, his eye drawn by the hunched silhouette of a well-fed rat as it skulked along a building's wall and ducked into a gap in the foundation. "And you need to concoct more rat poison, my dear. I've sold all that you've given me."

# CHAPTER 20

If Meddybemps's words had any effect on Bianca, it was that she allowed herself to slow when she neared Boisvert's neighborhood. She turned down Foster Lane, shivering a little from the damp and hating being plunged into near black. The Queen Moon hid behind the peaks of thatch roofs and offered scant light in the narrow lane.

As Bianca neared the dimly lit window of Boisvert's, she actually thought she might call on John. She paused to peek inside. Making out no more than the blurred glow of a wall sconce, she turned her ear to the window. No sounds ranged within; no conversation or clank of iron tongs leaked through the oilcloth. She rapped on the wood and waited, growing skittish as the city churches chimed the hour and a night watchman croaked, "Six of night and to all a good night." Time was wasting. And she had precious little of it.

She turned from the door. Her only thought now was to get home. The wind was coming up, and clouds raced across the sky. Pulling her hem above her ankles, she kept as near to the center of each road as she could. Her thin boots collected clay from the streets, weighing her down and oozing through holes in the leather. Despite the aggravation, she picked through the twisting, whispering streets, but unease seeped into her psyche. At one point she stopped and spun on her heel, suspicious she was being followed. After scrutinizing the shadows and finding no reason for alarm, she chided herself—fear had twined its way into her imagination. She quickened her pace and began to count her steps in an effort to control her apprehension. It worked, for soon she was back at her rent, standing before her calcination furnace, stirring the embers into a blaze.

She stood back, warming her hands, and thought about the inmates at Barke House. Banes was an odd fellow. But everyone had his peculiarities. Just because his left arm was half the length of the other was not reason enough to think him strange. It was his manner that troubled Bianca. He could be both secretive and forthcoming. She suspected he'd seen and heard more at Barke House than he was willing to tell.

Jolyn had said Mrs. Beldam was sympathetic to those in need. Instead of using young women, she now tried to help them. At least that was what Jolyn believed, but Bianca wondered what had caused her change of heart. And how could Mrs. Beldam keep the residence from falling into debt? She only requested the women earn a small pittance to help feed and house them. And the earnings did not come from carnal exchange. Though Banes had alluded to just that. Was he playing with her?

Bianca took an empty pot from the stove and stepped into the alley for water. A bank of clouds had moved in, obscuring the moon and stars. As she replaced the cover on the cistern, a flash of lightning needled across the sky, illuminating the alley. A rat skirted the stone foundation of the opposite building. Yet in that quick flash, Bianca glimpsed movement of something larger disappearing around a corner. She stared into the black, wondering if it was a dog or a man, when a clap of shuddering thunder sent her scurrying back inside. She slid the bolt and cursed the rusty hasp securing her door. For good measure, she moved a crate in front of it.

She stood a moment, wielding her pot of water and willing her jittery heart to quiet. She'd been in dire straits before, but her present circumstances unnerved her in a way she'd never expected. Her best friend was dead, and the loss left her feeling sorry and alone. She had always overcome obstacles in the past, but this grief was not easy to manage. It settled in the pit of her stomach like an immovable weight. She knew she couldn't ignore her feelings, but she needed to tame them. At least control them enough to find answers.

Bianca set the pot of water on the stove and poked at the fire. Poor Jolyn. She had never known the warmth of a fire on nights such as this. Left to fend for herself, she had slept in alcoves and abandoned buildings. Bianca had tried to get Jolyn to sleep in her father's alchemy room on the occasions that he was not there. But Jolyn always refused. "Your father is a strange bird," she had said. "Besides, I'd rather not sleep among pickled animals and ground bones."

Bianca had first met Jolyn two years ago. It was Bianca's habit to avoid Mass en route to her father's room of alchemy. Instead, she'd wander the riverbank and study the plants. Bianca was happiest in the twilight just before dawn, and usually she was alone at that time of morning. However, this day, she watched a girl comb through the mud, barefoot in the late fall. Bianca waited until she made her way up to the road. "Here," said Bianca, thrusting her shoes at the girl. "You need these more than I."

The girl took them and felt through to the hole in one toe. She waggled her fingers through the opening.

Bianca shrugged.

"What will you do?" asked the girl, looking down at Bianca's stocking feet.

"Never mind," said Bianca.

Another crack of thunder jarred her from her thoughts, and she looked around at her room. The board was strewn with bowls of forgotten and fermenting experiments. The shelves were better organized, but part of the copper tubing of her distillation apparatus still lay in a heap where Jolyn had pulled it down when she fell. Shards of glass lay half buried in the floor rush, and Bianca made a halfhearted attempt to pick them out. She collected the bowls on the table and the candles that had encircled Jolyn, and found the jar with remnants of the concoction she'd given her. Finally, she would brew the concoction and test it.

As Bianca settled on a stool next to the furnace waiting for the water to boil, she recalled her observations about Jolyn's circle of acquaintances.

Mrs. Beldam. Eyes of cool pewter and the carriage of a woman of higher station, but time had darkened her teeth, and lines crisscrossed her face like hatch marks in a drawing. Jolyn had believed she honestly cared for her, but Bianca wasn't so sure. Her obvious distraction at Cross Bones was not the picture of grief Bianca would have imagined. What did Beldam and Henley want from each other? The only thing she knew was that Henley supposedly pawned jewelry for her. What did they have in common? Jolyn. Mackney had said Henley wanted her ring. But why would Wynders speak with Henley? What did *they* want from each other? Bianca couldn't imagine. But she knew what *they* had in common. And that, again, was Jolyn.

Rain burst from the sky, pelting the windows and sluicing through wheel ruts in the lane outside. The red cat leapt from the rafters and leaned against Bianca, grateful for shelter and the fire's warmth. She fed him a few crumbs of leftover cheese and absently stroked his striped back.

Hopefully, Meddybemps would uncover something about Barke House. She hoped his many connections would prove useful and yield information about Mrs. Beldam and her past. She groaned, remembering his request for more rat poison. It was one concoction that sold predictably well. She checked her supply of apple seeds used in its recipe, thinking of all she needed to do and how her body ached with exhaustion. The fire crackled to a comforting glow. She turned her back to it while removing her sodden boots. Her muddy stockings sagged, and she peeled them off, exposing her cold white feet.

She sat by the fire and studied the remains of the dried herbs she'd given Jolyn, sniffing them to detect anything out of the usual. Perhaps it was foolish to take so bold a chance. What if she died like Jolyn? Well, at least it would be in the privacy of her rent and not a public swinging.

But a dead fool is no better than a live one, so she grabbed the flask of rancid goat milk and set it by, just in case. Just the smell of it caused an involuntary retch. She dumped the herbal concoction into the boiling water, stirring the brew and watching the steam curl into the air.

Over time, Bianca had learned that Jolyn's mother had been thrown in the Clink. Jolyn raked mud, trying to survive as best she could and save money to pay her mother's debt to set her free. But her mother died within a month of her arrest, having taken ill with one of the gaol fevers that spread like fire. Jolyn had bitterly quipped that her mother had vowed to get out of prison one way or another. Unfortunately, Jolyn had no other family.

Bianca thought back to her visit at Barke House, then tried to remember anything Jolyn had said about Pandy. Drawing a blank, she puzzled over Pandy's colicky humour. She was swirling the bowl of tea and inhaling its steam when another flash of lightning lit her room. The clap of thunder struck disconcertingly near, causing her to start, spilling some of her drink. A burst of wind blew her door open, and it struck against the crate with unnerving force. Bianca set down her bowl and went to find some rope to secure the door.

The rain poured inside, streaming from the eaves onto the threshold, soaking the floor. Bianca pushed aside the crate and leaned her weight against the door, lashing it shut. Finally she managed to keep it acceptably closed, though not without soaking herself in the process. Disgruntled, she tromped back to her stove and stripped off her bodice and kirtle, suspending them from a nearby beam to dry. She shivered in the chill and wrapped herself in a scratchy wool blanket, then went to the front door and shot the bolt.

Pandy had flushed red at the mention of Jolyn's suitor. Banes had witnessed Pandy's flash of temper, too. If Wynders had once loved Pandy, that would explain her anger. The girl was jealous. Bianca sniffed. Only two things caused a woman to lose her head—the loss of a child and the loss of a lover to another woman.

The wind continued to push against her alley door, worrying Bianca, but as she stared into the mesmerizing dance of flames, she recounted the few fragments of information she had been able to collect. Jolyn probably died from poisoning. Why would someone poison Jolyn? She could have died of natural cause, but that seemed unlikely. What could explain the trickle of purplish blood? Why would someone want her dead?

The fact that Jolyn had moved into Barke House and soon won the attentions of Wynders, who showered her with gifts and fed her all manner of unusual fare, troubled Bianca. Were his intentions true and from the heart? Or was there a reason for his interest in Jolyn?

Why did Jolyn become involved with Barke House? How did she come by it? Bianca racked her brain, trying to remember the details of Jolyn's decision. She couldn't remember and wondered if Jolyn had even told her. She blamed herself for being so preoccupied that she didn't devote but half an ear to Jolyn's stories.

Bianca thought about the abrasions on Jolyn's neck and her missing necklace. The muckraker accusing her of stealing a ring. The same muckraker talking to Mrs. Beldam at the funeral. The same muckraker talking to Wynders.

Bianca rubbed her temples and took a sip of tea. She thought back to Pandy's burst of anger. Banes had said she'd had Wynders's attentions until Jolyn came along. Obviously Pandy was hurt and jealous. If anyone had reason to want Jolyn dead, it would be Pandy.

The fire snapped, and the cat jumped in her lap. Bianca stared at the fire, rubbing its chin and imagining the faces of Pandy and the others as she thought. They seemed to float in the flames, their expressions appearing before her eyes. She concentrated on the feelings she'd gotten from their conversations, the unspoken words she'd perceived. She finished off the rest of the tea and set the bowl on the board. Like a shake to her shoulders, the sound of the bowl on the wood roused her from her thoughts. She picked it up and tipped it upside down. What had she done? Not a drop remained. She'd downed the remedy as casually as an ordinary cup of tea!

Her hand went to her throat, and she glanced down at the cat sleeping contentedly on her lap. How long had it been between Jolyn's last sip and the time she began to convulse? Bianca gulped and sat very still, her eyes wide with apprehension.

About a year ago, Jolyn had prevented Bianca from being run through with a dagger one dark night on the river's edge. It could have ended in a bad way, but Jolyn's bravery and selfless sacrifice were a testament to her character and how much Bianca's friendship meant to her. Bianca's eyes welled with regret. Jolyn had saved her life. And she had been powerless to save Jolyn's. For a moment, she let her tears flow, then squeezed her eyes shut and took a breath.

If she should survive this, she would be more careful. She would be as selfless and brave as Jolyn had been. And she would look to Pandy as the murderer. There was no greater cause for murder than hatred steeped in jealousy.

Bianca rubbed her stomach, wondering if her sudden nausea was her imagination. It had to be. She blinked and looked down at the cat. An active mind and imagination certainly had its downside. She spent far too much time in her head.

Another flash of lightning lit her room, followed immediately by a boom of thunder. The horn pane of her window rattled, then crashed to the floor. Bianca sprang to her feet, nerves skidding down her spine. The rain poured through the window, pounding the sill and floor, the wind pushing it sideways. Cursing in aggravation, Bianca found a plank of wood and jammed it in place. But as she stepped away from the window, the alley door blew open with such violence that it was as if the devil himself had thrown it open.

Bianca spun around.

The plank of wood clattered to the floor.

Again, sheets of rain poured into her rent, soaking the floor. But as she started for the window, a piercing pain surged through her skull, streaking and burning like a bolt of lightning. She staggered under its fierce and blinding force. The last thing she heard was the muffled sound of rain on the threshold.

# CHAPTER 21

As clouds swept over the Queen Moon, a man pointed his bow toward the quarantined *Cristofur* and, shoving himself free of the quay, heaved on his oars. With the clouds came wind, and the sea chopped at the hull, sloshing vile water on his fine leather boots. His cape was beginning to smell like wet dog, but he pushed away his distaste and concentrated on getting to the ship without swamping the foundering curricle.

His struggle caught the eye of the Rat Man floating in the shadow of the *Cristofur*, attracted there by the scent of vermin. The windfall he'd experienced when the ship first came to port had not lasted, but he was ever hopeful and always curious.

He noted the fine quality of the man's clothing, watched the plume in the man's cap become sodden and lose its bounce. He wondered why such a man did not hire someone to row for him. A storm brewed in the west, and the Rat Man lifted his nose and parted his lips to taste the weather on his tongue. It would not be long before the torrent was upon them. Why would this man take such a chance?

The *Cristofur* lowed and bobbed in the water, pulled at her cable and anchor like a restless colt. The few mates passed a flagon of gin on deck and sang bawdy sea shanties to pass the time. At least it kept the vermin away, or if not, the gin dulled their notice.

A lamp burned in the captain's quarters, where he and the first mate had taken refuge, drinking Spanish port. The door had been shut tight to keep out the stench emanating from the sleeping quarters, while the portholes were ajar as they preferred the reek of the Thames by comparison.

The man grunted and cursed as he rowed toward the *Cristofur*. His skiff dipped and shimmied in the choppy drink. Water breached the sides, soaking the man and weighing down the curricle, making it even more unwieldy.

The wraith chuckled at the man's perseverance. The only thing that could possess such a man to be out on a night like this was money. Though sometimes love could. But mostly money.

When the man neared the starboard side of the *Cristofur*, he called up to the drunken crew to put over a ladder. Finally, one of them stumbled forward and with some effort flung the brittle heap of rope over the side so that it hung tangled and twisted, completely useless. The man had to again yell for help. One by one the drunken mates appeared, some sneering, others taunting the merchant to figure it out for himself.

After a fair amount of bellowing from both parties, the rope ladder was righted and the man tied off his skiff and began to climb.

The Rat Man picked some gristle from between his pointed teeth and maneuvered beneath the captain's quarters, watching for the man's arrival. At a knock, the first mate released the hasp and allowed the man to enter. Setting formalities aside, the guest shrugged off his sodden cape, and the captain offered him drink as they discussed business. Numbers and tallies bored the specter, and he scanned the water for a snack before the man shifted the conversation more to his interest. The man reached inside his doublet, removed a leather purse, and plunked it in the center of the table. The ship's lamp swung like a pendulum over it, illuminating first the captain's face, the purse, and then the man.

"I would wish this to be filled with our sovereign's coin, but methinks it is not."

"I regret disappointing you. It contains rat poison."

"There are hardly any left to kill," said the captain, throwing back another drink. "Most swam for land when they smelled it. Only the fattest and laziest have stayed. They are locked away where they can dine undisturbed."

"My interest is to see the *Cristofur* off-loaded. You've a crew to pay, and I've an owner eager to deal. It pleases him not to see his goods waylaid."

"Indeed," said the captain. "It is not good business to pay a duty, then wait so long before collecting his profit. But we have the matter of a customs officer. Upon his inspection, we did not make a favorable impression."

"The poison should act swiftly enough. Bait the bodies and be done with it. We must get the *Cristofur* out of quarantine."

The captain leveled his gaze on the man. "I might remind you, there is the not so small matter of spreading contagion. We may well poison every last rat on board, but customs and medical protocol will require us to stay moored until the threat is over." His face bore a cynical but calm expression. The sea had hardened the captain. He was slow to register emotion and laid a matter of import out as stoically as giving an order. "Or until every last one of us is dead and gnawed to the bone."

The man masked his aversion by straightening his spine and adjusting his ruff. "I shall not let it come to that. Time is not the only way to end a quarantine."

The captain snorted and shot a glance at the first mate.

"Once the rats are dead, what shall we do with the bodies? We cannot make them disappear. We cannot dispose of them into the Thames. My crew would take issue with that. Besides, the customs officer is quite aware of the corpses."

"And you assume the customs officer cannot be bought?"

The captain raised his drink to their guest. "I apologize, my good sir. I did not realize we were in such capable hands."

The man suppressed a slight smile and finished off his quaff.

"Await the arrival of a dory where you may burn the bodies apart from your ship."

"The crew will like it not," said the captain.

"I need the *Cristofur* out of quarantine."

"Sailors are superstitious," said the captain, "and that is blasphemous, sir."

The man waved his hand dismissively. "It is more scurrilous to let them rot on board. When a sailor longs to feel the earth under his feet, a small fire can be easily overlooked."

The captain appreciated this man's cocksure attitude. Perhaps he would not regret this voyage after all. "Very good. We shall await the dory and a pile of oiled rags. And may I implore you to be quick on it. My crew grows restless, and I do not doubt they could scheme to make a float of my corpse and sail me safely to port."

The first drop of rain landed on the Rat Man's nose as he drifted beneath the captain's windows. A flash of lightning scorched the sky. The man watched the captain evenly and did not glance at the heavens and its warning. The Rat Man deemed the man an even greater fool than he had first thought.

The crew hooted at the gathering sky, and their calls were soon drowned by a rumble of thunder. The captain looked out the porthole. "If there is nothing further, I suggest you not delay." He smiled sardonically. "Unless you care to spend a night on board the *Cristofur.*"

Disguising his haste, the man stood and bowed, offered formalities, and departed the cabin. He got halfway up the stairs before realizing he had forgotten his cape, returning to the cabin, and snatching it off the chair. The captain waited until the first mate had bolted the door, then opened another bottle of port.

The Rat Man floated beyond the stern, listening to the crew mock the man shambling down the ladder. The clouds flickered from another streak of lightning, startling the man so that he missed a rung and slid down the rope in his attempt to hurry. His palms burned as the rope cut into them, and his desire to be done with the *Cristofur* distracted him from testing the bottom rungs.

His foot reached down, and he applied his full weight, only to find the rung and the one below it sliced in half. He fell, tumbling into the curricle, narrowly missing a swim in the Thames, and landed in a heap, staring up at the sky and the jeering crew slinging insults.

His head throbbing, he righted himself and fumbled with the bowline, releasing himself from the *Cristofur* and, he hoped, further indignation.

He had only cleared the ship's bow when the rain began to hammer. The crew dispersed, leaving the fate of the ship's agent to the unkind river and temperamental sky.

Despite hauling on the oars and generating his own heat, the man was chilled to the bone by the rain soaking through his already sodden wool cape. The wind whipped and howled, and the Thames lashed at his meager curricle, battling its inept captain for control. He knew he could not stop rowing, for the waves would capsize his little boat if they hit broadside. So he mustered his strength and resolve and entered into the match, knowing full well that if he did not succeed, drowning would be his consolation prize.

The Rat Man rode his mistress Thames like a seasoned lover. His posture erect, his black cape blowing and battered, he stood in his wherry as if all around him were calm. He feared no death or soaking chill, for he was beyond all that. Instead, he watched the struggle, amused at the monumental pitch of tempest—both human and non.

And who should be the victor? He'd place his bets on nature. In the end—she always won.

# CHAPTER 22

It had not gone well. Instead of luring him back into her arms, Pandy had driven him further away. Damn Jolyn anyway. If Mrs. Beldam hadn't taken her in, she might well have been the next Mrs. Wynders. She had thought, with Jolyn gone, he would have no further cause to reject her. Hadn't she indulged him like no other? Men—how short their memory.

Staring at the silhouette of London against the darkening sky, Pandy refused to spend the evening agonizing or listening to Kara's carping. If she could not have *his* attentions, then she would have the attentions of many.

She brushed her hair a hundred strokes—a shame to cover it with a rough linen coif, but until she was out the door she had to abide by the rules of Barke House and accept convention. Her lips and cheeks she stained with a squashed currant, and she laced her stays snug at the ribs and less so above.

To Kara's prying she said nothing, and before she left, she informed her bedmate not to expect her until late or perhaps not until morning.

Now she sat at the Dim Dragon Inn, entertaining a tankard of

ale and half a dozen men. Unfortunately, the ale was more interesting than they, and she stared fondly into her drink while the
men stared fondly at her. But she remained unmoved.

Her mood spiraled in an ever-quickening whorl. The one man
she wanted did not want her. She wished he could see her now,
surrounded by fawning and attentive men so keen to impress her.

But it was for one thing only and she knew that. None of them
had the tempered manner of Wynders or the finer dress to go with
it. There were all manner of charlatans and scalawags—a moneylender who preyed on yeomen and countryfolk new to town; a
jackman practiced in forging licenses for sellers and beggars; a
distracted dice cog and a card cheat, their eyes scanning the customers for gullible marks. And, most reprehensible of all, a lawyer.

The Dim Dragon Inn was suffering from a dearth of women
this night, especially ones with front teeth. Pandy should have
been heartened by the attentions of so many, and she had to
admit it was better than being ignored. Still, she sighed.

Pandy took a sip of ale as the lawyer tried to impress her with
his latest land acquisition and sale. The land, near Horsleydown,
was most probably a bog. He had managed to plagiarize a deed
and sell it to a land baron who sold it to a construction-minded
gentleman who planned to build another bear-baiting venue in
the obliging Southwark. Good moneys could be had by owning
such a place, and the recent success of the Bear Garden brought
out the money lust and fool in everyone. The man gloated about
his deal, which failed to impress Pandy as she noted his doublet
was soiled and smelled fusty, and he kept slapping the table
when her eyes wandered. She hoped for a savior, or a distraction,
someone at least worthy of her notice. It did not occur to her that
the pickings might be marginally better across the bridge. So she
sat with her eyes glazing over and her desire for attention waning.

Pandy had never had an easy way of it. She was contentious
and outspoken, though with Robert Wynders she had been more
subdued and agreeable. Not only had she seen him as a man of
money and influence who could rescue her from her surroundings, but she truly loved him also. But when Jolyn arrived, he had

lavished his attentions on her and promised the girl what Pandy believed was rightfully hers. In the end, though, Jolyn had gotten what she deserved.

"Pandy, what say you to a stroll along the Thames?" asked the moneylender, leaning in. His broad grin she construed as a leer. That, combined with a yellow tinge to the whites of his eyes, did little to convince her that this might be a good idea.

"I think not," she replied and settled her gaze on the door, which happened to swing open at that moment. A clatter of thunder accompanied the bang of wood against wall, drawing everyone's attention. Pandy was glad for the distraction.

Henley the muckraker stood on the threshold, his blocky body nearly filling the entrance. His dark eyes and darker countenance exuded weight and gave import to his arrival. He glowered at the denizens of the Dim Dragon, as if holding each patron accountable for some personal insult perpetrated against him. Obviously he was not well loved, and no one called out a greeting or an offer to join them.

Pandy was immediately intrigued. She'd never spoken to him, though she knew Mrs. Beldam had sought his help.

Henley slammed the door shut, and as men settled back to their ales and business, Pandy continued to stare at the dashing young rogue. Her stare did not escape his notice.

He strode over, removed his cap, and asked if he might sit. To the other men's chagrin, Pandy waved the clutch of clodpolls gone and welcomed the newcomer. He lowered himself opposite and ordered up an ale and bowl of stew.

"I've seen ye before," said Pandy, running a finger around the rim of her drink. She watched him unbutton his jerkin and settle. "At Cross Bones, at Jolyn's burial, talking to Mrs. Beldam of Barke House."

He neither confirmed nor denied it. Instead he watched her ambiguous eyes and waited for her to continue. He wondered if she was the sort to meddle—like that girl who had confronted him that afternoon. This was the second time today he'd been

sought out by one nearly his own age, and both had been attrac-
tive. He wanted to think it was his enviably good looks, but his
instinct warned otherwise.

"I live at Barke House."

The wench returned with his ale and bowl of stew and set it
down before him.

"So . . . ye know Mrs. Beldam." Pandy saw a glimmer of recog-
nition as he stirred his stew and blew on it.

"I know her," said Henley. He waited to see why she wanted
to know.

"But I've never seen ye at Barke House."

"I've no reason to go."

Pandy cocked her head. "But ye know Mrs. Beldam." Her
smile was sweet and without guile.

Henley's gaze traveled the length of her neck and beyond.
This girl was certainly lovely, and he didn't want to put her off in
case he might have a chance with her later.

"We've had dealings, aye."

Pandy took a sip from her pottle pot and watched him through
her long lashes. "So, what is it ye do?" Men were braggarts, and a
sure way to engage one was to give him the opportunity to spout
about himself.

"I trade what I can," he answered simply.

"Ye rake muck?"

Henley was loath to admit it—especially to a girl as lovely as
this. "I might find something on the flats, but I'm capable of
other things."

"Like what?" Pandy teased.

Henley's brow lifted. "We could leave here now, and I could
show ye."

A thrill ran down her spine. She'd caught his intent, and it
wasn't about business. "I hardly know ye." Not that she cared.

"We could change that."

Pandy took another sip to hide her smile. She was not inclined
to take up with the first man who dared her, but as she ran her

eyes across his broad chest, she liked what she saw. He might not be charming, but he had other qualities that made up for it. "You're bein' cagey," she said.

"Beth," he yelled, lifting his arm into the air, "bring this lass another ale."

Pandy tipped her head and grinned slyly. "I know what ye are about," she said.

This girl knew how to play the game. This time he let his gaze linger on the white curves of her skin disappearing into a russet velvet bodice. For the time being, this would be more enjoyable than slogging through muck. He would enjoy this sport.

"So, ye lived with Jolyn," he said when Pandy was settled in with her pottle pot.

Pandy took a long swill of drink. She sensed her judgment falter, but she was content for the moment, warm from the hearth, and the ale tasted better than the first two she'd been served. But maybe her tongue was just numb and everything seemed better. She nodded and glanced away.

"I knew her befores Barke House," he continued. "Knew her when she was a street urchin like the rest of us. Then, one day, she disappears from the flats. Seems she has taken a room at your Barke House. No one knew where she'd gone."

Pandy looked around, bored, but Henley went on, curious and enjoying the audience. "So's how'd she come by Barke House anyways?"

"Don't know," answered Pandy. She drummed her fingers on the table while continuing to glance around the tavern. Eventually, her eyes resettled on Henley, who was looking at her expectantly. She took another sip. "Mrs. Beldam took her in. I only knows they met at market and she offered Jolyn a place to stay."

"How'd you come by Barke House?"

"A girl told me abouts it." Her brow furrowed as if she were suddenly realizing something. The drink could no longer mask her contentious side. "What do ye care? I can think of more interestin' things to talks 'bout." She hoped this cove wasn't as thick as she was beginning to think.

Henley finished his stew and wiped his bowl with the end of his bread. "She had a ring."

"What's that got to do with me?"

"I was wonderin' if ye'd seen it."

Pandy's patience was at an end. She was hoping for a little attention, but all he could talk about was Jolyn. She finished her ale and slammed it down on the board. "It's gettin' late." She stood and rewrapped her shawl, clumsily winding it over her shoulders and chest in an effort to be warm for her walk back to Barke House. She hadn't expected the walls to move about her the way they did. She was starting to step away from the bench when Henley grabbed her wrist.

"Let me see ye home."

Pandy pulled her arm free, stumbling backward. Her head felt stuffed with wool, muffling the sound of her voice and the noise from the tavern. She wished she hadn't accepted that third pottle pot. "I can manage." She weaved between the tables, her unsteadiness drawing plenty of notice. She ignored the crude comments and slapped away groping hands, fighting them off to open the door, then pitched herself into the alley behind the Dim Dragon Inn. She had meant to go out the front.

She stood, swaying and blinking, squinting up the alley one way, then down the other. The back alley was as dark as tar, and the smell from rotting kitchen scraps melded with the musty reek of moldy, piss-saturated wood. Either direction was equally long and squalid, so she took a step, incensing a dog she had not noticed. Its head swung up from whatever it was gnawing, and its bared teeth and growl warned her off.

"I don' wan' your rotted meat, ye cur," she said, still possessing enough good judgment to turn and start up the alley in the opposite direction.

She took advantage of the dark to hike her skirts and leave a deposit of her own. As she crouched with her kirtle gathered in her arms, she felt the first pelts of rain on her face. "Aw, the bloody devil," she cursed. Nothing was worse than walking home in the rain. She stood, shook down her skirts, and laid a hand on a scummy wall to steady herself. Her head spun like a spindle, and she belched, frowning at the taste of muddy swill they called ale.

Above, the thin slit of sky sparked with lightning, and Pandy could at least see to the end of the alley and the lane it opened onto. What she didn't see or hear was a figure exiting the Dim Dragon Inn behind her.

Pandy stepped gingerly down the alley, as if she could avoid the mounds of offal, but the effort was wasted. She could have done just as well if she'd closed her eyes. Nothing was going to protect her hem and shoes from the hazards of traveling by foot.

By the time she emerged, the rain had begun in earnest, and she scanned the lane to decide which direction might provide the most cover.

Like a crab, she sidled along the fronts of buildings, wishing the teetering overhangs might offer some protection, but within minutes the slanting rain had soaked through to her skin. She had enough wits left to realize speed instead of cover should be her priority. So she stepped out from the buildings and trod heavily down the lane, glad for the occasional plank to lift her over the deepening muck.

Not only was she miserably cold and wet, but she had not succeeded in drowning her feelings for Wynders by finding someone else as worthy. And, it seemed, she could not escape the memory of Jolyn, which only served to further aggravate her. She cursed the dead girl, shook her fist to the heavens, and spouted a torrent of expletives. Anyone watching would think her lunatic.

But she was in Southwark, and most paid no mind to such a sight as it was as common as fleas on sheep. Except someone *did* take notice.

Pandy's linen coif stuck to her scalp, and she flung it to the ground, stomping it once for good measure. To the devil with convention and principles. She'd already condemned her soul to hell, so what was one more transgression?

She knew where Wynders lived. She'd followed him once and stood outside, watching his shadow move across the paned window to his wife's shadow. She'd sacrificed so much to be his. She'd consigned a life to the grave because of him. And all had been for naught. But there was a price to pay for his indiscretion. She'd already paid hers. And she would make sure he knew she was not one to be trifled with.

The cold and wet no longer chilled her. Instead, she burned with anger. Turning north, she set her course for London Bridge and the finer residences of Milk Street beyond. Even though she faced a long, miserable walk, she gave no further thought to it but instead focused on the end result. She would pound on his door and scream until all of London knew. What did she care about being dragged away by a night watch and taken God knew where? The fact that she had been wronged and would avenge her mental anguish was enough to extinguish any thought of better judgment.

But her cause, while understandable, mattered little to the one who crept up behind her.

# CHAPTER 23

Rescued from another world, Bianca blinked back into the reality of this one. From a soft, dreamless space she emerged into the hard dark of her laboratory. A rushlight burned behind several heads peering down at her, first four and then two. Their features were a blurred muddle of eyes and noses and concerned looks. She lifted a hand to her brow and was rewarded with a searing pain between her eyes.

"Lay you still. You've managed a bit of a strike on that crane. I'll not have you stand and fall until you are right." John gently guided her head back onto a mound of rush—a makeshift pillow—and pulled the wool blanket to her chin. "You were layin' in a heap when I found you."

Bianca grimaced, then turned her head to see where she was. He had fashioned a pallet of rush near the fire. Rain still fell, but a board was nailed in the window. The doors were shut, and the stoked furnace chased away a damp bite to the air.

"Is it morning?"

"It'll soon be light."

"What are you doing here?"

"You came by Boisvert's earlier." John checked a pan of boiling water and poured it into a bowl. He sprinkled in mint leaves and set it by to steep. "I heard a rap on the window, but you were already down the lane by the time I answered. I called after you, but you didn't look back." He blew on the bowl of tea and swirled it around. "So, I might ask the same question of you. Why did you come by?"

Bianca thought back to earlier in the evening. She remembered talking to Meddybemps and seeing a house marked with a cross of the plague. All else seemed a sea of confusion. "I don't remember why I stopped." She did remember why she didn't stay. The clouds were gathering, and the wind had started to blow. She raised herself up on one arm, then realized she had nothing on under the blanket.

John tossed her a nightdress. "I promise I didn't look . . . much."

Bianca glowered at him as she wiggled into it under the covers. "When did you get here?"

"I had to finish with the forge and by then the rain had started. I almost didn't bother." John crouched and handed her the tea. "This might help. I promise—no Capsicum peppers."

Bianca raised herself on her elbows and accepted the bowl. She smelled the steam just to be sure.

"Good thing I came along when I did," he said.

Bianca didn't say anything, but blew into the tea and took a sip.

"You should be glad I cared enough to see what you were about."

Bianca furrowed her brow, trying to patch together what had happened. She stared into the fire as if it might reveal the answer. She felt she had no time for rest, but her body told her otherwise. The drink soothed her jittery humours.

John stood and took hold of the fire poke, jabbing it into the fire. "Well, you could at least be grateful."

But Bianca was lost in thought. Had the concoction she'd made Jolyn knocked her out as well? Inadvertently, she had finished the entire bowl. She'd meant to try a little and wait for a reaction. Then the storm hit. The back door had blown open. . . .

"Right." John hung the fire poke and irritably dumped several dung patties into the furnace all at once. "Well, there you go." He whisked his wet jerkin off a beam where it had been drying, startling the sleeping red cat, which swiped at him. "Since you won't be needing me anymore," he muttered, stomping toward the door, "I shall not trouble you again."

Bianca blinked, rousing from her rumination. "John, wait! Where are you going?"

John stopped, then turned on his heel to face her. "It doesn't seem to matter to you whether I'm here or not. You could have caught your death of chill if I hadn't found you. If I don't mean anything to you, then why am I wasting my time?"

"John, that's not true. I do care for you." Bianca rubbed the back of her neck. "I don't know what happened. I'm confused." She set down the bowl of tea and threw back her blanket. "Stay," she said, sitting up. Her head throbbed, and she hesitated, waiting for the wooziness to pass. "Forgive me if I'm distracted, but I'm in a bit of a predicament." Surely he'd remember she was facing an accusation of murder and would not abandon her. She got to her feet, the cool dirt against her soles, and immediately the walls began to veer, then slide, and she started to topple.

John dropped his coat and caught her up in his arms. Her hair smelled of dung smoke, and her body felt thin and vulnerable as she leaned against him. But he resisted the urge to kiss her, though it took all his willpower not to take advantage of the moment. She was honestly befuddled and in no shape to be left alone. He might be furious, but this he quickly forgot as he urged her down on the makeshift pallet and sat beside her.

For a while they sat companionably as if nothing bothered them or could ever bother them. John's irritation waned, and he thought how easy they were together. She seemed as right to him as sunrise. How could he ever think of not knowing her? Of not caring for her? They'd depended on each other since they were twelve. He'd saved her then, too. But to be fair, she had helped him, too. If she hadn't developed a balm for a nasty burn he'd suffered at Boisvert's, he might have died from black blood. She was a talented chemiste, though frustratingly obsessed and driven.

"When I found you, the alley door was open and it looked like the pane had blown out of the front window. The floors were soaked."

"I was testing the remnants of the tea I brewed for Jolyn. I had taken a few sips to see how I felt. I had started a fire and was sitting, thinking. I guess I was lost in thought before I realized that I had finished the entire bowl."

"That is nothing if not foolish," said John. "No one here to help in case you fell ill?"

"I set aside rancid goat milk in case I needed an emetic. I was careful."

"Except you drank the entire cup." Once again, Bianca's pursuits had led her to a dangerous end. The girl could be as dense as marble in matters of common sense. John's throat tightened with exasperation. "You almost killed yourself."

"But I did not," Bianca replied simply.

"You must stop testing your liniments and medicines on yourself. Test them on someone else!"

"Are you volunteering?"

"Bianca, you have a mind for these medicines, but I don't fancy trying them out. Why don't you find someone with the ailments? It may benefit them. And you."

"But it might kill them. I've already been accused of one poisoning."

"Then find an animal. There are plenty of cats and dogs and pigs roaming about." He pointed to the cat skulking along the beam overhead. "Why not him? And you don't have to compensate an animal."

Bianca rubbed the back of her head, wincing at a tender spot. When she pulled her hand away, she found blood on her fingers. "Did I get this when I fell?"

John lifted her hair to check the gash. "You must have hit it on something. Maybe the furnace or the bench."

Bianca frowned, trying to piece together what had happened. She remembered the wind blowing open the alley door after she had secured it with rope and had moved a heavy chest in front of it. How could the wind have forced it aside? She looked over her shoulder toward the rear entrance. "When you got here, did you come in the alley door?"

"I came in the front. Your window was missing its pane, and you were lying on the floor. You didn't hear me when I shouted. I tried the front and got in. You hadn't bolted it."

"I *did* bolt it. I remember that."

"The back door was wide open."

Bianca squinted toward the alley and saw the latch and hasp dangling. "Did you move the chest back in front of the door?"

"It's the only thing to keep it closed. It's heavy, too. I can't imagine the wind could push it aside."

Bianca blinked. "Exactly," she said. "I could barely move it in place." Bianca pulled her legs to her chest and wrapped her arms about her knees. She tried to remember the events leading up to her collapse. It had been so sudden—the alley door crashing open, the windowpane blowing out. She rubbed her temple, remembering a strange feeling that she attributed to her imagination. Or had it been from the tea? Either way, it hadn't killed her. But she had seen the back side of her eyelids for a while.

She looked around the room, then took in a sharp breath as if seeing it for the first time. Indeed, she was becoming more herself and the fuzziness was beginning to clear. "John, someone has been here!"

"What do you mean?"

"Look at the table. Things are not where they were." She pointed to a stack of bowls. "Those were not on the corner like they are now. They were in the middle. And look at my shelves—those jars have been moved to the table. That's not where I left them."

John looked at the table strewn with crockery and Bianca's bizarre flasks and retorts. He could see no organization to the mess. "How can you tell?"

"John, I know!" Bianca stood and placed her hand on John's shoulder, waiting long enough for a slight dizziness to pass. She went to the table. "No, no. This wasn't how I left it." She looked up at John, baffled. "Did you move anything?"

"Nay, I just got a bowl and some mint for your drink."

Bianca gazed around the room, her eyes settling on the shattered remains of a jar lying in the rush. "Someone has been here."

"Who?" asked John, standing.

"I don't know."

"Well then, why?"

Bianca shook her head.

John followed her stare, studying the surroundings. The rush that usually covered the floor in an even thatch was kicked up and pushed into little mounds. He brought it to her attention. "Someone disturbed the rush on the floor."

Bianca looked about, then lowered herself on the bench.

John pushed aside the rush with his toe, revealing the packed dirt floor beneath. Nothing but shards of glass and pottery and the skeletal remains of a mouse littered it. He sat next to her, and together they blinked in silence, trying to put together a puzzle with too many missing pieces. After a while, John found some cheese stashed on a high shelf. He cleared a small space on the board and, with the small knife he always kept at his waist, sliced her a piece.

"I asked Meddybemps to find out more about Barke House," said Bianca, nibbling at her small wedge.

"You have suspicions?"

"I find it odd that Mrs. Beldam encouraged Jolyn to live at Barke House and soon aft this fellow Wynders tried to win her heart."

"I'm not surprised a man would have designs for her. She was lovely."

Bianca lifted an eyebrow. "It is too much of a coincidence. And then, there is Pandy."

"Jolyn never said much about her."

"True. But I'm beginning to put some pieces together."

John retrieved the blanket, then removed his boots to stretch his legs toward the fire. "Like what?"

Bianca pulled the blanket over them. Her head throbbed mercilessly, but she took some comfort in leaning against John, who tucked her in close and draped his arm over her shoulder.

"I paid a visit to Barke House. I wanted to speak with Mrs. Beldam. Banes told me she wasn't in. Pandy came down the stairs and was as flighty as a robin. Wouldn't answer me with anything other than sarcasm. I gathered she was not particularly fond of Jolyn."

"She's jealous."

"Most certainly. The moment I mentioned Jolyn's suitor she couldn't get out the door fast enough. And then Banes told me that was a touchy subject for her."

John pushed the hair back from Bianca's cheek, exposing her neck. He wanted to kiss it, lay his lips on her skin and inhale, but he knew what kind of reception that might get. He knew better than to distract her when she was thinking out loud. Still, he found its graceful curve distracting and forced himself to look away.

"Remember when Banes came by for Mrs. Beldam?"

"Aye."

"Remember what he came for?"

John shook his head. "I didn't pay any mind."

"He came for purgative."

John shrugged. "I suppose that's fairly common for a house of women."

"For a house of women of ill repute," said Bianca. "But Jolyn told me Barke House was reformed."

"All good intentions, but probably not easy to succeed."

"Perhaps, but Mrs. Beldam had rules. Besides, I believe only two things can wound a woman's heart enough for her to seek revenge."

John perked to hear what these could be. Any information regarding the behavior and thinking of the fairer sex was worth listening to. "Do tell."

"First, losing a man to another woman," said Bianca. "I believe Pandy may have been in love with Wynders."

"It's plausible."

"And the second, of greater consequence"—Bianca removed John's hand creeping down her arm—"losing one's child."

"Pandy had a child?"

Bianca shrugged. "Someone needed the purgative."

"I understand the cause for rage. But to murder?" John snuffed with doubt. He rested his hand on her thigh beneath the blanket. The heat from her skin warmed his cool fingers.

"Put the two together," said Bianca.

"Bianca, you don't know that she was his lover."

"Banes all but confirmed as much."

"But you don't know if she was with child."

"Aye. But what if she was with *his* child?"

John moved his hand toward her inner thigh and watched her from the corner of his eye. "Banes's visit to buy purgative *is* suspicious."

"That's why I think Pandy could have murdered Jolyn."

John nonchalantly kneaded her thigh. "Could she have poisoned Jolyn with the purgative?" he asked.

"I don't know. It might explain the cramping, but I'm not sure it would kill her."

"Perhaps a coincidence. She very possibly could have suffered from something else being slipped into her food."

"Mayhaps. But remember her blood took on a purple tinge. The only way I'll know for sure is to test the purgative and see if it changes the color of blood."

John tilted his head, then shook it. "Promise you won't test it on yourself." He knew she'd do what she pleased, but he hoped she'd be more careful. "Besides, you don't want to make it easy for Constable Patch."

"Meaning I'd deny him the pleasure of seeing me hang?"

John couldn't resist the wry look on her face. He kissed her long on the mouth and let his fingers tangle in her hair.

Bianca felt as if her ideas were finally making sense. It wouldn't be long before she had the proof she needed to bring Jolyn's murderer to justice. She gave over to John's seductive weight. She lay against his chest and let him brush his nose along her neck, nuzzling her to her clavicle.

But then, visualizing the measured tick of a pendulum, she remembered that time was not standing still, and she pushed away from John.

John started to protest, then thought better of it. His first priority was Bianca's welfare, and he remembered why he had ventured here in the first place. She would not be glad for what he had to say. He hesitated, thinking how best to tell her. How could he not alarm her? In the end, though, he knew she'd prefer his being direct. "Bianca," he said, "Constable Patch came by Boisvert's asking for you." He hated seeing her face become tight again. "If he finds you, he will arrest you."

Bianca stood up and savagely jabbed the fire with a poke. "I can't let that happen. I can't prove my innocence from gaol."

"Leave here, Bianca. It's only a matter of time before he returns."

"But I can't avoid him forever. I have nowhere to test my purgative except here."

"Why not use your father's room of alchemy?"

When Bianca had developed her balm for the French pox, she had done so in her father's room of alchemy. She had to sneak around when he was not there or when he was too preoccupied to care what she was doing. Even though she was beginning to become known for her medicinals, he continued to regard Bianca's and her mother's work as "the meaningless dawdling of simple minds."

"No," she said, without any hesitation. She gave John a scorching look. "I'll have to secure the doors better." She looked at the alley door, thinking. "It shouldn't take me long to test my idea. I just need a little time."

"Bianca, come with me to Boisvert's. You can perform your experiments there."

"You know very well Boisvert would never stand for that. He likes me, but he would never stand for me running experiments at his forge."

John racked his brain, trying to think of what to say or do to convince her to leave her room.

But with the threat of execution looming, Bianca's mind simmered with possible solutions and explanations to absolve herself of the crime. "Something else troubles me," she said. "I went to the Dim Dragon Inn yesterday. I was looking for a muckraker named Henley. He was at Cross Bones when Jolyn was buried."

John became sullen and didn't answer.

"Remember she had mentioned a muckraker who accused her of stealing? Henley was that fellow."

Relieved, John answered, "She never said what he accused her of stealing, did she?"

"Apparently, it was a ring. I saw him with Mrs. Beldam at Cross Bones, and when I asked him what business he had with her, he said he had pawned some jewelry for her."

"That's not unusual. Mrs. Beldam has to make money somehow."

"I suppose. But as I was leaving, a man wearing a pheasant plume cap arrived. I had sold rat poison to him earlier. I waited, then stole back into the tavern and hid in the shadows, curious why a man of such standing should frequent the Dim Dragon. He could certainly afford a finer establishment across the river in London." Bianca tucked her hair behind her ears. "He was talking with Henley."

John shrugged, uncertain where her logic was leading. "That doesn't mean anything."

"Meddybemps had followed the man to Barke House. And when I visited Barke House, I asked Pandy if Wynders had been by. I might just as well have told her she had a face like a mule, she left in such rage. Isn't it odd that a muckraker who hated Jolyn and a merchant she loved would associate with each other?"

"Bianca, the Dim Dragon Inn is frequented by all sorts. Rascals and the well intentioned. That two men should know each other is not cause for alarm."

"Why do you discount everything I say?"

"I am not discounting everything."

"You just did it again."

John took a breath to say something, then thought better of it. "All right," he said. "Suppose the two of them are rascals. What do you suspect?"

"Don't be condescending."

"I'm not!" He stared up at the ceiling while he composed himself. He knew she was anxious and touchy, and he tried to conjure enough patience not to lose his temper. After a moment, he tried again in a more level tone. "Tell me what you suspect."

Bianca's irritation was more with herself than it was with John. She knew it, and yet she struggled to stay reasonable. Someone had bludgeoned her and then ransacked her belongings. He had rifled through her sacred space, where she lived and worked. She felt violated, accosted. Maybe the intruder had meant to kill her; maybe he thought he had. Was it a warning? Not only did Constable Patch want her dead, but now it seemed someone else did, too.

The comfort she felt with John vanished, and her instincts told her she should be out pursuing Pandy and peppering the girl with questions. And she had to see if the purgative would turn a person's blood purple. She stiffened. What was she doing arguing with John while irreplaceable minutes of her life ticked away?

"John, you need to leave."

"What?"

"Leave and let me get on with it."

"Get on with what?" John's voice rose in frustration. "Why do you do this? I try to help, and you reject me."

"You can't help me right now."

"I'll do anything you need. I'll go with you to find Pandy. I'll sneak into Barke House and watch Mrs. Beldam without her knowing. Tell me what to do and I'll do it."

"I have told you. I need you to leave me be."

John stood abruptly. "What are you going to do?"

"John!"

Only she could do what was needed to save herself. It was written on her face. If he insisted on staying, he would only further alienate her. She had been in dire straits before, and if she survived this adversity, he had little doubt another predicament like this one, or even worse, would happen again. It was Bianca. He didn't expect her to live a sedate life, though he wished she would—at least just a little bit.

He took the fire poke from her hand, then stoked the fire so she'd have several hours of warmth before her. With the blaze crackling hot, he found his jerkin and shrugged it on. He did admire her self-reliance and grit. She had not always been so brave but had shed her fears like a dragonfly sheds its skin, emerged a confident young woman, certain of no one but herself. Without a word, he kissed her, and as he felt her skin warm his cheek, he silently wished that someday she would believe he was just as worthy of her faith and trust.

On the surface he would do as she wished, but as he edged out the door of her room of Medicinals and Physickes, he was already contemplating how best to protect Bianca from Constable Patch.

# CHAPTER 24

Banes was accustomed to doing Mrs. Beldam's bidding. For as long as he could remember, he had lived at Barke House, where his earliest memories consisted of watching scantily clad women lounging about. A steady stream of men had paraded through its halls, never staying long and always hazarding Mrs. Beldam standing guard at the door.

Accustomed to being shooed off, Banes was often given chores to distract him or was led away by the ear when he lingered at closed doors, listening to the strange sounds emanating from within. The clandestine nature of what went on intrigued him. He was inquisitive and took exception to being chased away. So he learned at an early age that stealth could satisfy his curiosity.

Jolyn's death had disrupted the routine at Barke House, and he was as much affected by it as he was baffled. Mrs. Beldam was her usual curt and efficient self, and while she did not openly mourn Jolyn, he sensed she was troubled by the girl's absence. She seemed more distracted, more irritable than sad.

As for Kara, the girl was more sedate when she arrived for

morning porridge, but she left to go about her day without much fanfare and kept her disparaging remarks about Pandy to herself.

If Kara seemed quietly troubled by Jolyn's absence, Pandy was practically delirious with jubilation. She had bounced out of Barke House last night in spite of her tearful encounter with Wynders earlier in the day. If there was one thing that fascinated Banes about women, it was their unmitigated spirit to sally on. In fact, Pandy was a study in dogged pursuit of unrequited love. Perhaps she had sought to soothe her bruised ego last night and had had a rowdy time of it, for she had not yet risen to eat. Banes cheered. If she did not show her face soon, she would suffer a good lashing from the missus's tongue—a comeuppance to look forward to.

Banes finished dipping the last of the dirty bowls in a bucket of water and set them to dry. Having finished his chores, he returned to his room and sat cross-legged on his little tuffet of straw, leaning his head against the wall. His eyelids grew heavy from lack of sleep, and he closed them, hoping Mrs. Beldam might be tired, too, and leave him be for a while.

He was still chilled from last night. The storm had soaked through to his skin, and Mrs. Beldam had shown little sympathy to his grumblings. He rubbed his sore arm. His whole body ached.

It had been an unusual request. When Mrs. Beldam told him to dress in dark clothing and handed him a ramrod of wood, he accepted both without question. He was inclined to covert activity; he was comfortable with such. But where would they be going? He had a feeling he might know.

The lowering sky had borne down as they made their way through the back alleys of Southwark. If not for the lightning, he would have had to navigate by running his fingers along the buildings. He did not question the missus but somberly followed her in silence, listening only to Southwark and the sound of their breathing in the hollows of its streets.

When they turned onto the familiar, quiet lane, his curiosity was piqued and his presumption was confirmed. Perhaps he would soon learn why the missus had a sudden, unshakable interest in Bianca Goddard.

To their benefit, the sky had cooperated. It billowed and belched, blew and bayed. And under its bluster they made entrance to Bianca's room of Medicinals and Physickes.

The two of them had heaved a chest out of the way, and when a crash from the front conveniently distracted the young chemiste, he had watched in astonishment as Mrs. Beldam bludgeoned the girl in the back of the head.

As Bianca slumped to the floor, the blood seeping through her black hair, he wondered if Mrs. Beldam had killed her. He opened his mouth to object but thought better of it since Mrs. Beldam still held the ramrod and had a wild look in her eye.

He bent down to see if Bianca was breathing and saw her chest shallowly rise and fall. Her face looked so appealing in the dim light of the furnace. He glanced up at Mrs. Beldam, who'd dropped the wood and was busy running her hands along the shelves as if feeling for something. Cautiously, Banes reached toward Bianca's lips and traced their curve with his fingertips. What would it feel like to press his lips against hers? They looked so warm and inviting—she wouldn't even know.

Mrs. Beldam grabbed a candle and stool and clambered onto the wobbly thing to have a better look at the upper shelves. Banes saw his opportunity. One kiss could never hurt anybody. He leaned over and lowered his mouth to hers.

"Banes!" screeched Mrs. Beldam. "Help me!"

Banes jolted upright. He scrambled to his feet and smoothed down his shirt to collect himself.

"Search the table. Look through every crock and bowl."

"It might help if I knew what I was seeking." He had yet to learn what this late-night foray was about. Surely she did not expect him to read her mind, too.

"A ring," said Mrs. Beldam, pulling down a jar and peering into it.

"A ring one might wear on a finger?"

"Aye!" She shoved the jar back on the shelf and pulled down another.

"Why would you think Bianca has it?"

Mrs. Beldam turned an exasperated eye on Banes. "Because this is where Jolyn died. She may have stripped her of her possessions."

The day of Jolyn's death, when he had arrived to buy purgative, Bianca had appeared in a state of shock. Her face was splotched and puffy from crying. She was too bewildered to be interested in any jewelry her friend might have owned. But he kept his opinion to himself and made a feeble attempt to search the surface of the table. He inched along, admiring the intricate copper sculpture Bianca had erected. He found its twists and turns intriguing and imagined the path a liquid would take from the beginning of its process to the final spout suspended over a beaker. He wished he could ask the young chemiste what the elaborate contrivance was for, but alas, she lay crumpled by the stove.

Mrs. Beldam shoved the last jar back onto the shelf. "It has to be here," she said, scouring the room with her eyes. She kicked aside some rush on the floor in frustration.

Banes poked his finger into a jar of sweet-smelling powder and cautiously tasted it. "Why is this ring so important?" he asked.

Mrs. Beldam bristled. "Survival. And if ye want to keep on at Barke House, we'd better finds it."

Banes studied the missus through the twists of copper. He observed her grim expression and the deep creasing of her forehead. He couldn't remember a time not knowing her, but she was not his mother. She had always made that insufferably clear. When asked how he'd come to live at Barke House, Mrs. Beldam responded with a fantastic tale—an almost mythic one, so that for years he had thought he was destined for greatness. But age and time had trampled that notion.

She said he was found floating in a basket on the river Thames, hidden in a patch of reeds. A girl had brought him back to Barke House. If not for Mrs. Beldam's generosity, he'd have certainly perished. Despite his deformity and the urgings of others, she had resisted drowning him and cared for him like he was her own.

A Jew who frequented Barke House compared his story to that of Moses, so Banes fancied himself akin to the heroic prophet. Like Moses, he had been found on a river and his life had been spared, but unlike Moses, he had not heard the voice of God through a burning bush. At least not yet.

For years, Banes was content until one of the men frequenting Barke House noticed him. He had Banes hold out his arm so he could examine it. He turned Banes's hand over carefully, as if it had been made of butterfly wings. "Make a fist," he demanded. And so Banes did.

"Press your palms together." But that was more difficult. All the time the man's eyebrows lifted with interest and studious consideration. Then, pressing his fingers into the withered flesh of Banes's limb, the man announced he was missing a bone. He showed Banes his own arm by comparison.

Until then, Banes had not shied from his grotesque appearance, but the man's intense examination drew the attention of the women of Barke House, and they had gathered round. At first they watched with polite curiosity. The man did seem to know something of a person's anatomy. Then one of them had tittered and another had quipped, and as he looked from face to lovely face, it was not acceptance that he saw in their expressions. It was something akin to distaste. It was revulsion. He no longer felt special. His deformity had made him unique, and his realization of people's true feelings wounded him. Banes had learned to feel shame.

Being surrounded by desirable women did not result in a growing comfort or ease with the opposite sex. That women were beautiful only heightened his feelings of ugliness and self-loathing. He began to shy away from people, preferring to make himself scarce. He would recede into the shadows, as if to make himself invisible, rather than elicit someone's notice and hurtful comment. But Banes never abandoned his ability to meet a person's gaze once he drew it. He did not shrink from appraising stares if they were offered one-on-one. It was as if he dared that person to look on him. His level stare was his armor. He could meet those eyes with the coal-black gaze of his own.

Bianca had been different. When he first arrived at her room of Medicinals and Physickes, she had welcomed him as any other. She watched as he accepted her philter and clutched it to his chest as he paid with his good hand.

"You make do as well as any man with two," she had said. There was no mistaking to what she was referring. "We all have defects, some more evident than others. I imagine your worst difficulty is overcoming people's ignorance." She had treated him no more and no less than any other, and thereafter, he looked forward to fetching whatever Mrs. Beldam needed from her.

Bianca's words had stirred him. He began to take his place in life and not avoid it. He still retained some of his insular inclinations, but that was changing, and he regressed only when he was feeling insecure. So it was with some anguish that he was party to Mrs. Beldam's ill treatment of her.

"By 'survival' what do you mean?" Banes had circled around the table and was standing near Bianca, keeping a worried eye on the girl, who still hadn't moved. "How can a ring serve our well-being?"

"Ye have a roof aboves your head and foods to eat," said Mrs. Beldam, brushing off her hands and straightening her bodice with a smart tug. "It doesn't come without cost."

Banes knew better than to expect a forthright answer. Hadn't their whole survival depended on lies? Barke House was no longer a house of ill repute—but what *was* it? Men no longer frequented its halls as they had done when he was younger. But men did come round. And one man in particular.

"Has this something to do with Robert Wynders?"

Mrs. Beldam abruptly turned away so he could not read her face.

Banes thought back to the strange confrontation between Wynders and Beldam in the kitchen. He wondered if the ring was the missing link between the two. What did it signify? What possible value could a ring have for the two of them? He dropped his gaze to Bianca and was surprised to see her stir.

"She's coming to!"

Mrs. Beldam pushed past him. She glowered at Bianca and was about to nudge her with the toe of her boot when Banes put out his hand to stop her.

"Shh!" he hissed.

A soft groan escaped Bianca's lips.

Mrs. Beldam looked about in panic, her eyes finding the rod lying on the floor. Banes watched in horror as she started to lunge for it, but he got there before her and grabbed it. "Are you mad? You'll kill her! Do you want to be hanged for murder?"

Mrs. Beldam tried to snatch it away, but Banes stepped back and held out his misshapen arm to stop her. She recoiled from his touch, as if his fingers had scorched her chest. Her eyes dropped to his deformed arm. The contempt she felt for him was evident on her face.

"I suggest we leave," said Banes, trying to sound reasonable and hoping Mrs. Beldam would relent.

Mrs. Beldam looked down at Bianca motionless on the floor, then turned on her heel and marched toward the door. She stopped as if she'd had one last thought. A bowl on a table next to the door had caught her eye. She brought it to her face and studied its label, then peered inside. Unhappy with its contents, she cursed and hurled it at the wall.

Now Banes pondered. He sat in his room, wondering why Mrs. Beldam let him stay at Barke House if she hated him so. Other than to fetch her potions and clean—what purpose did he serve?

He scratched a fleabite on his calf. For some reason, the missus wanted Jolyn's ring. Perhaps it explained why Wynders had favored the girl. Why he lavished gifts and attention on her. But if Jolyn had a ring they both wanted, why didn't one of them just steal it? Mrs. Beldam could be an expert conniver—he'd witnessed that plenty of times. But why hadn't she succeeded? She could have gotten Pandy to steal it. Or, for that matter, why hadn't she enlisted him?

Banes lay on his pallet of scratchy hay and closed his eyes. His troubled thoughts kept him from drifting to sleep. If it was true that Jolyn had died of poisoning, who, then, had poisoned her? A rising feeling of unease roiled in his gut. More than one person had wished ill for Jolyn. More than one person had wanted what she had.

But more worrisome was that more than once he had fetched powders for Mrs. Beldam—the last being purgative. Had he unwittingly procured a poison that had killed Jolyn? His eyes blinked wide as he stared at the ceiling above him. A grip of nausea turned his stomach. He rolled to his side and retched into the rush.

His squeamish stomach would not be calmed. He lay back, staring at the ceiling, sweat trickling down his temples. His head pounded, growing louder and more insistent, until he realized it was not of his own making but came from the front door. Mrs. Beldam called for him to answer it. Banes staggered to his feet and grudgingly made his way to the front vestibule. He took a breath to steady himself before unlatching the lock and pulling it open.

The queasiness in his gut took a turn for the worse.

"Aw. I sees someone *is* home at the ignoble Barke House." Constable Patch peered in at him. "If you woulds be so kind as to summon Mrs. Beldam."

# CHAPTER 25

If a shadow could be cast on a foggy night, her silhouette would have resembled a hunchback's. Bianca gripped a bulging satchel slung over her shoulder and solemnly crossed London Bridge toward Wool's Key.

Despite the threat of arrest, she had spent the day in her room of Medicinals and Physickes fashioning traps made of woven reeds and vines. She had secured her doors and worked by the light of a wheezing tallow, mindful to appear "not at home" to any who called. Twice she had escaped through the alley and circled back in a wide arc, spying her door from a safe distance. Two women had separately knocked, and she recognized each of them as customers but did not chance engaging them for fear that Constable Patch might suddenly appear.

Her fingers expertly wound the strips into pliable but sturdy cylinders, each the perfect size to contain and subdue her prey without them snarling and biting their neighbors. She'd made seven cages, a sufficient number. Any more, and the serrated blades of sedge would have sliced her fingers raw.

Was this the best way to proceed? A mental picture of Pandy kept her company while she weaved the cages, as did the red cat sleeping on an overhead beam. Questions whirled in a jumble of unanswered theories. At least testing the purgative might be a start and an end she could finish. If the purgative tinged blood purple, she would have cause to believe someone at Barke House had slipped Jolyn enough of it to have killed her.

She kept a wary eye out for loobies and miscreants, difficult since the smoke from chimneys hung low about her, trapped in the dense fog off the Thames. The two blended into a thick, putrid brew difficult to breathe and see through.

Emerging from the bridge, she cut through a short alley onto Thames Street and skulked toward the Tower. She disliked going near its walls and did her best to avoid looking at the sinister edifice even when safely on the other side of the river in Southwark. The Tower was the scene of Anne Boleyn's and Catherine Howard's executions and nearly that of her own. But that was over a year ago, and she was better served to focus on what lay ahead.

The water stretched before her, and as she neared its banks, the prows of moored merchant ships appeared, then disappeared in the gloaming mist. She was at Wool's Key, with its winches and abandoned pulleys. The damp had coated the steps of the pier, making them slippery, so she gingerly descended to the river's edge.

Still bearing the unwieldy satchel, she paused to peer into the murk. This was as good a place as any for catching her prey.

She dropped the satchel and withdrew a net she'd filched from behind a fisherman's rent. She spread it out and worked the tangles loose, picking out clumps of mussels and mud until it lay smooth. Bianca sat back on her heels and slipped her fingers beneath her scarf to warm them against her neck. They felt drained of blood, cold as twigs in November, but against the heat of her skin, they burned like she had just plunged them into a stove.

Soon the noses of curious rats poked from under the steps, catching a whiff of rank mussels piled next to her. Bianca hadn't expected such a quick response. She slowly gathered up the net and crouched, waiting motionless for the rats to move closer.

They seemed to come from everywhere. Before long, a dozen swarmed over the mussels. They fought and rasped, and she nearly lost her nerve. Bianca almost abandoned the idea, but with a clipped yelp, she threw the net over the feeding rats.

Cursing and muttering, she gathered its ends, sweeping the vermin into a neat bundle and cinching it closed. She held them up, a teeming, roiling mass of fur and teeth. The thought of reaching in and pulling them out to drop in their respective cages seemed a delicate matter, not to mention wildly disagreeable. Then she noticed a bollard of dense wood. She wound her arm like a windmill, then whacked the bundle hard against it.

Unfortunately, one whack was not enough. She had neither stunned nor silenced the awful brood, so she smacked them again.

Improvement.

Bianca repeatedly beat the rats against the bollard and pier, anything that offered resistance. At last she rendered them senseless and dropped the sack on the pier to catch her breath.

Not a single rat stirred. However, they would soon rouse, and when they did, she wanted them secured in their individual cages. Bianca opened the satchel and dumped the reed cylinders out on the pier. Working quickly, she pulled a rat out by its tail and dropped it in a cage. She tied the opening closed with a length of jute, then poked the rat with her finger to be sure it was alive. The rat bared its teeth, and she dropped it in her sack.

She grabbed a second cage and a second rat, and it wasn't long before she had all the rats she needed secured in the makeshift cages. The remaining rats she kicked into the water. Bianca pulled the satchel closed, pausing to blow into her fists to warm them. A dog barked in the distance, and at her feet the river sloshed against the wood pier. She thought how cold she was and rewound her scarf about her neck, tucking the ends into her bodice to keep her chest warm. With a grunt, Bianca hefted the satchel onto her back. Soon she would be back in front of her stove. She was taking a step toward the stairs when an orb of yellow light caught her eye.

The light moved along the riverbank in an easy arcing swing of someone walking. On closer inspection she saw three men, one carrying a lantern and a pair of oars and another dragging two cumbersome sacks. The third followed, lagging behind the others as he stepped carefully through the muck. Bianca crouched, fearing they might see her, but the men were intent on locating a particular skiff, one dragged to shore and guarded by a lock and chain.

The man with the sacks hefted them into the boat, then lifted the heavy padlock and asked for the key. The man holding the lantern tossed the oars into the skiff. He held the lamp aloft, illuminating all their faces as he fumbled through a pocket then withdrew a key. Bianca sucked in her breath.

Wynders.

Anticipation shot through her veins.

"Row to starboard," Wynders said, handing him the key. "The captain is expecting you, though I suspect you will have to rouse them. If they are any less sotted than the other day, I'd be smacked. These mates are long on drink and short of temper. Quarantine does that to a crew." Wynders glanced at the third man catching up to them, then continued his instructions. "They'll set down the bodies, and you lay them on the oil rags. Use the rush lights to set it ablaze. And don't set the *Cristofur* on fire in the wake of it."

The man grumbled something inaudible, and Wynders answered, "I'll meet you when she's out of quarantine and pay you then." He stepped back as the man dropped the chain on the mudflat and dragged the boat into the water.

Bianca stayed as still as stone, watching the rowboat fold into the fog. How he'd find his way to the *Cristofur* in this thick she couldn't imagine.

Wynders led the other man to a wall next to the quay, where

they sat atop their perch, with the lamp in between. If it weren't for the glow of light, Bianca would have had a difficult time locating them. She could see they kept their attention on the river and spoke little, but how long would it be before they noticed her?

Bianca glanced about anxiously. A coil of rope nearly as high as her shoulders was her only chance of staying hidden. She crouched behind it and worried the rats might start to hiss and the sound would give her away. She lowered her head at an unnatural angle, trying to hide. Her neck cramped, but she would not leave without her traps, nor could she chance Wynders spying her.

A rat nosed her foot. She pushed it away with the toe of her boot, but it came back, threatening to climb into her lap. She jammed a fist in her mouth, smothering a shriek that inched up her throat. Glancing at Wynders, she quickly plucked the thing by its tail and hurled it in the water. The men looked toward the splash, and Bianca quickly ducked and held her breath.

In a moment, she dared a peek and saw that they hadn't moved. Her neck ached from hunching, and she forced herself to resist the urge to stretch. Instead, she concentrated on the sound of the river lapping at the pilings. She waited.

The persistent rat found its way back on the pier. Bianca was about to snatch it up again when an eruption sounded across the water. An orange-red burst of flames scorched the night, cutting through the miasma, revealing the hull of a merchant ship. The blaze flickered and reached skyward, a hot searing fire bellowing smoke that raked her nose with the smell of charred wood and something abominably foul. Bianca buried her nose under her arm and watched until the churning inferno was eventually subdued by fog.

Wynders and the man saw it, too. They stayed until the fire died, then hopped off the wall. Wynders took up the lantern.

A gut feeling told her to follow.

Bianca blew into her hands to warm them, then lifted the satchel of rats. She was settling her foot on the first step of the quay when unexpectedly the whole structure shuddered. Bianca froze until the rumbling stopped, but three words came to her. Had she remembered them carved in stone on a building or etched on a grave? Peculiar how they suddenly came to mind, or were they whispered in the vaporous night? She spun around and scanned the water, but all was silent and dark, shrouded in mist.

"*Fortes fortuna iuvat.*" She couldn't say from where the words had come or why she had thought of them. But she knew what they meant. Fortune favors the brave.

# CHAPTER 26

Bianca followed inconspicuously—or as discreetly as a girl could toting a satchel full of hissing rats. She followed the men from the wharf up to Botolph Lane, where it appeared Wynders handed the man a pouch. She saw them part ways and decided to follow Wynders toward Wool's Key. Warehouses lined the waterfront, and he entered one of them. She sneaked as close as she dared, then flattened herself against a wall where she could peek around the corner from a safe distance. She wasn't sure what she'd learn about Wynders, and certainly, as the night wore on, she was no closer to discovering what killed her friend. But perhaps if she knew more of this man's business and his habits, she could piece together his intention.

The massive oak door muffled the sound of his movements, and Bianca wondered if she should even stay. She didn't know how long he would be, or whether he'd come out anytime soon. There were no windows or openings to peep through. She set the bundle of restless vermin next to her and kicked it once to silence them.

The night air needled through to her bones, and her nose ran from the cold. She rubbed her hands together to thaw them, wishing she had remembered her gloves. Mercifully, she did not have to wait long before Wynders emerged.

He drew the door shut, securing it with a length of chain and a lock. Testing it for security, he reworked the chain and lock, then took up his lantern.

Bianca plastered herself against the wall as he walked past, unaware. She held her breath until he turned and was out of sight.

She hurried after to gauge his direction, assuming he probably headed home for bed. She watched until he turned a corner where wealthy merchants and tradesmen lived, then returned to the warehouse. The door had been secured with a chain that allowed barely more than a hand's width of opening, enough for Bianca's thin frame to slip through. She sucked in her breath and squeezed inside.

No light penetrated the interior. She hesitated, allowing her eyes to adjust, when she whiffed a putrid odor permeating the air. An undercurrent of musty sacks of grain merged with a caustic stench. She buried her nose in her scarf, trying to smother it.

She was able to sense wooden chests stacked before her and touched them lightly as she stepped past. Along the walls, the barely visible outlines of crates towered above. She moved warily through aisles jammed with containers and barrels, wishing she could see well enough to know what their labels read. Her nose clogged from dust as thick as smoke. More than once she removed her scarf and took a mouthful of the odious air, then rewrapped her mask of rough woven wool.

An odor that would have repelled the fainter of heart did not deter Bianca, who long ago had grown accustomed to noxious fumes. However, this smell was not one with which she was familiar. Her eyes burned and her throat seized, but she had to know its source.

The smell grew stronger as she made her way into the cavernous expanse of warehouse. Her surroundings grew darker still, and she tripped, stumbling into a crate, jostling it loose. It gave way, jarring the surrounding crates. She lost her balance but managed to land on her rump while throwing her arms over her head to protect it. An object rolled from the top of a disturbed crate, landing square in her lap. She shrieked, frantically brushing it off, imagining the worst. It rolled to a stop, and she eased her breathing when it didn't move. Tentatively she reached out and felt a long bundle of twigs. A rushlight.

Where there was a torch, there must be a flint, but without a light how could she find it? She snickered at the irony. "Oh for a flint to chase away the black." She was about to toss aside the useless torch when she remembered she might have one. She was forever misplacing her flint when she was lighting her dung fires, only to find she'd dropped it in her skirt pocket. She reached in her pocket and smiled.

The dark receded from the smoky flame, and Bianca now had the means by which to navigate. She pushed ahead in the direction of the foul odor, grateful the smell of the burning rush managed to help mask it.

She wove her way through an aisle of crates labeled with ports of origin and destination. She stopped to read one label written partly in foreign tongue. Familiar with the look of French, she knew it was not that. She'd seen plenty of the script at Boisvert's, and John was practiced in it. No, this looked more floral, more Latin. Italian. She searched the end of the crate and read, *"Porto di origine, Genova."*

The rushlight would only allow her so much time, and she chided herself for her curiosity. Sometimes it did little to advance her cause and much to delay it. She pushed herself forward to the back of the warehouse.

As she neared a platform of barrels, she heard a strange sibilation—a hissing noise, a skirmish. She stopped cold. The rasping grew. She took a cautious step forward. If her skin had not been attached, she would have jumped out of it when she heard a scratching, then a thump.

She held the torch aloft but saw nothing. It was then that she heard a noise come from behind, and she whirled around, sweeping the rushlight in a wide arc.

But for her chest heaving, she stood still as stone. Her imagination was not making this easy. She wondered if Wynders had returned. She held the scarf over her nose and gulped a mouth of putrid air.

Eventually she convinced herself the sounds were coming from in front of her. She crept forward between the walls of grain sacks towering overhead. The stores of grain made a formidable barrier, and she stepped toward an opening, focusing on the dark gap. But a sudden scurry and weight on her boot made her jump. She swept up her kirtle and swung the light, searching for its source. A rat ran along the bottom of the sacks of grain and disappeared into the dark. She paused to catch her breath, then continued forward, inching closer to the opening, the torch lighting her way. Now a whisker's length from the gap, she jabbed the torch around the corner and followed, peering past its orb of light.

For a second she couldn't fathom what she was seeing. It was surreal, like a night fright brought to life. She threw her hand over her mouth.

There, in various stages of decay, lay more than a dozen corpses. Strewn in sinister repose, some lounged as if sleeping off too much drink, some lay with limbs askew, and some were rump side up. If their poses were not macabre enough, even more disturbing were the rats feasting on them.

Hundreds of vermin hissed and ripped off skin, crawled and sated themselves. Some yanked while others pulled. The bodies jerked and their limbs moved as the vermin tore them apart, feeding like maggots.

Bianca's stomach heaved. She turned and ran for the door to the warehouse, running like a madwoman through the aisles of crates and barrels.

She tripped—narrowly avoiding setting the place on fire with her torch. But even that didn't slow her down. She stopped to vomit, not caring she soiled the hem of her kirtle in her haste to keep moving.

Was this what Wynders had come to check? For what purpose

did he warehouse the dead? If Bianca had had more nerve, she might have stayed long enough to see that the bodies were all men. If she had had a stronger stomach, she might have stayed long enough to note their dress. But as it was, she had seen enough to realize Wynders did not want these bodies found. And for Bianca, that was plenty.

She reached the entrance and pushed against its massive oak frame.

It wouldn't budge.

Frustrated, she drove her shoulder into it, trying to force open a thin gap so she could squeeze back out. Still, the door remained secure.

The chain had been secured more tightly since she had gotten in. Wynders must have returned. Did he know she was there?

Bianca let loose a scream that shook the gibbets at Aldersgate. Stealth and covert snooping be damned, she wanted out.

# CHAPTER 27

John never tired of polishing coins. Being surrounded by money and touching it was a pleasure, but Boisvert's unwarranted harping quashed any joy he was having bringing a shine to silver. The metallurgist lectured him on women's wiles as if he had never seen a female and had been pent up in a monastery all his life. Not that Boisvert's sage words fell on deaf ears; it was just when it came to Bianca, his advice wasn't relevant.

Bianca was and always would be unique.

From the moment he first saw her picking pockets at Cheapside, he knew she was the one for him. They had been only twelve, but Bianca had filched his heart as sure as she'd lifted sausage from under a butcher's nose.

John knew he was destined for disappointment along the way, for he was schooled in the harsh realities of life. His father had been killed in a tavern brawl, and his mother had abandoned him for a Danish sailor. Left to fend for himself, John begged for scraps at an inn on Old Fish Street Hill and slept in an empty barrel in the back alley. He had a good heart, as good as any rascal who'd had to live by his wits to survive.

If he hadn't helped Boisvert one night after the French metal-lurgist escaped the point of a dirk, both Boisvert and John would have fared much worse. Boisvert was new to London and igno-rant of its customs and cuisine. That night Boisvert had ingested one too many ales and slices of dubious kidney pie. He bragged too much of Frenchwomen and French ways, and so, when he tripped out the door to weave his way home, it wasn't long before he found himself at the end of a menacing blade. John watched as Boisvert was robbed, then kicked senseless for throwing up on his assailants. Wondering if the man had any coin left on him, John ventured out of his barrel and searched his pockets. When Boisvert's eyes fluttered open, John saw an opportunity to rob the man's rent once he helped him home. It was with some effort he got the pudgy greenhorn home to Foster Lane, and once he did, the metallurgist thanked him with a preemptive slam of the door.

John vowed never to help a Frenchman again.

Nothing would have come of it if Boisvert hadn't sought his young rescuer to become his apprentice. When he found him, John followed as if called by Christ himself. And he never regret-ted it.

Except when Boisvert preached about women.

"Boisvert, contrary to what you believe, Bianca does not want to be taken care of. She has her own rent."

"My friend, you are so naïve." Boisvert shook his head with the arrogance of an experienced romancer. "It is not that the *fille* doesn't want to be taken care of. Every woman, *sans exception,* wants that. It is because she doesn't want . . . you."

"Oh, I know she does. I know she wants me."

"How so? You do not live with her." Boisvert watched John for a reaction. "It is a curse, this love. It is true what they say—that this 'love, she is blind.' You saw it come, but you do not see it go."

"Boisvert, Constable Patch is after her!" John threw down the polishing cloth. "She's a wee preoccupied of late."

"But can you tell me before this happened, before she saw a noose dangling, did she treat you as you wanted?"

John hated when Boisvert posed questions. It always got him thinking in ways that made him squirm. Bianca and he were different. They didn't have to be crawling over each other to show how much they cared. Though, he had to admit, a little more crawling would have suited him.

"Bianca would never fawn over *any*one. She hasn't the time."

Boisvert tsked. He hung a metal mold on a hook next to the forge. "Then, that is a problem."

"Perhaps for you. If Bianca acted like she couldn't live without me, I wouldn't want her."

Boisvert looked on him with overt skepticism, which only further incensed John. The Frenchman had succeeded in wearing him down. He was worried about Bianca, and getting prodded by Boisvert wasn't helping to allay his fears.

"Boisvert, I've had enough." He lifted his jerkin off a hook and, ignoring Boisvert's protests, headed out the door.

John had no intention of monopolizing Bianca's time. He only wanted to peek in her window and see that she was safe. The last time he had done that, he had expected to see her working on one of her concoctions, not sprawled on the floor naked and unconscious. An uneasy feeling slithered down his spine as he wondered what he might find this time.

She had told him that helping her meant leaving her alone. Only she could do what was needed to save herself from a swing at the end of a rope. It bothered him to leave her, and he had done so reluctantly. John believed that Bianca would be able to avoid Patch for a day, and so he was able to go about his work at Boisvert's without much worry. But John wouldn't stay away forever. He sought his own reassurance in this matter, and he would help without her knowing.

He crossed London Bridge and passed into the seedy borough of Southwark, feeling his disquiet grow along with the number of stray dogs and runagates eyeing him.

Once he turned onto her lane, a whiff of Morgan's Lane stream worked its foul magic. His breath caught in his throat, and he pinched his nose closed. Bianca was made of sterner stuff than he, living in Southwark.

When John arrived at Bianca's moldering front door, he hesitated, uncertain whether he should knock or just peep through the window and leave her alone. But the decision was made for him when he found the window still boarded. He'd have to risk her anger by knocking. This he did, to no response.

"Bianca," he called, trying the door.

John circled around to the alley, knowing the back door and lock were probably still broken. After budging the door, he managed to push his face in the wedge and called her name.

Still, no response.

He kicked the spongy wood slats and loosened the flimsy rope securing it. Once he was inside, the only light came from the dying embers in her calcinatory furnace. He scanned the room, checking between the tables to be sure she wasn't on the floor again, then found a tallow in a basket near the front door. He lit it in the stove and waved it about. Definitely no Bianca.

Where *was* she? Had Patch arrested her? He refused to believe it. She was too wily to let that happen—at least not without a fight. He studied the room for signs of struggle and found none. Just the normal jumbled mess of her experiments.

He scratched his ear, puzzling where she might have gone, when he saw lengths of grass reeds spread upon the table and a half-woven basket. He picked it up and turned it over in his hand. This wasn't a basket; it was a cage. The uneasy feeling in his stomach doubled. He knew what animal a cage this size was meant for. And he knew where she'd go to get it.

# Chapter 28

If there was one thing Meddybemps enjoyed more than swiving, it was intelligencing. He was as happy as a pig in mud to combine the two. And for such good cause. He'd hate to see Bianca dangle at Newgate. Knowing her was far too fun.

He knew nearly every Southwark stew and proprietor thereof. Most were past bloom and preferred running the business, leaving the more physical exertions to their bawds. They were nearly all like walnuts to crack, but Meddybemps had a way about him.

So it was that he had encouraged the attention of Maude Manstyn off a twisting lane near the Clink. Her house did a good business, being one of the first stops for freed felons on their way to making more mischief. Meddybemps figured she had seen it all and any gossip worth knowing she would have heard about. And, as an older but still desirable woman, Maude was not averse to the occasional romp with a worthy pizzle.

It was hard to say what information he could wheedle out of her. The secrets kept between sister proprietors often remained that way. No one wanted to end in prison for any reason—the time and lost income was too inconvenient. These women were shrewd, and they knew how to survive. And that usually meant keeping their counsel and that of their neighbors.

Plied with a little Spanish port, Maude's tongue loosened, and before long she was responding favorably to Meddybemps's expert handling. Not only did she coo at his ministrations like a plump pigeon, she also enthusiastically answered his questions while kneading his bare bum.

"Meddy, don't tease me so."

"Luv, I've no mind to tease." Meddybemps twirled a finger where it counted.

She raised her hips, pushing his head between her legs. "Then torture me!"

Meddybemps grabbed her hips and tilted her pelvis, his wandering eye no longer freewheeling. "You've known Jane Beldam for as long as you've been in Southwark."

"Aye, that," she agreed.

"And she was once a trull herself?"

"Oh, aye!"

"At the same stew as yourself?"

"Nay!" Maude placed her hands on either side of Meddybemps's head and pulled him toward her, but his head popped up to peer over her smooth belly.

"Then where?" he asked.

Maude frowned. "Jane was at Barke House first and last. She rose through the ranks, as they say." She shoved the crown of his head down with the heel of her hand, but he popped up again like a rabbit from its burrow.

"How did she become a madam of the games?"

"Fool man, like anyone does. She outlasted them all." Maude boxed his ears and pushed him down again. "Meddy, I'm losing my patience."

The storied streetseller rewarded her with just enough attention to keep her interested. "Do you know Robert Wynders?"

"Aye!" she responded, with unbridled enthusiasm.

"What is the connection between Jane Beldam and him?"

"Meddy!" she shouted in exasperation.

"Maude!" replied Meddybemps. He resisted her moony eyes until she answered him.

"He was her daughter's lover!"

"What is the crime in that?" he mused, absently running a finger along her inner thigh. It was not atypical for a man to take pleasure. "Ahh," he said, as a thought occurred to him. "Was he married?"

"Oh, AYE!" she shrieked.

Now they were getting somewhere, though, he had to admit, she made it difficult for him to keep drilling her—with questions. For the moment, one of his objectives would have to suffer, and never one for letting business get in the way of pleasure, Meddybemps dispensed with the interrogation.

The two of them bounced on the bed in wild abandon. Maude slapped his bum like the flank of a spirited stallion, ignoring concerned inquiries at the door. The denizens had never heard such caterwauling from Maude. It was enough to make seasoned whores turn pink about the ears.

But they ignored everyone. They whooped and howled, shrieked and growled. And when finally Meddybemps rolled off Maude in utter exhaustion, he, the bed and even the house itself sighed in relief that that was finally over and done with.

Meddybemps lay with his arms splayed, gasping and staring at the ceiling, his mind empty and his body spent. He should get up and take a hard piss, though it was only a rumored preventive for the French pox (alas, too late for him anyway) and the itch. Instead, he resigned his "health" as a lost cause and enjoyed the tranquility of the moment. Slowly, as he regained his senses, his visit's other purpose crowded out his feelings of bliss and demanded attention.

"That a married man takes a lover is not unusual, nor is it so shocking," said Meddybemps, returning to the subject.

Maude lay beside him, her eyes closed. "True. But Wynders had cause to keep it quiet."

Meddybemps turned to face her. "And the cause being?"

"Methinks it's my turn to be coy."

"Maude!"

"Meddy?"

"Don't torture me!"

Maude's eyes opened, and she smiled archly, turning to look at him. "It'll cost you, luv."

Meddybemps hadn't an ounce of vigor left to pluck. Surely she couldn't be serious. But the look in her eye spoke otherwise. "Have pity," he said. "I am not the stuff I once was."

"Nor I. But be cheered you'll leave with no fewer coins."

With a moan of appreciation and exhaustion, Meddybemps accommodated. It was a bit of a struggle, but once he got past a slow start, they were once again shaking dust from the rafters.

This time, Meddybemps didn't wait to question her. "What of this scandal?" he asked as he teetered over her.

"Meddy!" she shouted.

"Maude!" Meddybemps retreated, a man expert in the taunt and touché.

Maude squirmed. "It is rumored she was with child," she said in exasperation.

"Wynders's child?"

"AYE!"

Meddybemps rewarded her while he pondered, splitting his wits between the two. He stopped to catch his breath. "What became of the girl and her child?"

"Disappeared."

"No one disappears never to be found. They might leave and go somewhere. Surely that is the explanation."

Maude pulled him toward her, and they took up where they had left off. "Supposedly he forced Jane to send her daughter away to France to wait out the child's birth. Perhaps she serves the nuns that took her in. No one has seen or heard of her since. She's long since been forgotten."

"Indiscretion comes at a price—both for Wynders and Jane Beldam."

"It would have been dangerous to let the girl stay at Barke House."

"Dangerous?" asked Meddybemps, thinking of his overtaxed genitories. "How so?"

"Jane's daughter was a bug of Bedlam, they say. Discretion was at issue. Best to keep the pregnancy and birth a secret. You see, Wynders's money did not come from his earnings in business."

"Meaning?"

"He married it, silly man."

"But how could he force her to leave?"

"For coin, what wouldn't a person do? And for Jane it was an opportunity. Not only could she rid herself of a troubled child, she could make money doing it."

"So, the girl never returned?"

"It is not my interest. I trouble myself no more over it. Jane's conscience is her own concern."

Meddybemps stopped in distraction. "Yet Wynders still frequents Barke House."

Maude reminded him of his task. Her stamina was truly a source of wonder. "Perchance Jane Beldam still has sway," she mused. "They are like two bulls squaring off. They circle and move with their eyes fixed on each other. Neither dares to step first."

The information gave Meddybemps something to ponder, and while his brain was occupied with that puzzle, his pizzle was occupied with another. He rocked and galloped to the finish, then fell off Maude and rolled from the bed, grabbing his pants. "Well, no one gossips about a man's virtues."

Maude smiled knowingly. "They do here."

# CHAPTER 29

John wasn't about to search for Bianca. He knew she sought rats for her experiment, and while part of him thought he should help her, the repulsed part of him knew that he couldn't. Nor would he try to stop her. Bianca would do as she pleased, and it was useless to try to convince her otherwise. His stomach complained. It protested as much from hunger as from the thought of Bianca on the waterfront, trapping rats.

Finding little comfort in these thoughts, he resolved, instead, to settle his hunger at the Dim Dragon Inn with a detour of food and swill. The fog was settling, and a meal would give him a chance to warm himself and think.

He pushed open the door beneath a sign of a blue beast and stepped into a wall of cheap smoke and stale air. A few patrons lifted their gaze, but most continued their business, unconcerned. John found a space within sight of the door and settled between two bleary-eyed patrons.

"A tankard, luv?" asked the tavern wench when she got to him.

"Aye, and stew." John watched her saunter off, and saw the

blocky rogue he recognized as the muckraker who'd caught Bianca's interest at Cross Bones. He eyed him suspiciously and decided to speak with him after he'd polished off a draught.

John couldn't have chosen a better post from which to watch the sullen brute. From his vantage he observed the muckraker shovel mash and gravy into his mouth and down a pottle pot of ale. Then down a second one. Conversation burred around him, but he remained uninterested and insular, averse to camaraderie or social revelry. John felt no stab of jealousy. The rascal was purely business.

After John filled his gut and slaked his thirst, he squeezed his way over to Henley, who was now intent on devouring his second plate of food. After standing for what seemed an awkward length of time with no acknowledgment, not even a simple lift of the eyelid, John spoke.

"You are the muckraker Henley."

The muckraker responded with a twitch of the eye before speaking. "Is that a question or a statement?" He continued eating without glancing up.

John wedged himself in between two men sitting opposite and stared intently at the hulk until he stopped chewing and returned the stare. "I don't suppose you might tell me what it was you wanted from Jolyn Carmichael."

Henley snorted and dug into his dinner for another bite. "I don't suppose I would," he said with his mouth full.

"Methinks it might be important to someone who could be taking the noose for a murder she didn't commit."

Henley chewed with his mouth open, studying John as he did so. He swallowed, then wiped his lips on his wrist. "Not my concern."

"I could make it yours," replied John, congenially. He patted a breast coat pocket as if a groat nestled there with his name on it.

Henley's gaze dropped to the pocket, then rode back up. "Show me."

John was not about to remove what lay in his pocket, certainly not in a public venue. The apprentice might have lived a less dastardly life under Boisvert's tutelage, but it didn't quash his cunning. He ticked his head. "We can finish talking outside."

An eyebrow lifted as Henley considered him. Without a word, he laid his fork beside his platter and rose from the bench. John felt suddenly puny by comparison but led the way to the back alley.

When the tavern door closed behind them, John turned.

A look of surprise, then mild amusement spread across Henley's face. It wasn't a coin in John's pocket. His eyes fell to a dagger, its point now firmly against his stomach.

"I would like you to answer my questions," suggested John. He would not have undertaken such a risk if he hadn't judged his odds favorable on its success. He had watched Henley down the second ale laced with sleeping philter he'd bribed the tavern wench to dispense. He could see the brute's eyelids grow heavy with befuddlement and hear his voice begin to slur.

John shoved him up against the wall and pricked the buttons off of Henley's jerkin, the better to encourage cooperation. He cut the cloth beneath and poked the knife into the paunch of gut, drawing a line of blood.

"Mrs. Beldam of Barke House wanted something from Jolyn Carmichael. If you want that mash to stay put, you'd best tell me what that something was."

Henley wobbled unsteadily. He'd already lost the strength in his arms. They hung useless at his sides like two timbers waiting to be moved. He fought to control his legs to keep from falling into the muck and piss of the alley.

But John was persistent. He flicked his wrist enough to make Henley yowl at the burn of blood.

Henley drew in a sharp breath, his sense dulling by the second.

"Tell me! It'd be a shame to take a nap in this squalid bed." Henley's head was beginning to swim—John could see it dip on the muckraker's thick neck. He'd soon lose his chance to get an answer. "Say it!" John abandoned the soft gut and drew the blade under Henley's chin. He pressed the metal against his windpipe, effectively collapsing it.

This got Henley's attention. His eyes flew open, rolled down at the blade, then over to John leaning into him. But his strength was at an end. He started to crumple, and his legs buckled from his great bulk. John rode down with him, not wanting to slit the rascal's windpipe before getting an answer. He released the pressure off Henley's throat.

"A ring!" Henley wheezed. He gulped and, with a final breath, gasped, "Wynders's ring!"

# Chapter 30

Bianca threw herself against the chained door and screamed loud enough to set every dog in Romeland barking. Perhaps the commotion might draw notice—she hoped so. At this point, she didn't care if she was arrested for trespass; she just wanted out. The nightmarish sight and smell had thoroughly unnerved her, and she rattled the door like a madwoman. Exhausted, she slid down the implacable door to her haunches.

"Now what?" she asked the dark. She relit the stump of rushlight and peered back into the gloom. At least Constable Patch couldn't throw her in gaol if he didn't know where to find her. She sniggered. But no one else knew where to find her, either.

Times like this required resourcefulness and calm. Unfortunately, both had escaped her. The thought of rats chewing her apart renewed her calls for help, and she banged and kicked the door until her thin leather boot wore through and her toes ached. She considered setting the door on fire, but what if it asphyxiated her before it burnt down? Well, at least she'd be dead when the rats gnawed her bones.

Bianca slumped against the door. Which would she prefer? Death by rats—or noose?

She waved the rushlight in a wide arc and wondered how long it was before daylight. Maybe her chances of being rescued might improve if she waited. She shook her head. She had no choice but to wait. Surely someone would pass the warehouse or even open it. But what if that person was Wynders?

Aye, what if?

Realistically, he had no quarrel with her—well, aside from the trespassing. He probably had no idea she was accused of his betrothed's death. He only knew her as a chemiste. After all, she'd sold him rat poison for his ship. She winced, thinking of this man's problem with rats. For as many as there were in this warehouse, one could assume he was importing them.

But why stow bodies in a warehouse? Why not dispose of them at sea? Unless he couldn't. Unless they died in port. Was he hiding them? Hiding them to get through quarantine and skirt the custom authority's health inspector?

The rushlight flickered, then smoldered and died. She tossed it on the floor and pressed her heel into it. Utter darkness. She felt her way atop a crate and drew her knees to her chest, wrapping her arms around them. She would renew her shouting with the day's first light. For all of her desire to slow time down the past few days, morning now couldn't come fast enough. She buried her nose in her scarf and forced herself to think on other things.

She thought back to Wool's Key and pondered Wynders sending a man out to a ship. A man toting soaked rags that blazed even in the fog. The smell had not been unlike the one here. Only that smell had been acrid with the reek of charred flesh. The smell here was of dead bodies. Dead, decomposing bodies.

Whatever stores or goods that ship held in its hold, Wynders wanted them out. He probably had taxes to settle, debts to pay. Not to mention the lost income having goods sitting in port, moldering and losing value.

So, what had been his attraction to Jolyn? She was beautiful and clever—what man wouldn't take notice? Did he feel the only way to bed her was to wed her? Bianca sniffed. The lengths men would go in order to have a woman. But perhaps he never planned to wed her. What if his motive was only to get close enough to poison her? Bianca shook her head and began talking out loud to drown out the sound of the feeding rats. "Why did you promise marriage? Why did you raise her hopes?" Bianca could think of no worthy cause besides love. She closed her eyes and thought. Did he plan to marry or to murder her? Bianca rubbed her temples. Two extremes, but there was one thing they both required: intimacy. "So why would you want to marry, then possibly murder Jolyn?" Bianca asked the dark. And then a thought occurred to her. "Unless Jolyn had something that you wanted. Something that you valued more than her."

What was it? Henley wanted her ring. Did Wynders and Mrs. Beldam want it, too? And that led Bianca back to whoever broke into her rent and searched her belongings. What was he after, and why did he think she had it? But perhaps Jolyn's death and the break-in were unrelated. Perhaps the thief was merely looking for money or something of value to steal. She hadn't noticed any-thing missing. Certainly, her store of silver filings and coins from Meddybemps had been left untouched. Whatever the thief wanted, as far as she knew, the thief had not taken.

Did the thief think she had the ring? Or did he want her dead? If the latter were true, the intruder could have finished her off. Had he been interrupted? Perhaps the thief had merely wanted her out of the way while he went through her room.

Bianca tried to concentrate, but she found it harder to ignore the hideous sound of feeding rats. She held her hands over her ears, trying to muffle their horrible rasping. How much longer until morning? Her sanity was dwindling.

With renewed fury, Bianca leapt off the crate and rattled the door. She jammed her fingers between the slats of board and leaned back with all her weight. One of them gave a little but not before drawing blood from her fingertips. She ignored the pain and wrenched the slat with a savage burst of strength. The wood squealed as it splintered in half, revealing an opening.

It was a small opening, and she crouched to press her face against it, inhaling fresh air and closing her eyes in appreciation. Her back hurt from crouching, but so be it; at least now she could breathe.

Once revived, Bianca felt some measure of calm restored. She cocked her head sideways, laying one ear on her shoulder so she could see out with both eyes, and opened them.

"For a girl accused of murder, your preoccupation with the worst London has to offer never fails to astound me."

"John!"

"Bianca," answered the young silversmith.

"Get me out of here!"

"And if I do? Tell me how I might benefit."

"John, this warehouse is full of rats."

"So is London."

"They're feasting on corpses!"

"Unpleasant. I assume you didn't enter by choice."

"Never mind how I got here. Help me!"

John stood back and studied the chain and padlock. "I don't suppose this could be easily picked." He withdrew his knife and pushed its tip into the keyhole of the shackle. He wormed it about with no effect and, after a moment, gave up and scratched his chin. "Do you have a thin piece of metal about you?"

Bianca pushed her face into the opening. "Are you daft? Why would I have that?"

"A young lady should always have something to jab into a man's groin or eye if the situation calls for it."

"I'm not a violent person."

"You should be."

"John, get me out of here."

"I need something to work against. Something thin and strong that I can shove into the hole for resistance."

"Thin like what?" asked Bianca. She was beginning to wonder if she might be stuck in the warehouse until Wynders came back.

"Bianca, if I get you out of here, will you marry me?"

"If I live that long!"

John was momentarily stunned by the thought. He couldn't seem to help himself. He might be mad to love her, but it was an affliction he gladly undertook. He blinked at Bianca and pushed his lips through the opening. For as ridiculous as it was, Bianca met his lips and managed to convey an acceptable kiss that did nothing to get her out any sooner but inspired John nonetheless.

"Patience. I'll be back before you miss me." And with that, he was gone.

Bianca leaned against the door. She could barely tolerate another minute. The sound of feeding rats grew louder, perhaps because she was focusing on it. She crouched again and peered through the slat. Where did he go? She turned her head, trying to see, then sat back. Had she really agreed to marry him? She would have said anything to get out of there, and apparently, she had. Her heart pounded against her ribs. Certainly, there were worse things than marrying John. She'd worry about that later. She sat back and covered her ears, murmuring one of Meddybemps's patters until John returned.

A chorus of angels couldn't have sounded as sweet as John picking open the lock, and when the chain clattered to the ground and John pushed open the door, she nearly trampled him. John had expected as much and caught her up in his arms. "I deserve better than that," he said. Bianca showered him with kisses, and when those ran out, she lingered in his arms.

"How did you find me?"

"I stopped at your room to check on you. You left a trap on your table, and after our last conversation I sorted out what it was for. I imagined you paid a visit to Wool's Key." He could see Bianca appreciated his concern, but he neglected admitting he didn't want to help her trap rats. "I was near the Dim Dragon Inn," he continued, confident she read his nonchalance as belief in her ability, "and thought I'd have a bite."

Bianca listened intently.

"I settled in, and who should walk in but that muckraker."

"Henley?"

"I don't believe you had much success talking with him, so I had a go at it."

"And did you manage to engage him?"

"I did."

Bianca pecked him on the cheek. "Should I ask how you managed to speak with him or skip to the good part?"

"It depends on what you consider 'the good part.'"

"I can tell you're keen to tell me both."

"I paid the serving wench to pour sleeping philter in his ale, and offered to pay him some coin for a few answers in the privacy of the alley. My knife can be very persuasive."

"Sleeping philter?"

"Labeled as such and borrowed off your shelf."

Bianca cocked her head. "Clever knave."

"I am," said John, pleased. "Apparently Henley was after Wynders's ring."

Bianca nodded in satisfaction. "Did you ask him why he wanted it?"

"He passed out before I could ask."

"But how did you know I was in the warehouse?"

"After I left Henley, I crossed the bridge back into London and turned toward Wool's Key. I saw a man with a pheasant-plumed hat heading up New Fish Street, when suddenly he turned around and stopped as if he'd forgotten something. I thought he fit your description of Wynders, and he was acting suspiciously, so I decided to follow him. I trailed him to this warehouse. He stopped and pulled a chain tight against the door, securing it with a padlock. I then shadowed him home, or at least I assume it is his home, then returned to look for you on the river. When I did not see you, I wondered what could be in the warehouse. Since it was close by, I decided to find out. You saved me from crossing the bridge to check your room for a second time."

Bianca planted a boisterous kiss on his lips. "A more cunning cove I'll never know," she proclaimed. She pressed her ear against his chest and listened to the muffled thud of his heartbeat, as strong and as steady as hers. Indeed, there were worse things than marrying John.

# CHAPTER 31

Bianca sat up and reached for her nightdress. The red cat noted her stirring and sauntered over from his spot by the furnace.

She had escaped into sleep as soon as her head reached the pillow, and when John kissed her out of a dreamless slumber, it took her a moment to surface and realize where she was. His hand lightly traced the skin of her thigh, and she let him pull her close. She felt safe under the weight of his body, and his loose hair surrounded them like a curtain of flowing gold. For a time, she escaped her world of troubles for one of content.

She had never known the touch of another man nor did she want to. John was her anchor, her abiding confidant and partner. But love could be fickle. The king would soon have a sixth wife, and she wondered if her parents had ever found happiness together, if even for a moment.

If her father gave her any thought, which Bianca doubted, he would have been ashamed she had so dishonored him. But he had no money, and she no dowry, and in Bianca's mind, his opinion mattered not a whit.

"So what shall you do now?" asked John, rising to his elbows and watching Bianca drop the gown over her shoulders. He could still see the outline of her body through the thin fabric.

Bianca shifted her attention to her predicament and what tasks lay ahead.

"First, I shall test the purgative and the rat poison on my rats. Those are the two powders I regularly sold to Banes. If either should tinge their blood purple, I'll have my answer as to what poisoned Jolyn." The cat wound itself through her legs, and Bianca bent over to pet it, then turned to the fire and tossed in a dung patty.

It wasn't the response John was hoping for. Still, every night must come to an end. "What if neither dyes the blood?" he asked.

"That would pose a more difficult problem."

"You have your work cut out," said John, rolling to his knees and standing. He was less modest than Bianca and made sure she got an eyeful.

She did. But Bianca felt time's persistent breath blowing down her neck. "John, I have to get my work done. I haven't much time."

"And you will have even less if I do not help."

Bianca preferred working on her own but agreed he could be of use. "All right," she said. "I need water from the cistern." She thrust a pail at John, then swiped his pants from off the floor and stuffed them in the bucket.

John grabbed her arm, but she slipped from his grasp, leaving him to get dressed while she did the same.

She set about clearing space at her long table and erecting the rest of her distilling apparatus. Joining the twists and curves of copper helped her concentrate and prepared her mind for experimentation. She imagined her idea beginning as a single drop, forming deep within her subconscious, flowing, turning, traveling to the final conclusion.

John set down the pail of fresh water and looked to Bianca for more direction.

"Set two pots to boil." Bianca left her distillation apparatus and wandered over to the caged rats, deciding how she would test the purgative and poison. She could bait apple and feed it to them, but the effects would take too long. She didn't have time to wait for them to digest a meal. A liquid solution of each powder would be best. She prepared scraps of parchment to label the cages so she'd know when and how much she'd given each rat. Three rats were set aside. Not only would they be her standard, but if some part of her experiment failed, she would have spares if needed.

John scratched his head. "How are you going to do this?"

Bianca was deep in the throes of working through the steps in her mind and didn't answer.

John fell silent, irked she was ignoring him. But if he'd given it any thought, which he did after a moment, he'd remember how Bianca came to her science. She'd spent years assisting her father in his alchemy and had learned by observing. Rarely did Albern Goddard offer a comment or explanation about what he was doing, and most often, if she asked, she'd get a sharp retort and long rebuke not to trouble him with her trivial questions.

So John clamped tight his mouth and stood by to observe Bianca in her single-minded quest.

As for Bianca, it was almost as if John wasn't there. She thought through how she would prepare the solutions; then, with capillary tubes of delicately blown glass she'd filched from her father, she would open each rat's mouth and administer an equal and exact dose. Once that was completed, the two of them could sit and observe the results.

As the water boiled and burbled, Bianca measured the purgative into a flask and set it aside. She scooped a measure of rat poison and prepared a separate solution.

"I can't have these two confused," she said. "I have no time for mistakes. For all I know, Constable Patch might be on his way over to arrest me right now."

"All the better that I am here. I can answer the door while you make an escape."

Bianca smiled ruefully. "I can't avoid him forever."

"But you can avoid him long enough to find the answer to what poisoned Jolyn."

Bianca poured boiling water into the vessel of rat poison, then swirled it. She appreciated John's confidence in her, though she knew experiments didn't always work smoothly. Hopefully, this one would because she only had one chance to get it right. She didn't think she could ask John to repeat an experiment by himself. She set the rat poison well apart from the purgative and lined the cages of rats along the edge of the table.

"I still believe Pandy had the most cause to see Jolyn dead," she said, collecting the capillary tubes. "She was in love with Wynders before Jolyn came along."

"That doesn't explain the ruckus over the ring."

Bianca poured the boiling water into the purgative. "But I don't know for sure that the ring is the missing motivation. The only thing we know for sure is that Henley wanted it."

"Wynders's ring."

"Wynders's ring that Jolyn found." Bianca set down the flask to cool. "And probably a ring Wynders wanted back," she said, returning the pan to the furnace. "I haven't any proof Mrs. Beldam wanted the ring. But she liked jewelry. I wonder if Henley played Mrs. Beldam against Wynders? Perhaps he wanted to hold out to the highest bidder."

"You don't know if Henley was working with or against Wynders."

"For certain, there is a story behind that ring," agreed Bianca. "But I don't believe Henley got it back from Jolyn. He never admitted he sold it—did he?"

John shook his head no. "So where is it? Who has it?"

"That I would like to know." Bianca swirled the solution, thinking. "Why all this skulduggery? Why didn't Wynders or Beldam just buy it from her and be done with it?"

"Because Jolyn believed the ring brought her luck. You know how superstitious she was. No amount of money could convince her to sell something she believed had changed her fortune for the better. Selling it would commit her to an uncertain future. Not after all she'd lived through. She finally knew some comfort and hope."

Bianca considered this. "I still think Pandy had the most cause for seeing Jolyn buried. It was obvious to me she had strong feelings for Wynders. There is no greater cause for revenge than a broken heart."

"You watch too many plays," said John. He stoked the furnace and prodded it with a fire poke.

"I wish that were true." Bianca peered into the flask, then held it up to see if the powder had dissolved. "I spend all my time here."

"You don't have to," said John, softly. He watched her carefully.

"John, right now, I have no choice. I'll never be able to live in London if I don't prove my innocence. I don't want to live in fear of my life," she said, exasperated. She stirred the flask of rat poison for a moment, then addressed John in a quiet, somber voice. "Please don't press me."

John's heart pained. To be honest, he didn't know which would be more painful, suffering Bianca's rejection or seeing her hanged at Newgate for murder. For now, neither was certain, and he would do whatever it took to prevent either from happening. So he dismissed any more talk of the two of them and attempted an easy smile. "Understood," he said. He avoided looking into her eyes—they had such power to unnerve him, and he needed spine. "Now, tell me what to do."

Bianca's own feelings were a torture of hope and regret, but she set them aside and refocused on her chemistries. "Time to dispense the solutions." She found the glass capillary tubes and swirled the solutions, ensuring they were completely dissolved.

"I want to start with the purgative." Bianca set apart a total of four cages for her experiment. "Two rats will be given purgative, and two rats will be given rat poison." She poured off enough solution to draw up liquid in the tubes, noticing the rats moving back and forth, obviously sensing the need to escape. One tried gnawing through its cage but stopped, no doubt finding the reed as sharp as a knife's blade.

John held up a trap and looked at the rat inside. "How are you going to get them out?"

Bianca glanced around the room. "I think I need something to hold them with, perhaps a cloth so they don't bite us."

John searched among the shelves and table. He found a rough square of woven jute and held it up.

"That will work," said Bianca. "I've been looking for that." She snatched it away from him. "You've already proven yourself useful."

The rats gnawed at their cages. Bianca pinched her lips, steeling herself. "I'm going to show you how to use the capillary tubes, and you'll feed it into their mouths."

John's smile looked doubtful.

"You can do this," she said in answer to his dubious expression.

Bianca drew up a column of liquid and held a thumb over the open end. "There isn't much to drawing the liquid." She handed John the tube and let him practice. "When you're ready, I'll pry open their mouths and you'll have to be quick about dispensing the fluid."

John drew up the dissolved purgative and released it a couple of times. "I'm ready," he said.

Bianca held the square of thick jute in one hand, hesitating before taking up a cage. She hated rats.

"Bianca?" John was about to ask if she had changed her mind when she shook off her hesitation.

She grabbed one of the cages and thrust it open, dumping the rat onto the table. She covered its back with the thick jute and squeezed its torso. Holding its legs tight against its body, Bianca turned it over so its throat and little pointy chin were exposed. "Have you drawn the purgative?"

John didn't like rats any more than Bianca, and the sight of her holding one made him squeamish. She wasn't exactly the kind of girl he'd bring home to Mum, if he had a mum or a home to bring a girl to. But Bianca never failed to intrigue him and he could never claim her dull. "Aye!" John quickly drew up the liquid and stopped the end with his thumb.

With her free hand, Bianca pinched the rat on either side of its mouth, forcing its jaw open. "Now!"

John positioned the tube over its mouth and released his thumb. The column of fluid flowed silently and evenly down the rat's throat.

Satisfied, Bianca shoved the rat back into its cage and secured the small hasp. She wiped her hand on her kirtle. "That's one," she said, labeling the cage and setting it by.

John wiped his hand along his leg. He hadn't gotten but a drop of purgative solution on his skin, but still . . .

"Again?" he asked.

"By the time I get to the third rat, we'll be used to this."

John had his doubts but kept quiet. How could anyone get used to this? Hopefully, the end result would be a dead rat because, in his mind, the only good rat was a dead one. But John realized this was Bianca's inquiry, and ultimately, if she got an answer from all her effort then he would be glad.

Bianca grabbed the second rat and John fed it the purgative.

"There," said Bianca, satisfied. She labeled the two cages and set them aside.

"Now for the rat poison." Bianca readied another two cages and John swirled the solution.

The two of them continued, with Bianca prying open their mouths and John dispensing the poison.

"So, our little friends will die, and then you will slit them open and see if their blood is tinged purple?" asked John.

"If their blood tinges purple, I'll know whether it was the purgative or rat poison that killed Jolyn. If the purgative turns blood purple, then I know for sure that someone at Barke House poisoned her. If it is the rat poison, then both Wynders and the denizens of Barke House are suspect."

"But Wynders bought rat poison from you after Jolyn died."

"True, but the recipe for rat poison is standardized in London. Wynders could have had a stash of it. What separates my rat poison from others is a smell of terebinth derived from pine. No one would mistakenly ingest it."

"So if rat poison tinges the blood purple, then Wynders is our man."

"In my mind, he would be the stronger suspect."

John thought for a moment. "What if both solutions turn blood purple?"

"I don't believe that will happen. But it could. In which case, I am no closer to figuring this out."

"And if neither tinges her blood?"

"Then . . ." Bianca's voice trailed off. She shrugged. "I will look in a different direction." She scratched her head. "I'm certain Jolyn could never have ingested my rat poison. The smell of terebinth resin cannot be easily masked."

John agreed the smell was potent. A sharp whiff made his eyes sting as he worked to draw up the fluid.

Bianca sat and observed the cages of rats. She hoped it wouldn't be long before she'd see the effects of her physickes on the animals. It was midmorning, and she couldn't help but feel anxious. Every minute and every hour that passed, her sense of hope dwindled. Constable Patch was never far removed from her mind.

John wandered the room in search of something to sit on and found a stool in a corner that was covered in crockery. He was setting the bowls and cucurbits on the floor when something caught his eye.

"What's this?" he said as he tugged the corner of something half buried in straw. "Bianca!" He held up a brown leather glove. "Wasn't this Jolyn's?"

Bianca snapped out of her stupor. "Where did you find that?"

"It was covered in rush. It must have gotten lost in all the confusion."

Bianca abandoned her vigil and took the glove from John. She ran her hand over its soft leather and thought of her friend, whom she missed dearly. "I'm glad to have something of Jolyn's." She smiled wistfully, then dropped her gaze to the floor. "The other one must be near."

The two of them brushed back the rush. After a moment, John found its mate pushed against the wall.

"I can think of her when I wear them." Bianca pulled them on, but as she worked the second glove over her hand, her brows knit together.

"What is it?"

"I can't get my finger in. Something is in the finger." She felt at a lump and turned the glove on end to shake it out.

A sprinkling of fine white powder collected in her palm; then out plopped something hard and weighty and gold. John plucked it out and held it up.

They looked at each other, and their eyes grew wide. "The ring!" they exclaimed.

John turned it over in his hand. "This is the first time I've ever seen it this close." A crest in the shape of a shield was etched in relief. One third of the crest held three tridents. Another third held a cockatrice. A cross graced the bottom—all four ends split decoratively like flowers. "It may be a family crest."

Bianca examined the design. "Do you know what any of it means?"

"I know some symbolism. Boisvert makes casts for coins, and the patonce, or flory cross, means conqueror. You must have seen it on half-groats."

"I never paid attention. What is that dragon with the rooster head?"

"It is a cockatrice. A small but deadly creature of evil. A single glance can turn one to stone. Only a weasel is immune to its power."

"How appropriate," said Bianca. "It has to be Wynders's. Or if not, then it has something to do with him." She looked at the powder in her hand.

"What do you suppose that is?" asked John.

Bianca passed her nose over it. She blinked, then went over to the solution of rat poison and compared its smell. "Terebinth resin." She ran the powder close under John's nose, and he screwed up his face.

Bianca nodded in confirmation. "Rat poison."

# CHAPTER 32

Banes hoped to reach Bianca before Constable Patch found her. He had been unable to leave Barke House after Patch left—Mrs. Beldam had him put fresh candles in the sconces and empty the chamber pots.

"I wouldn't put it past that girl to kill her. She came lookin' to speaks ta me," Mrs. Beldam had told Patch. "But I wouldn'ts see her. I've heard she's a murderer."

If Patch believed all Mrs. Beldam had told him, the constable would want to speak to Bianca. Finally, Banes had gotten the chance to warn her. He delayed an errand for Mrs. Beldam and detoured to Bianca's room of Medicinals and Physickes.

Banes was disappointed when greeted by John, with his broad shoulders and supposed concern for Bianca. Banes thought he would have abandoned her given the trouble she was in. That kind never amounted to more than a passing fancy. In matters of consequence his sort wasn't long on loyalty. Banes's eyes narrowed.

"I need to speak with Bianca."

It was bad enough that John hesitated, but when the rascal

made him wait outside, it was more than Banes could stand. He resented being treated with such ill regard, especially when it came to information concerning Bianca's well-being. He didn't wait but pushed open the door, smacking John on his backside.

"Banes," said Bianca, looking up in surprise.

But it was Banes who was the more astonished. Strewn on the board were a half dozen rats splayed open with their greasy little guts glistening in the candlelight. Bianca stood over them wielding a scalpel, her hands and forearms spattered in blood. She looked as unholy and godless as any sight he could imagine. What *was* she doing? Performing some sort of heathen ritual? Her hair hung about her face, unkempt, and dark circles shadowed her eyes—eyes that shone with unnatural effulgence.

Banes staggered to a stop, uncertain what to say. He knew an expression of shock had overcome his initial desire to appear in control and detached. His eyes darted to John and back to Bianca.

"Banes, I've been trying to determine what killed Jolyn," she said, straightening and brushing the hair from her eyes, leaving bits of fur stuck in it. "The coroner found a trickle of purplish blood on her chin. I've been testing solutions to see if any can turn blood purple."

Banes stared down at the row of rats in disgust. "You used rats?"

"They're abundant these days."

Banes certainly could not disagree. One would have had to be blind not to notice the many vermin crawling the streets of Southwark. Still, the gruesome sight of this left him speechless, his mouth agape.

"I believe I know what killed Jolyn."

Banes blinked. He could barely form the words to ask, but he had to know. "Was it a solution you sold to me?" He watched her face for signs that she thought him guilty, or at least complicit.

Bianca ignored his question and posed one of her own. "Banes, have you ever seen Wynders's ring?"

"Ring?" There it was again—that cursed ring. Probably the

same one Mrs. Beldam wanted. Wasn't it the reason for clubbing Bianca over the head in the middle of the night? Banes was relieved she had survived Mrs. Beldam's assault, but he couldn't bring himself to tell her who was responsible for it and why. Shame kept his mouth shut. He had never meant her harm. The girl was in a world of trouble as it was. He shook his head, unable to meet her eyes. "Nay, I've never seen it."

"My hunch is that it is of importance to him," she said, watching him carefully. "And I believe someone at Barke House also wanted it."

Banes shifted his weight and glanced up at John. The two of them stared at him expectantly, but he stifled the urge to tell what he knew. Secrets were best left alone, even if telling them could absolve him of blame. Besides, he had to live somewhere, and Barke House was all he'd ever known. He wasn't going to risk losing food in his gut and a pillow at night. Surviving outside of Barke House with his deformity would be difficult, his life fraught with abuse. He'd be reduced to a beggar's life.

Banes sensed Bianca's curiosity stemmed from knowledge she had about the ring. He didn't know if it was in her possession, but he took the chance to ask. "May I see it?"

Bianca shot a look at John. They were wondering if they could trust him. Banes held his breath, waiting, but offered no more assurance. Personally, he never trusted anyone, so why should they trust him? Loyalty was something best left to those who never lied.

"Why would you think she has it?" asked John.

Banes played coy. "I don't," he said, hoping his voice didn't betray him. He couldn't bring himself to say that Mrs. Beldam had thought so.

"I suspect its value is worth more than its gold." Bianca started back to her experiment, neither confirming nor denying they had the ring. Banes interpreted her evasiveness to mean that they had it. He could scarce blame her for not admitting it. He was scanning the room, wondering where it was hidden, when a loud banging shook the door.

Banes startled, remembering why he was there. "Bianca, I came to tell you that the constable is looking for you. That may be him."

He might as well have told her that she had black hair. She showed no outward sign of alarm, and in fact, she calmly nodded for John to open the door.

As if the display of gutted rats was not enough, in walked a knave dressed in the rough cloth of streetsellers and smelling just as bad, sporting a red beret at a rakish angle. The sleeves of his jerkin were too short, and his arms looked as thin at the wrist as they did at the forearm. Banes might not have had two normal appendages, but at least the one good arm had some muscle to it.

The cozen swept off his cap with a flourish and extended a leg forward in a theatrical bow. "Bianca, my dove. I'd not suspected a coterie of young men charmed by your wiles." One eye rolled toward the table of eviscerated vermin, and the other swam in appreciation. He returned his hat to his head and advanced on Banes, extending his hand. "And with whom might I have this pleasure?"

Banes stared at the rascal's hand but did not shake it.

"Meddybemps, this is Banes," said Bianca. "Of Barke House."

"Barke House," repeated Meddybemps, withdrawing his hand and noting Banes's snub. He stepped back to get a measure of the peculiar lad. "Indeed."

For his part, Banes presumed the man some kind of charlatan or counterfeit swank. Perhaps a dealer in dice or even an itinerant quack. Whatever he might be, it wasn't reputable.

"Banes, Meddybemps sells my salves at market."

That explained the man's unctuous manner, thought Banes.

"I suppose you've come for more salves," said Bianca, looking hard at Meddybemps.

The look was not missed by Meddybemps. He played along, forestalling divulging the information he'd gleaned from Maude Manstyn until after Banes left. "Indeed. I've had plenty of requests for your rat poison." He glanced at Banes, whose eyes were trained on him. "So, my turtle," Meddybemps asked, perusing the display of rats in various stages of dissection, "what have I interrupted?"

"I'm trying to determine what poisoned Jolyn."

Meddybemps smiled at Banes. "You look alarmed, Banes. Are you well?"

Banes hated being the focus of attention. He felt his neck grow warm and wished they'd change the topic.

"You must be privy to an eyeful living at Barke House," said Meddybemps, his own eye wobbling as if imagining as much.

Banes did not respond to Meddybemps's prodding but instead edged toward the door. "I need to be getting back," he said and withdrew to the street. But he was not inclined to return to Barke House just yet. He snuck next to the front window that had been boarded up since the storm. It afforded him a crack through which he could watch and hear what they said.

"Did you learn anything?" asked Bianca, once the door had closed behind Banes.

"I did." Meddybemps strode to the furnace and warmed his back, which only served to roast his clothes, further diffusing their rank bouquet.

"Mrs. Beldam and Robert Wynders have had a long association. Wynders married Sarah Chudderly, the daughter of a merchant named Thomas Chudderly. Chudderly imports silks and velvets from Genoa. He sells only to those who can afford his fine textiles, most notably His Majesty and his court. Every altar, throne, and royal bed in this kingdom is draped in Chudderly's Italian cloth."

"What is Wynders's background?"

"That I do not know. Suffice it to say, Wynders knew how to be at the most propitious place at the most auspicious time. No doubt he was beautiful and charming in his youth, and able to endear himself to the daughter of a rich merchant." Meddybemps lifted a knowing brow.

"And now he works as a ship's agent?" Bianca looked skeptical.

"A ship's agent for Chudderly's fleet." Meddybemps helped

himself to a chair next to the fire. "Perhaps Wynders possesses the right combination of grift and couth to prove himself indispensable to the firm."

"So, his fortune was not got by his own hand. He married it," said John.

Meddybemps nodded. "Most assuredly. And, as a result, Wynders must walk a fine line of propriety lest he risk losing his position and his money."

"Restoring one's reputation is harder than losing it," said Bianca.

Banes listened intently. It seemed to have no bearing on him personally; however, Wynders had been frequenting Barke House for as long as he could remember. To know something of the man's secrets might prove useful.

"How did you learn this?" asked John. He was peeling the leaves off a fallen sprig of marjoram.

Meddybemps readily admitted his method in lurid detail. Bianca endured his detailed account as a matter of course with the randy streetseller. She was not innocent of his past. When she was a child, she used to follow him around, fascinated by his cart of talismans and trinkets. He prevailed on her curiosity and propensity for sweets to watch over his cart while he visited Maude Manstyn and others—mostly lonely widows and disaffected wives, including her own mother. But their dalliance had been more recent, having occurred while her father busied himself with his reckless involvement with men destined for treason.

Bianca's father had ignored her mother's warnings that his participation would lead to his undoing. In fact, she had argued, his participation could lead to the entire family's ruin. But her opinion mattered little. She was his property, and as such, she was expected to accept and obey his decisions, bow to his authority. Bianca had seen her father beat and humiliate her mother on more than one occasion. The neighbors were of no help. They believed that she must have provoked his anger.

So when Meddybemps came around and offered her mother a little affection, she accepted it against Bianca's protest. Her mother risked being severely punished. She could have been burned at the stake. Bianca warned Meddybemps to leave her mother alone. But her mother preferred being punished as an adulterer rather than a traitor—for she would have been accused of treason if her husband was convicted.

Bianca's parents reached an unhappy impasse. Each refused to stop their behavior, and Bianca was unable to convince either of the danger of their deeds.

It was unfortunate Bianca had suffered a disreputable education in the more ribald side of love, but she had managed to form her own set of morals from the experience—and while not exactly lofty, she did seem to know her own mind when it came to the subject of "docking."

"An acquaintance of Maude Manstyn's who, shall we say, served the needs of the more mannered class was quite forthcoming," said Meddybemps. "I shall spare you those details, but I learned a great deal from her . . . and, of course, Maude." Meddybemps's eyes skipped in fond remembrance. It took him a moment to relinquish his reminiscing and continue. "Wynders has a somewhat checkered past, I'm afraid." Meddybemps scratched under his cap.

"Is there a connection with Barke House?" asked Bianca.

"Indeed."

This piqued Banes's attention. He watched Meddybemps more intently.

"It seems he had relations with Mrs. Beldam's daughter."

"When was this?" asked John, tossing aside the marjoram stem.

"Years ago. Long enough to be forgotten by some, though not so long that it doesn't matter now." Meddybemps savored reporting scandalous news. He cocked his head, coyly dispensing bits of tittle-tattle. "Perhaps you might say it is a rare man with money who does not spend it on women. And I would resoundingly agree. But this 'affair,' shall we call it, continued long enough for Beldam's daughter to be got with child."

"That is neither unique nor unexpected," said John.

"Aye," said Meddybemps. "However, Wynders—imprudent behavior aside—still ascribes to the pope's religion. He may not have wanted the child, but he could do nothing to prevent its birth."

"He could have denied paternity," said John.

"Unless he was forced to admit it," said Bianca.

Banes gawped at the news. How had he—a resident of Barke House for as many years as he could remember—never heard about this? Aye, he knew Mrs. Beldam had a daughter, but no one spoke of her, least of all Mrs. Beldam. What had happened to her? And why was Wynders still visiting Barke House? Why was Wynders beholden if he could simply walk away?

Banes pressed his ear firmly against the crack. He felt he should know more. He searched his memory for answers, but he could not make sense of this. Had Beldam's daughter visited without him knowing? It was certainly possible, given the number of women passing through Barke House.

"I wonder if Banes knows any of this," said Bianca.

Banes startled at the sound of his name. He shook his head. He didn't recall ever seeing or meeting anyone purporting to be Mrs. Beldam's daughter. He absently rubbed his foreshortened arm.

But hadn't he regularly fetched purgatives from Bianca for just this purpose—ridding women of unwanted babies? In fact, the last portion had been intended for Pandy. He had overheard her admit as much to Wynders—at least that is what he assumed. And Wynders had responded coldly. But maybe her child wasn't his after all. Perhaps Pandy had hoped to trap him. Banes stood back and thought. Had he misunderstood her intent? The possibilities made his head ache. He thought back to what he had seen and heard. Then, something else occurred to him. Something that made his blood chill, and it wasn't just the sudden tap on his shoulder.

# CHAPTER 33

Constable Patch hobbled up the lane, leading his minions. The two ruffians had agreed to assist him for the promise of a beer afterward, but also, more importantly, for his dropping charges of swindling visitors at the entrance of St. Bartholomew's. They had told gullible travelers that a relic of skin from the saint was enshrined therein, and for a penny they could kiss it for eternal good health. They now loped behind the constable, mocking him silently behind his back as he led them through the alleys of Southwark to find that murderess Bianca Goddard.

Patch muttered unintelligibly, skirting a mangy goose and a copious puddle, arguing with himself that he could not be sure the girl wasn't a witch impersonating an apothecary. But he had no proof of this, so for now, he must be satisfied with the simple claim of murder.

If he succeeded in nabbing the villainess, he'd be one step closer to a possible commission in a better-paying district of London. The aldermen appreciated constables practiced in bringing miscreants to justice. They believed the need was greater on their side of the river, though Patch knew that assumption was patently untrue. Yet on the other side of the river lay "civilization" and the men with money and the status to go with it. Merchants and livery fancied living in a less-nefarious borough, and were willing to hire those who had proven themselves worthy of such commissions.

Worried the two scalawags might prove useless, Constable Patch spun to face them.

"I'll not 'ave ye burgle this arrest," he said, catching them in an obscene gesture. He fixed them with hard stares as they staggered to a stop, inches from plowing into him.

One of the men spoke up. "Sir, if ye mean 'bungle,' we don't have a heart fer it. Nor would we filch a single strand of straw in this venture. We've a mind to see a murderer hanged. Aye, we would. We has a vested interest in treachery of all kinds."

Constable Patch's eyes narrowed as he considered this. "Let me be clear, it is not my treachery but hers."

The one scalawag nodded vigorously and was joined by his partner. Their two heads bobbed in unison. He said, "Sirs, we do as ye likes. Character is for God to judge, not fer the likes of men such as we."

Constable Patch pulled his beard as his eyes traveled up and down their persons. Two filthier, stinking knaves he'd never seen, but he knew the difference between men who wanted ale and men who needed it. They were the latter.

"This one is a clever sort," Patch said. "She is as deceitful and conniving as any woman," he added, unable to conceal his bitterness toward the fairer sex. "I would not put it past her to weevil her way out of this."

"Aye, sir," said the second man, the one most smelling like a goat. "Like a maggot in a sack of grain, she is."

"Or a worm in fruit," said the other.

Constable Patch wondered why they were drawing comparisons to insects. But his was not to ponder the logic of criminals. "Be ready to nab her and we'll make quick about it. I should hope we'll find her alone, but if not, I can't imagine a crowd of admirers stuffed into that small rent. To be sure, I feel I must arm you."

The men exchanged looks and bobbed their heads again with enthusiasm.

"For ye," he said, handing one of them a length of rope, "the means to bind her wrists."

The rope dangled from the man's hand like a limp snake.

"Let me see ye bind your friend's wrists." Constable Patch was none too sure the rascal knew the first thing about such matters, and he was leaving nothing to chance.

Sure enough, the man proceeded to weave the length in and out and around with no sense of how to tie a secure knot. The rope hung loosely in a tangled lump. Constable Patch grabbed the useless snarl and proceeded to give him a proper lesson. He momentarily questioned whether it was wise to educate lowlifes in the finer points of criminal apprehension, then decided these fools hadn't the wits to use any of it once he'd finished with them.

After he was satisfied the man could not completely botch his assignment, he gave the other a short dagger. "I assume ye know how to use this."

The man looked as if he'd been given the Holy Grail. He turned the weapon over in his hand, studying its blade. After a long whistle the man looked up and smiled.

"I'll be expecting that back," said Constable Patch, to be sure the rascal had no delusions. He resumed his trek, touched his trusty anlace in its scabbard for luck (and a measure of assurance), then continued his grumbling and instructions.

"After we deliver the miscreant to gaol and she is safely disposed behind iron bars and three foot of stone wall, then we may breathe our ease that we have successfully delivered the dangerous killer off the streets of London."

"But this is Southwark," said the rope-bearing knave, trying to be helpful.

Constable Patch stopped in his tracks. He threw the rascal a look that would silence a guinea hen. "I'll not have ye right me.

By your office ye are nothing more than a drunkard at best and a charlatan at that. Ye do not have the office to right me wrongs or wrong me rights. Keep your tongue until spoken to, and dare ye not wag it before." He looked the two up and down with a scouring glare, then resumed his walk, grumbling all the more and kicking a goose out of his way.

The two men said nothing more, but followed the foultempered constable through the grounds of a disbanded rectory to the area of Gull Hole.

Bianca Goddard's room was down a narrow lane catty-corner to a yard of chicken coops, the sound and smells of which greeted them before they even turned the corner.

"Fie, I've not met such foul fowl in all me life," said the man with the rope. He scrunched his face as if it should help filter the stink and prevent his eyes burning. "I'd not be a chicken farker if I were given a hundred crown."

Constable Patch pointed out that this was an odd observation coming from a man who smelled of goats. He glanced over his shoulder and found the other cuffin still enamored with the dagger, waving it about with great sweeping swathes and engaging in a duel with an imaginary assailant. Constable Patch stopped.

"Before I get theres, I needs ye two to look mincing. I'll not have ye cringing and parrying behind me back."

The two men planted their feet together and threw their chests forward. They squared their shoulders as best they could, just like the king's guard. The goat smeller wet his palm and slicked his hair away from his eyes. They each attempted a menacing stare.

"Ye goose this, it'll be you who's buyin' me the drinks." Patch could not hide his contempt as his lips pinched in disgust.

The two bobbed their heads in agreement.

Constable Patch muttered under his breath and turned the corner, where he was met by an unexpected sight. He stopped and put his arm up to keep his crew from stumbling over him. He was pleased to note it worked. He put his finger to his lips and, with stealth, tiptoed forward.

When he was within a step of the undercooked abomination of a young man, he drew himself erect and tapped the lad on the shoulder.

Banes whirled about and, seeing Constable Patch, took off running.

"Shoulds we run after?" asked the goat smeller.

But the lad had the advantage of youth and nimbleness and turned the corner before Patch got out a word. "Forgets it," he said. "He's already gone."

Disappointed, Constable Patch pressed his ear to the door, listening for voices. Satisfied he heard the squeak of a female, he pounded the door.

He waited, listening for movement; then, when he heard an approaching footfall, assumed a pose of authority. The door swung open, and he found himself faced not with the murderess Bianca Goddard but with that irksome streetseller Meddybemps. The impertinent barnacle had the gall to smile.

"Ah, Constable Patch. To what do I owe this honor?" Meddybemps nodded in mocking deference.

"Honor? You, Meddybemps, speak to me of honor? I do not care for ye, nor do I owe the likes of ye an answer. Step aside."

The smile slid from the streetseller's face. "I suppose manners are a lawman's failing." He stood aside and let through Patch and the posse of bootlickers trailing behind.

Constable Patch scanned the room, ducking beneath the clusters of hanging herbs to better see. The putrid smell set his eyes watering, but there was Bianca, sitting on a stool with a blood-stained rag in her lap. Her hair needed a comb, and her eyes looked puffy, as if in need of sleep.

Unfortunately, she was not alone. That wheaten-haired fellow was next to her. He and Meddybemps looked as if to shield her, and Patch was glad at least for arming his minions, feckless though they were. He believed he had justice on his side, and that steeled his confidence—along with the thought of a promotion.

"Bianca Goddard, with the power vested in me by the just and honorable citizens of Southwark . . ." He took a breath and began his long-winded pronouncement like the wheezing exhale of a bellows. With nose pointed to the rafters he recited and embellished his speech. He had nearly finished when he glimpsed the disemboweled rats lined up on the table. He stopped midsentence and gawked. "My God," he exclaimed. "What manner of evil *are* you?"

"I've discovered what poisoned Jolyn." Bianca walked over to the table and pointed to several rats whose veins had been slit open. "The coroner discovered Jolyn's blood was tinged purple. I was able to re-create the effect. It was rat poison that killed her."

Constable Patch stared down at the display and the alarming purplish tinge of rodent's blood. "This is your confession," he affirmed.

Bianca shook her head. "I'm merely showing you the cause of her death, not who caused it."

"But ye are practiced in rat poison."

"I do deal in such."

Constable Patch glanced over his shoulder at his appointed guards, who seemed even more horrified than he. They clamped shut their hanging jaws and watched him with bugged eyes.

"I taint my rat poison with tincture of terebinth resin—a noticeable additive."

"Noticeable—how?"

"As in its odor. A smell of pine."

"Are ye saying she would not have eaten it?"

"I am saying it would have been difficult to mask the odor in food."

"But a murderer can be clever," said Patch. "If one has the desire to see another dead . . ."

"True," said Bianca. "Desire has its own life, separate from our moral, conscious one. It can drive one to ignore consequence. It has no remorse. It feels nothing but the satisfaction that comes with completion."

"It is not surprising that murderers feel a certain satisfaction."

"But motive is the means to satisfaction. Murder is always an act of passion. It can be born of jealousy, retribution, or defense. The reasons are varied, but the intent is always to end the murderer's own personal suffering."

Constable Patch looked on in amusement. This girl could certainly weave a tangled tale. "Pray tell, what do ye suppose was the motive?" he asked.

Bianca placed the stained rag on the table next to the rats. "Jealousy."

Constable Patch searched her face. Was this her confession?

"Jealousy over another lover," added Bianca, showing no indication of her own guilt.

"Another lover," Patch groaned. "How pedestrian." He'd never understood how love could incite a person to murder—especially when one considered the inevitable consequence. Was love worth the cost of a public hanging? "And who do ye suppose this other lover to be?"

"Jolyn was the last woman to receive Robert Wynders's attention. But before Jolyn, there was another. A woman who suffered his poor treatment and was driven into a jealous rage. A woman living at Barke House, abandoned by Wynders and forced to watch him lavish affection on Jolyn. A woman with no choice but to take purgative to rid herself of the consequence of their failed passion. She did this in the hope of winning back his flagging attention, but it did not work. Left with no other choice to staunch her outrage, Pandy murdered Jolyn."

Constable Patch's brows shot up. "Pandy?" He glanced round. "Hmph. An interesting concussion." He studied the expressions of John and Meddybemps. Apparently the crippled lad hadn't informed Bianca Goddard of the news. Strange he had kept it quiet. After all, Banes had been there when he had visited Barke House to tell Mrs. Beldam.

"That is an interesting theory," he continued, "though highly unlikely."

John spoke. The color had drained from his face, leaving him as pale as Bianca. "What do you mean, 'unlikely'?"

Constable Patch answered genially. How likely would a murderer become a victim so soon after committing a crime? Patch pulled the hair on his chin and watched Bianca's face carefully when he told her.

"Pandy Shaw of Barke House is dead."

He was not disappointed.

# CHAPTER 34

Bianca recalled her mother's counsel, "Imagine the worst possible outcome, then work backward." Sage advice when the worst scenario was something other than death.

"Are you going to die if you learn to stuff a goose?" she had asked when Bianca had preferred to run the streets with John. Bianca had grudgingly agreed to help her mother with the cooking that time, and she had learned a useful skill—if ever she wanted to serve roast goose.

However, in this particular case, the worst scenario *was* death. It was not imagined. On the contrary, it was inevitable.

Bianca had not been able to convince Constable Patch of her innocence—nor had anyone else.

Despite the futile protests of John and Meddybemps, which included a scuffle and fistfight, Bianca had been bound at the wrists and marched from her room of Medicinals and Physickes. Constable Patch led the way as two dubious guards alternately pulled her along. To her annoyance, one was particularly keen to nudge her forward with the point of a dagger he brandished at her backside.

Bianca sought to engage the constable in conversation in the hopes that the guards might stop tugging and prodding her. "Pandy must have known something," she said. "Otherwise why would she be stabbed?"

Patch ignored her. Nothing could dissuade him from throwing Bianca Goddard in the Clink and trying her for murder.

"Am I to be tried for Pandy's death, too?" she asked.

"Maybes there is something ye's not telling us," he said over his shoulder.

Bianca opened her mouth to protest, then wondered if he meant for her to be tortured once she was confined. Her knees buckled and she nearly fell but was caught up by the elbow and dragged forward by one of the guards.

Constable Patch turned to see what had happened, and his expression hardened. "Don't tarry, now. Ye'll have plenty of time to think on it once yer confined."

But Bianca's imagination got the better of her, and she heaved the contents of her stomach onto the guard.

"Gak! I'd not agreed to this," he said, letting go of her arm and looking to rid his sleeve of her sick. Finding nothing suitable, he proceeded to examine the damage she'd done, then snatched the dagger from his mate and scraped the fabric with its blade.

His mate protested, and when Patch saw what was happening, his neck bloomed an exceptional shade of rose.

"Hand over that knife," he said, unable to stand by while his favorite dagger was irreverently used to scrape sick. He snatched it away and pointed it at the ruffian's chin. "I'll not have ye abuse me edge." He nicked the man's jaw to prove his point, spit over his shoulder, then handed the blade back to the other. At least his companion had had the good sense to hang onto the prisoner so as not to lose her.

"Constable Patch," said Bianca, desperate to dissuade him from taking such a narrow focus on the murders, "have you looked into the business dealings of Robert Wynders?"

"He is of noble employ with the Chudderly fleet, I knows that. It does not concern us."

"But it does," said Bianca. "I saw him send a rower to a moored ship in quarantine last night. I watched to see who would be setting out from shore at that late hour. It wasn't long before a fire raged in the skiff next to the ship's hull."

Constable Patch marched on, although his pace slowed.

"Wynders was on shore. Once the fire died, he turned and left. If it were an accident, he would have acted alarmed."

"Dids ye follow him?"

Bianca knew she had piqued his interest and seized her opportunity. "I did. He went to a warehouse in Romeland. After he left, I slipped inside."

Constable Patch stopped. She thought he might say something about entering a property where she had no business. Instead, he encouraged her. "Go on."

"I found something quite disturbing. Something of great import to the citizens of London."

"If ye thinks ye is going to tempt me with something that has no bearing on my parish ward, then ye are mistaken. If it is of no interest to Southwark, I've not a care for it."

"It does interest Southwark. What happens in London happens to Southwark. After all, we are two sides of the same river. The king might even want to know what I found."

Constable Patch spun about and lowered his face inches from hers. "I'll not have ye play me, girl."

"Sir, I do not toy."

"The consequences of which could be worse," said Patch, his eyes narrowing in warning. "You've been duly reminded. But pray, do tell."

"The smell was not of this world."

"Odd *ye* should say it."

"I heard snarling and rasping. It was dark as pitch, but I found a rushlight. Crates from Italy and bales of woolens and silks crammed every inch of the warehouse. I picked through the stacks to the interior." An involuntary shiver skipped down her spine as she recalled the memory. "What I saw should not be taken lightly." Bianca took a breath, watching Patch to be sure she had his attention. "The back of the warehouse was over-run with rats. Hundreds of them. All fighting and feeding off a pile"—Bianca opened her eyes wide and leaned forward—"of rotting corpses."

The two guards exchanged glances.

Constable Patch's upper lip quivered. "Well nows," he said, "when ye says a 'pile'—exactly what does ye mean?"

"I cannot say for sure. I did not stay to count them. Perhaps thirty . . . or more."

Constable Patch blinked.

"I cannot imagine for what purpose Robert Wynders stores bodies in a warehouse. But if he does have a reason, there is a risk posed by doing so. Is he fattening the rats of the city and sending them forth to multiply?" Bianca could see she had given the constable pause. She was not going to abandon her advantage and made sure he'd have plenty to think about.

"Wynders came by my room of Medicinals and Physickes to acquire rat poison for his ship two days ago. I gave him a measure suitable for ridding a merchant vessel of a problem. But, sir, the amount I gave him would not be nearly enough to vanquish the problem in that warehouse." Bianca noticed Patch was stunned into silence. His mouth opened and closed as if he were a carp gasping out of water.

"What if they overrun the city?" she said. "Why, you have to be blind not to notice their increased numbers."

"It is true," said one of the guards. "I has noticed. I have seen with me own eyes the bands of vermin on the streets of late."

The other guard nodded while Constable Patch recovered enough to tug the wiry strands of his beard. He skittishly glanced around as if this talk of rats might actually summon them. "Wells," he said, "it is not my jew's diction." He tossed off the responsi-bility, but Bianca could tell he was troubled. Whether he pursued the tidbit for his own glory, she did not care. But if she must hang, at least she would not take the information to her grave.

"I've got a murderer to deliver. I'll not have ye waylay me fur-ther from my public duty. Come ahead, now. We haven't all night."

Constable Patch turned and with a purposeful stride set off, but Bianca saw him glancing this way and that, as if checking the lane for errant vermin.

A mantle of fog crept up from the Thames, and Bianca thought how she might never again see the sun once she was thrown in a cell. She sighed, and a harsh reality sank in. Would the next time she saw the sky be the day of her execution?

Her conveyance stirred the interest of curious passersby. A girl set down her yoke of buckets to watch them pass. Theatergoers, dray drivers, and goodwives all noted the entourage and drew their own conclusions—some quietly and others not so. Though her emotions churned, Bianca forced herself to lift her chin and meet their stares. She believed in her innocence even if no one else did, and she wanted others to see it in her face. She had little hope, but she clung to the notion that she'd be vindicated at trial.

The high tower of St. Mary Overie disappeared beneath the fog's unsavory broth. Day was fading, and Bianca imagined that once inside the Clink, it would be blacker than any dark she'd ever known.

On they trudged, their boots sucking in the squidgy mud and Constable Patch's mumbling the only discourse between them. Bianca hoped Patch was thinking about what she had just told him. Her conclusion that Pandy had murdered Jolyn for revenge had fallen on deaf ears. But even if she was correct, no matter of argument could convince Patch otherwise.

She needed to untangle the threads of her logic and rethink where they took her. Whatever her conclusion, ultimately, the judge would decide. She had to be convincing, and the only way to be that was to be right.

They arrived outside the moldered stone enclave, and Bianca gaped up at its menacing façade. Small arched windows dotted the front, the iron crossbars bleeding rust down the stone. Inmates stretched wasted arms through the gaps, their palms outstretched for alms or a crusty end of bread that a pedestrian or relative might charitably press into it.

"Those are the lucky ones," said Constable Patch, gesturing to the prisoners begging.

Bianca knew he was right. No doubt the constable had a less jovial welcome in mind for her. They came to a halt, and one of the guards threw her forward. She stumbled into the muck, coating one side of her kirtle and sleeve. Patch glanced down at her unsympathetically, then pounded the hulking door.

"Stand her. I can't kick her through the door," he said.

A moment passed, and the door groaned open, and standing in its shadows was an ox of a man wearing a stained rough coat with a bollock dagger tucked in his leather girth. "Ah, Patch," said the gaoler, his ring of keys jangling from the crook of his elbow. His broad face perused their party. "Whats ye gots fer me today?"

"A murderess," answered Patch. "And mayhaps a witch—but a delinquent just the same."

The gaoler scrutinized her with round pinholes for eyes, then stepped back and addressed Patch. "Such a young bess to be settin' about murderin'. 'Tis a shame. Catch them up with babes to feed and a drunken cuff of a husband, I don't blame them none." He tsked. "What's her story?"

"Poisoning another young bess, she dids."

"Ooo, jealous of a lover?"

Constable Patch leaned in. "Ye may remember the alchemist Albern Goddard?"

"Ach! A puffer set to poison the king. I remember him well. Not every day a man would chance that."

"Her father he is."

The gaoler reared back and studied her. He looked as if this presented Bianca in a new light. "Wells then. I am privileged. I mights be able to makes some coin from this." He clapped Constable Patch on the back. "Ye always looks out fer me, Patch. A worthy public servant."

"See that she is treated suitably for a murderer," added Patch. "Methinks she may not be tellin' all she knows." He paused as a shriek from the depths therein grew in intensity and disconcertingly echoed off the walls. "A confession helps the cause."

The gaoler tilted his head. "That cause being?"

"Mine," said Patch.

The gaoler handed Patch a torch and led them down a hall. Sconces sputtered from drips snaking down the limestone walls. They descended stairs to an underground section even more dank and dark. The smell of mildewed straw mixed with the ammonia of human waste and sick. Even Bianca reacted to the putrid air.

It wasn't just the stink of human suffering that was so disconcerting but also the sound of it. Disembodied moans and ignored pleas accompanied their passage, occasionally interrupted by the treacly cackle of madness or bloodcurdling shriek.

Constable Patch and the gaoler trundled on. Bianca supposed they'd grown accustomed to the place, though she could sense the two guards were doing their best to appear untroubled. Finally, the gaoler stopped in front of a welded iron door and searched through his ring of keys, trying one in the rusted lock and then another. After several misses, he found the appropriate key and the door creaked open.

Constable Patch swept the smoking torch in an arc, illuminating the interior. It was a small hold. If Bianca could have raised her arms from her sides, she might have touched opposite walls while facing the door. It was more deep than wide.

"Go on now," said the gaoler. He pushed Bianca forward and swung the iron door closed behind her.

"Am I to be kept bound?" Bianca held up her wrists.

"Until a time when I send a man to shackle ye," replied the gaoler.

"Sees that ye treat her fittingly," Constable Patch said. "No special considerations."

"When will I be tried?"

"Whenever they deem fit," said the gaoler, snorting in laughter. Patch chuckled, and the guards offered wan smiles.

The party left, their torchlight fading, and Bianca's only light was a guttering tallow in the passageway. She squinted at her surroundings, choking down a rising panic. The cell was a desolate, putrid affair, windowless and damp from the Thames. No rush or mats covered the dirt floor, nothing to push into a pile on which to sleep or even sit. She had no stool to sit on, and definitely no chamber pot was provided for her necessaries. The only adornment was a pair of chains hanging from a wall, ending in manacles.

She stood next to the iron bars, taking advantage of what little light there was, and immediately set about trying to wiggle her hands free. With her teeth, she rotated the bindings knot side up. The tallow sputtered, reminding her that time was running out. She held up her wrists to study the knot. Tug the wrong bump, and instead of loosening the bindings, she would tighten them.

Bianca visually traced a length as it looped over and under, then brought her wrists to her mouth. With her teeth she tugged at the binding, then dropped her hands to see if it had loosened.

As she tilted her wrists toward the dim light, a final *ftt* signaled the candle had expired, plunging Bianca into darkness.

Probably she could have seen more with her eyes shut. There was no telling if she had loosened or tightened the knot. When she wiggled her wrists and hands, the bindings felt just as tight as before.

Bianca sank to her knees, leaning against the door, not caring how filthy the floor was beneath her. Her legs ached, but she needed to rest them—though it occurred to her that maybe she should walk before she was clapped in chains. Tears flowed, and she sobbed inconsolably. If her mother knew, she would be sorely disappointed and utterly bereft.

Her mother was a stubborn woman, and even though she had behaved brashly with Meddybemps, Bianca did not resent her for it. She had seen her mother so unhappy that even with Meddybemps's reputation she could not blame her for what small measure of enjoyment she had exacted from their fleeting fancy. She loved her mother, and she loved Meddybemps. But her mother knew what the randy streetseller was about. And she did not care. Nor did she concern herself with what influence he might have on Bianca.

Bianca held herself to a higher standard, in part because her mother expected it. And she could not bear to disappoint her mother. The thought of being hanged in humiliation without her mother ever knowing her side of the story made her insides churn.

"Stop that whimperin' over there. You think you is the only one sufferin'?"

Bianca took a jagged breath and stifled her sobs. "Who's there?"

"You answer first."

"I'm Bianca Goddard. I deal in medicines for the good citizens of Southwark and London."

"Bianca Goddard. You don't says. Why I've bought your salve for me fever from Meddybemps, I has. Could do with some now, I coulds. You haven't any on your person, 'ave you?"

Before Bianca could say one way or the other, he answered for her. "Phaa, wouldn't do me no goods, anyways. You couldn't get it to me." He grumbled something unintelligible, and Bianca heard the clunk of something heavy fall on the ground.

"Are you strung up?" Bianca called.

"Nay, they tethered me. Just me ankle. They got me draggin' a cannon shot. I takes to carryin' it 'cause me ankle is raw to the bone."

"I'm sorry."

"So am I. But I guess it could be worse."

Bianca had her doubts.

"So why is an herbalist in the Clink?"

"I've been wrongly accused of murder."

"You and maybe half the lot in here. It's always the way of it. The guilty dance free, and the innocents are made examples of. They've got it back arsewards, but the catchpoles are a drunken, cheatin' lot. They is the ones doin' the public an injustice. But that's just my opinion, and they care not a whit. Why should they? They does a great business haulin' in whoever they want."

"You haven't cheered me," said Bianca.

"Well, forgive me if I don't spout accolades and dance a jig.

I'm a bit hindered draggin' the *Mary Rose*'s armory about me foot. Anyways, it's not me place to plump you up."

As her neighbor yammered on, Bianca grew more determined to free herself of her bindings and of him. She brought the rope to her mouth and ran her tongue along it, tracing the knot until she found the spot where she had last worked.

"I's been here near I can tell maybe two months now," said her neighbor, without prompt. "Course you can't tell day from night down here, and I am no judge of time's fickle passage. But sometimes I can get the keeper to tell me."

"So, what is your name?" asked Bianca, trying her wrists to see if she'd gained some slack.

"Aw, that's right. I didn't say, did I? Simon Slade, I is. Master locksmith."

"*Master* locksmith, you say? Perhaps you overreach."

"Aw, now, no need gettin' tart with me. I ain't the cause for your troubles."

"I apologize. But I should think a master locksmith might have made some progress on his shackles."

"And with what? Me teeth? Should I chew through an inch of iron? A man can't make progress without a pick or the likes. You think I haven't studied this contraption? I've looked it right side up and left side down. I'll thank you not to disparage me or me trade. A smith needs tools."

"So why are you here?" Bianca went back to tugging her knot. She was encouraged to find it beginning to give.

"I'm here as is you. Wrongly accused."

"Wrongly accused of what?"

"Assault."

"Assault of what?"

"Not what—who. A cozen most deserving. He had it long in coming. I jus' had the bollocks to do him."

The rope began to loosen, and Bianca's glum mood began to lift. "How did he earn your harsh opinion?"

"He was makin' outs he was a taxman for Romeland and needed

to get in warehouses, claiming the owners were in arrears for more than a year. He aimed to take possession for the royal coffers. He was none such character. He took possessions all right, he did. And a number of locksmiths were charged for abetting his sham. I'm not the only one sittin' in a hole because of 'im. I'm lucky to be here in the Clinks instead of Newgate. One must count their blessings."

Bianca couldn't think why one prison would be preferable to another; they were all miserable. But then this was the first one she'd seen from the inside, and she didn't savor the thought of a promotion to Newgate, where public hangings were far more enthusiastically attended.

"Well, I am sorry to hear it."

"As am I," said Slade.

The knot loosened, allowing Bianca to work free of it, and with a hoot of victory, she flung the wad of hemp to the floor and stomped it.

"Why so merry? There be nothin' to be glad of down heres."

"I am free of my bindings." Bianca rubbed her raw wrists and swung her arms about to wake them up.

"Well, enjoy your freedom now. It's only temporary. They'll soon clap you in iron."

Bianca ignored his dire prediction and could only think how glad she was to have the use of her hands again. She scratched every itch and felt her way to a corner, where she relieved herself, being careful to avoid stepping and dragging her skirt through her waste. She then went to the iron lock of the door that kept her from total freedom.

She felt its cold, unyielding metal and worked a finger into the keyway, feeling its metal wards. Bianca interrupted her neighbor's rants, for he had gone on about his maladies, poor luck, and complaints about life.

"Slade, how might one go about picking a lock?"

"One hires a master locksmith."

"Tell me what I must do."

"Why should I?"

"Because if I pick this lock open, I shall help you."

"I've heard that before."

Bianca played to his better nature. "Slade, if you have any chance—no matter how slim—wouldn't you try? Do you want your foot to fall off from rot?"

"I hate to piss on your party, lass, but unless you have a pick or the actual key, you won't get nowheres."

Bianca had neither. She sank to her haunches, leaning against the door.

Surely John or Meddybemps would get her out. She wished she'd told John where to find her latest earnings or her silver filings to sell. Any turnkey could be had for a bribe—even one disposed to do Constable Patch's bidding. All she needed was a little more time and the chance to prove her case without a doubt.

After all, she'd confirmed it was rat poison that killed her friend. The purgative, if given in a large enough dose, might have killed her, but it didn't tinge blood purple. Because of the press of time, she'd had to strangle those rats in order to kill them and check their blood.

Bianca stared into the dark and concentrated. Both Wynders and Banes had bought rat poison from her. But Wynders bought his after Jolyn had died. She visualized Banes and ran through her observations. She had read his face when he first saw Jolyn dead. It wasn't deceit on his face but bewilderment. She didn't think Banes would poison Jolyn. But how did Banes feel toward Mrs. Beldam? He was cautious—she could see that. Did he fear losing his place at Barke House? Or was there something else? He might not like the woman, but he protected her.

Bianca's head throbbed. Her stomach growled with nerves and hunger. She fought exhaustion and forced herself to rehash her conversation with Meddybemps and Banes before Constable Patch had arrived to arrest her.

Robert Wynders was a philanderer who had gotten his position by marrying the daughter of a wealthy merchant. Apparently, Mrs. Beldam's daughter had a child with him out of wedlock—a threatening situation. If it were known, Wynders stood to lose his marriage and position. Humiliation and ruin are strong motivators.

But why did Mrs. Beldam and Wynders both shower Jolyn with attention? The only thing Jolyn had besides her beauty was that ring. A ring that Bianca was sure they both wanted.

Were they in league with each other? They both wanted the ring—but why?

What was the ring to Mrs. Beldam? Had it something to do with Mrs. Beldam's daughter? Bianca rubbed her neck and stared into the black. The ring had power for Mrs. Beldam. Power over Wynders.

The sound of someone descending the stairs roused Bianca from her thoughts.

"Mayhaps they've come to clap you in chains," hissed Simon Slade.

"Mayhaps they've come to beat you silent," said Bianca.

Slade snickered. "You got a black wit, lass. You better watch yourself if you get out of here. Though I'm thinkin' you never will."

An orb of light advanced, illuminating the sneer of the gaoler stopping in front of Bianca's cell. A guard accompanied him—a man specially bred to instill fear and loathing in those who were the unfortunate recipients of his skills.

"Here she is," said the gaoler. "The daughter of that alchemist who set about tryin' to poison the king last year. Ye remember the likes of 'im—do ye?"

"Aye, sir. Such treachery," said the man, tsking. "It must run in the blood."

"Be not gentle. Constable Patch thinks there is more to learn."

The guard studied Bianca as he fingered the lash at his side.

"Whats I told you, lass?" crowed Slade from his cell.

The gaoler stepped away from Bianca's cell to address her

gloating neighbor. "See as ye stops your mouth, Slade, or we'll
'ave another go at ye." He then reappeared and gave a black look
at Bianca. "Where's ye bindings, girl?"

Bianca shrugged. "They fell off."

The gaoler raised an eyebrow. "Dids they now?" He addressed
his unappealing companion. "See's ye teach her we don't appre-
ciate noncooperation."

# CHAPTER 35

A measure of guilt niggled Banes's conscience as he headed back to Barke House. He should have told Bianca that Pandy had been murdered; then maybe she would have taken her chance to flee while she could. Once Constable Patch and his guards had entered her room, he had snuck back to the window to watch what transpired. As it was, Constable Patch gloried in Bianca's ill-conceived account of Jolyn's murder. Banes hated seeing Patch revel in smug satisfaction.

He kept remembering Bianca's look of puzzled dismay when Patch set his guards on her. To his credit, John had put up a good fight. His effort had left him with a nasty gash on his arm. Meddy-bemps did not intervene, but Banes did not suppose the sly street-seller would sit idly by while his business partner sat in the Clink. What the skinny knave was up to he did not presume to even guess.

So Banes had left armed with information. Information he intended to use.

His primary obstacle would be getting Wynders and Mrs. Beldam in the same place at the same time. He wanted to be able to

see them both when he asked his questions. If he could confront
them together, he could watch them squirm—actions being more
telling than anything they would say, which would likely be lies
anyway.

As a thick mist settled in the lanes of Southwark and night
began to fall, Banes grew more alert and conscious of his surroundings. London's seedy sister was never a blithe stroll even
on a sunny day. Soon winter's final gasp would give leave to
spring, but for now, winter's spell would not relent.

Banes slowed as he approached Barke House. He studied its
exterior as if he might see through its walls to its inhabitants.
Surely he would find Mrs. Beldam, and he might pose his questions to her regardless of Robert Wynders's absence. The fear of
being shut out of Barke House weighed on his mind. Where
would he go? How would he survive? But more pressing and unpleasant was the notion of perpetuating a lie. To him, confrontation was worth that risk.

Carefully, he lifted the latch and opened the door, spitting on
the hinges to quiet them. The candle in the vestibule had not
been lit. He stood in the dark, motionless, listening for the
sounds of women, conversation, a clatter of crockery in the
kitchen. But all was quiet. Almost eerily so.

He felt the shelf above for a flint and lit the candle, the light
warming the edges of his shadow as it sprang monstrous on the
yellow walls. Then he heard it. A man's voice. He moved from
the vestibule and stepped cautiously toward the kitchen.

Robert Wynders loomed over Mrs. Beldam. His sheer physical
bulk filled the room so that he looked cramped within its four
walls. "You have no grounds to prove anything. You have nothing."

Mrs. Beldam's jaw was set in an air of defiance. A wave of revulsion washed over Banes. Was she? Could she be . . . ? He
winced in disgust, unsure if he wanted the truth.

"Banes," she said, discovering him lurking in the shadows.

Wynders looked over his shoulder. "Leave us."

A jumble of thoughts crowded Banes's head. It was as if he
were seeing the two of them for the first time. Look at her thin

build and ruddy complexion. Were they not like his? And Wynders's black eyes—did they not match his own in shape and color? He shook his head, trying to dislodge the awful thought from his mind. The realization was too raw, too painful.

"Get out," said Wynders, taking a step toward him.

Banes had not come this far only to be dismissed. For once he believed his need was far greater than acquiescing. He had questions, and he had to know for sure. They both wanted what he had, and he would use it against them. It was the only thing the two of them cared about. "I know where the ring is," he said.

Mrs. Beldam and Wynders froze, as if doused in cold water. But neither spoke nor moved.

"You both want a certain ring, and I know where to find it."

Mrs. Beldam and Wynders stared but offered not a word.

"I can tell you where it is, but you must tell me why you both must have it."

Mrs. Beldam looked askance at Wynders and stepped beyond his reach, putting a table between them. "I will tell ye, so long as ye don't tell him where it is." Her eyes slid to Wynders, then back again.

Wynders was twice the size of Mrs. Beldam—he could certainly manage to get the information out of her later. It didn't matter to Banes which of them knew. He wanted the truth, and to hell with their personal dispute. Banes agreed.

Mrs. Beldam slowly inched her back along a sideboard. Her eyes flicked toward Wynders. "It belongs to your mother," she said to Banes.

All these years she had told him he had been abandoned. "My mother? It belonged to my mother?"

"She is lying. It belongs to me," said Wynders.

Banes remembered what Meddybemps had said, and deep within his soul he knew the awful truth. "You want the ring back because you gave it to my mother. And I am your son."

"That's right," said Mrs. Beldam. "Ye's the bastard's son." She relished saying it.

"The ring was not a gift. They stole it from me."

"Ye was dead drunk, ye fool," said Mrs. Beldam. "We took it as payment. For getting her in a bad way with no intention of bein' honorable about it."

"But you are my grandmother." Banes stared at her incredulously. "Why did you lie to me? Why did you tell me I was abandoned? That I was found in a basket along the river?"

"I hads to keep his secret so's not to humiliate him."

"Humiliate?"

"Did ye think he'd want it known, with your arm as strange as feathers on a fish?"

"I did not ask to be born with this arm."

Mrs. Beldam shook her head. "None of us ask to be born at all. But ye takes what ye gets, and ye learns to manage. He used your mother for his pleasure. And you is his perversion."

The words stung like a slap across his cheek. "But look on me. Am I not like him? Do I not have eyes as dark and a nose of similar shape? Is my hair not like his? The similarities cannot be denied. You don't need a ring to prove it."

"I could haul ye out for all to see, but I'm not so sociable. Besides, why would I ruin our agreement when possession of the ring is proof enough? I don't needs to embarrass anyones."

Banes stared at Wynders, his resentment filling him with abject bitterness. This was his father. And the man despised him. Wynders must have wondered how *he* could have created *this*— this aberration of a son. Wynders rejected him—he was an embarrassment. A person to loathe and despise.

"Nows," said Mrs. Beldam, suddenly seizing a knife off the sideboard and pointing it at Wynders. She carefully stepped toward Banes, keeping Wynders at arm's length. "Suppose we leave now, and ye take me to the ring."

Banes no longer felt inclined to do Mrs. Beldam's bidding. He was not finished asking questions, and he played his advantage. "Tell me what happened to my mother."

"She's well taken care of," said Mrs. Beldam, tugging Banes's shirt and encouraging him toward the door.

"Tell me where she is." Banes jerked away from her touch.

"She's in the care of nuns," answered Mrs. Beldam, exasperated.

"Where?" insisted Banes.

Mrs. Beldam considered using the knife on him instead. "There's time for that later."

"She wouldn't know you," said Wynders.

"A mother never forgets her son. She'll know who I am."

"You're as daft as she is," muttered Wynders.

"What do you mean? What did you do to her?" This was his family—his father and his grandmother—and they despised him. Even worse for him to imagine, they despised his mother. And for what? Because she gave birth to him? He could think of nothing but his anger and the mistreatment of his mother—in his mind, an innocent victim of Wynders's wanton passion. His rage unleashed, Banes launched himself at Wynders.

But Wynders had seen the boy tremble with mounting anger and expected Banes to lash out at him. He threw Banes against a wall, cracking his head and sending a shower of crockery crashing down on top of him. Wynders turned to face Mrs. Beldam.

"Ye wouldn't dare touch me," she hissed, stepping backward. She swiped the air with her knife. "Not with the boy knowing who ye is now."

Wynders had waited years for this moment. He had never been angry or clever enough to scheme how to end their vile confederacy. He had stalked her and had imagined slipping a blade between her ribs. He had spent sleepless nights envisioning how it might feel to finally be finished with her. But he lacked the audacity. He was not, by nature, a malevolent man. However, years of marriage to Sarah and, by association, Chudderly Shipping had changed him. To Wynders, there was no reward for behaving with exemplary restraint. His dalliance with Mrs. Beldam's daughter—a petulant retaliation for his ill treatment at Chudderly—had resulted in another "marriage," even more noxious and regrettable.

He swung his arm up and knocked the knife out of Mrs. Beldam's hand. It skidded across the floor, coming to a stop near a bin of grain. Mrs. Beldam chased after it, and Wynders struck her jaw with his elbow and the full force of his weight. The blow knocked her cold. She fell—hitting her head on the bin of grain with a sickening thud. Wynders stared down, then rolled her over with the toe of his boot. Satisfaction warming him as if he'd just sipped a robust brandy.

He stepped over Mrs. Beldam's body to retrieve the knife. "Get up," he said, pointing it at Banes.

Banes had watched from behind the slim safety of a table leg and now clambered to his feet. He stood unsteadily, waiting for the humours in his body to level out. A glimpse at the threatening blade didn't help.

Wynders gripped him about the collar and pulled him within an inch of his face. "I want that ring, and you will take me to it." He pushed Banes ahead of him, through Barke House toward the front door.

At the vestibule, Wynders shoved Banes at the door, upsetting the small table next to it. Banes stumbled, reached for the table, and fell, pulling it down on top of him.

"So where is the ring? Who has it?"

Banes's side ached, and he staggered to his feet with pained stiffness that he hoped would not be mistaken for stalling. "Bianca has it. I'm certain."

"Did you see the ring in her possession?"

Banes rubbed his bruised side and met his stare. "I know she has it."

On the street, under the cover of darkness, Banes and Wynders joined others hurrying along, eager to reach home or some derelict establishment. Banes hobbled beside Wynders, wondering if anyone noticed his battered appearance. But then again, nothing seemed out of the ordinary on the streets of Southwark. When the two had gotten free of Barke House and Morgan's Lane, Wynders stood at its intersection to take his bearings.

"How best to Bianca's room of Medicinals and Physickes?"

Banes reluctantly answered for fear of another slam against

something hard, this time a building being the most convenient surface. "I do not believe you will find the ring there."

"You said it was in her possession," said Wynders. He pulled Banes up again by the scruff of his collar. "Do not deceive me, I warn you."

"Nay . . . sir," he said, the sound of the formal address tasting cold on his tongue. "I do not purposely mislead you. I am certain Bianca is in possession of the ring, as I have said. But what she has done with it, I do not know."

Wynders drove him into the stone building.

"I told you," Banes gasped. "I do not know if it is on her person or whether she has hidden it."

"So, we shall go to her room of artifice and convince her to tell us."

The pain in Banes's side reminded him of the transient nature of life. "I do not tell you this to enrage you," he said. "But she is no longer there."

"Then tell me where she is."

"On promise that you will not strike me."

"Tell me!" Wynders's patience was at an end.

"Sir," said Banes, blanching as he said it, "she is in the Clink."

# CHAPTER 36

"John, have you forgotten what sense there is in patience?"

"Would you have me complacently watch a pot boil while she hangs for a murder she did not commit?"

"My lad, you misunderstand me." Meddybemps whisked a pan of boiling water off the furnace and dipped a square of linen into it. He cleaned the gash on John's arm, then dabbed on a healing ointment from Bianca's shelves. John had been wholly brave and, in Meddybemps's opinion, too brash defending Bianca from arrest. "I do not expect you to stand idly by, but I do caution you to consider your choices rather than act with heedless abandon."

"What would you have me consider?"

Meddybemps rinsed the linen cloth, then ripped it apart and wrapped it several times around John's wound. "Firstly, consider the culture of said Clink."

"How so?"

"You are but one lad. Granted, you are a strapping one by all counts. But one lad against a three-hundred-year-old citadel does not a successful venture make. Do not presume you should win against her stone walls."

"What would you have me do?"

"You cannot enter into this with no forethought. Chiseling a hole or tunneling your way to Bianca's cell will not work."

"I haven't the time."

"Nor does blade or brute strength work unless you have an army behind you." Meddybemps uncorked his wineskin and took a swig. "Bianca is kept by men much like me who care not a piss for public duty. These men speak the language of coin. Moral standard is mere pretense. But to play a bribe . . ." Meddybemps's errant eye quivered with import. "To play is not only typical—it is expected."

"But I have nothing with which to bribe."

Meddybemps smiled, offering John his flask. "Do you not work for a silversmith?"

John took a long drink and handed back the wine. "Are you asking me to filch coin from Boisvert?"

Meddybemps looked disappointed. "Is Bianca not worth the risk?"

"Meddy, if I should end in the Clink, who should come and rescue me?" He shooed the red cat off the table. "You?"

Meddybemps dropped onto a stool and rubbed his eyes. "That would be difficult since I plan to accompany you." He peered up at John. "And since I intend to partake in this madness, I have no intention of standing behind bars." Meddybemps scanned the room. "John, Bianca is the daughter of an alchemist. And while she denounces his maniacal methods, she is still curious enough to consider them." His gaze settled on the shelves of crockery, and his face brightened. "If I know Bianca," he said, standing, "and I believe that I do, she will have a stash of ingredients that delight the smattering of alchemist blood that I am sure courses through her veins. She cannot deny that from which she is wrought."

John gazed around the room. "What would she have of any

value?" He pointed to the row of dissected vermin. "Rats?" he asked, cynically. "Or this maze of copper tubing? How about this stack of crockery?" He pulled a human skull off the wall and held it up. "I'm sure a guard from the Clink would want this."

Meddybemps ignored John and started going through the jars on the shelves, lifting lids and peering inside. "Puffers love metals. Surely you know the theory behind their obsessive search? The philosopher's stone and such?"

"Of course I know something about it. I am a silversmith's apprentice and in love with an alchemist's daughter." John sniffed that Meddybemps should think him thick.

Meddybemps pulled out a box and lifted its lid, then put it back on the shelf. "I also gave her a bag of coins from selling her balms at market. Mayhaps we shall find it."

Resignedly, John followed suit and started looking through the paraphernalia on the abutting wall, an area mostly blocked with discarded cucurbits and stills. Probably she had pinched them from her father's room of alchemy when he was unawares. After examining every bowl of desiccated plant parts, he started pulling down plugged bottles of a selection of powders, the labels for which fluttered to the floor. He hoped Bianca would remember what they were when and if she ever returned.

Meddybemps chattered to himself, and John ignored his rhymes and patters flowing as easily as ale at the Dim Dragon Inn. Between the two of them, they exhausted every piece of crockery and had nothing but raw noses to show for it.

John stepped down from a stool and sat. "Nothing. Not even her stash of coins." He watched Meddybemps continue the search, undeterred. "Truly, Meddybemps, don't you think if she had anything of value, we would have found it by now?"

Meddybemps hopped off the chest he'd been standing on. "Bianca is not so easy to figure. She is at once predictable and confounding." With hands on hips, he gazed about the room, puzzled. "I am certain she would not be entirely without something." He rubbed his temple in thought. "Did you see any stone chips or rocks?"

"Nothing of merit." John's patience was wearing thin. "Meddy, I'll not spend another minute searching through her belongings. She's sitting in the Clink, and I'll not abandon her there." He stood, roused by his own words. If he had to rescue her by himself, he would.

Meddybemps scratched under his red beret, his eyes rolling like goose eggs. "Hey non," he said after a moment, as if the most wondrous idea had sprouted in his head. He turned and looked down at the chest he had been shoving about and standing on. "What's this?" He crouched and tried to open the hasp, but a rusted padlock held it closed.

"You know anything about locks?" he said.

"Only how to spring them," mumbled John.

"So obvious as to be ignored . . ." Meddybemps hefted the wooden chest to the table and studied its hinges. "If we pry these off, perhaps we can lift the lid."

John grumbled. "She wouldn't stash valuables in that decrepit old box."

Meddybemps searched the shelves for an iron rod or bar that he could shim beneath the hinges. With a yelp of triumph, he found a metal stirring spoon with a sturdy handle and wedged it under the hinge. A solid yank later, he had prized the rusty device from the wood and was searching through the contents. "What say you?" Meddybemps lifted a pouch of silver for John to admire. "Enough for a bribe, I'd say."

John snatched the pouch from the streetseller and stuffed it in his breeches.

"And who knows Bianca better than anyone?" gibed Meddybemps as John headed for the door with a grudging scowl.

They hoped that with nightfall the turnkey might be more easily plied by crooked method. The prison was as Meddybemps presumed, a wholly corrupt system, and what was one more illicit deal among many?

John was careful to extract just enough silver to entice and convince, while leaving some to pad for any unforeseen glitch in their plan. Neither of them relished being anywhere near the Clink, and the idea of entering it set them ill at ease. They hurried along in silence, each harboring thoughts of what Bianca might suffer if they should fail, but neither one daring to mention it.

The Clink was well known for the brutality of its guards and its unwholesome conditions. One might avoid the rack and wall shackles for a stint at a gristmill. But that was only marginally better as the inmates there were whipped and starved and forced to keep moving until they dropped. Either way, there was no shortage of cruelty at the Clink, and they sorely hoped they could rescue Bianca from any such fate.

When they were within sight of the infamous prison, Meddybemps seized John's arm and pulled him to a stop. "Let me do the speech making, lad. Your eyes are as wild as a scared rabbit's. You'll do best to take a long breath and count to ten first." Meddybemps tightened his grip. "Go on, now. Do as I say."

If he looked like a scared rabbit, what did that say for Meddybemps, with those errant eyes skittering around? John sighed, then took a breath, but didn't feel any better afterward. "Come on now," John said, exasperated. "We haven't got all night."

It appeared the inmates had been shut away for the evening; no one begged at the windows, and the edifice stood black and silent. Meddybemps adjusted the angle of his cap, and they tentatively stepped up to the massive arched entry and looming oak door.

John lifted his fist and knocked.

"Lad, a polite rapping will not do," said Meddybemps, staring up at the stolid stone façade, imagining the disturbing din of prisoners beyond. "I doubt they heard you."

John complied, and in a moment a hulk of a turnkey stood before them, clutching a roasted leg of mutton. He chewed openmouthed and peered down at them. John stared up at the chomping, grinding teeth, stupefied. He'd never witnessed mastication so explicit. From grinding flesh and the overproduction of saliva, to the man's lips, glossy from fat, John followed the life of that one bite to the swallow. Stymied, John took a step back and pushed Meddybemps forward. Meddybemps was unimpressed; he'd seen worse at the Mad Cow near Butcher Row.

"Good night, sir," he said, sweeping off his cap in a grandiose gesture. "How might you fare this evening?"

"I fare as well this night as any other. What's your mischief?"

Meddybemps smiled. "Mischief? Sir, do I look as though I would misdemeanor?" Meddybemps glanced at John, well placed behind his back.

"Nay, a stringy lad as you would not hazard here unless it be for purpose. You come for pleasure? I've a few bawds worth your coin."

Meddybemps seized on an idea. "Aye, well. You are a shrewd businessman, I can tell. As well as a worthy sentry." A little bootlicking never hurt.

"Dispense with the bloat and say you what you mean. I've no mind for exchanging pleasantries."

"I shall not delay, but instead with lightning speed shall I waggle my tongue and say to you what it is that I would say if given more time than this in which to say it . . ." Meddybemps felt a jab to his spine and sputtered, though he regretted having to stoop so low, "We would like to sample the affections of a girl who was taken in this day."

The turnkey squinted down the acreage of his nose and snorted. "The twos of yous," he said, scrutinizing them. The corner of his mouth turned up conspiratorially. "At once?"

Even Meddybemps couldn't sustain such a notion. "Nay, no," he answered, shaking his head. "Naw, we are mannerly." He glanced at John, and though it pained him, said, "First one and then the other. We are not greedy." He wondered if John might carve out his kidney with the dagger in his boot later.

John was riled. He wouldn't mind being intimate with Bianca, alone, but the thought of Meddybemps . . . with Bianca . . . Well, even if it was just a ploy to gain entrance, the idea of it made him seethe.

"Well, there is no free pleasure. An' then I have to take her down."

John stepped out from behind Meddybemps. "What say you— 'take her down'?"

The turnkey scratched an armpit as he studied John. "Aye. Take her down. An' after I just gots her up." He turned his cheek, indicating a long scratch of newly clotted blood. "She's as mean as a badger."

John's heart sank. He could hardly bear the thought of Bianca in manacles suspended on some wall; much less waste another minute dickering with this fellow. He pushed Meddybemps aside and thrust out a hand of silver. "Sir, take this and show me the way."

The turnkey noted John's haste and grew thoughtful. He knew that where there was some, there was sure to be more. "That is hardly enough for her worth, or mine."

John dug into his pouch and offered more filings, to which the gaoler lifted an eyebrow, still unimpressed.

Finally, John emptied the pouch into his palm, shaking out every scrap, crumb, and particle of silver, then tossed the purse on the ground.

This interested the ward. He held out his mammoth hand.

Meddybemps looked on in horror as John conveyed the precious metal into the gaoler's massive paw. "You fool," he muttered to John under his breath.

The ward pocketed his swag and grinned. "You have entrance," he said to John, sweeping his arm in a gesture of welcome. "But," he said to Meddybemps, poking his chest, preventing him from following, "you shall wait your turn."

John stood motionless in the gaol's chill, waiting for the turnkey to take him to Bianca. He stood expectantly, gazing at the man, who tore another bite from his snack of mutton.

"What?" said the ward, irritably

"Would you lead me to her?"

"I haven't the time." He picked a piece of meat from a tooth, then waved the leg past John's shoulder. "That ways," he said. "You'll find her."

"But you must unlock the cell," said John.

"The guard below will do that."

John started down the hall, glancing back to see the gaoler swilling from a wineskin, unconcerned. He thought if he had the means, he could have freed every prisoner along the way without the turnkey even noticing. As it was, those not asleep in their cells called after him, some pleading, some taunting. John tried muffling their disquieting chorus with thoughts of Bianca and forced himself to focus on a rushlight blazing at the end of the corridor. It lit a stone stairwell twisting away into darkness below. He followed the stairs down as they turned ever tighter, like the shell of a snail.

At the bottom, the reek of human sweat and waste hit him like a mallet. He hesitated, girding himself for what might lie ahead, and continued on. The dimly lit corridor hindered his vision, and he called for Bianca, hoping she would hear and perhaps answer. But the only response was a din of moans and appeals from inmates hoping he'd find them a suitable replacement.

He reached the end of the corridor and, not finding Bianca or a guard, retraced his steps. His eyes had adjusted to the dark, and he peered more carefully into each cell. The thought of Bianca shackled to a wall or beaten unconscious followed his every step. When he came to where he had started, he noticed a second corridor intersecting with the first. He called out for Bianca and received a chorus of replies even more desperate than before, until one voice sang out above the others.

"Bianca, the alchemist's daughter," it said.

"Do you know Bianca?" John stopped, listening which direction to go.

"The poison runs thick in her blood, and she'll end here again, mark my words."

"Who goes there?"

A madman's cackle pierced the air. "I go nowhere."

John turned toward the voice. "What is your name?"

"Simon Slade, am I. Master locksmith and most innocently condemned citizen of this king's realm."

His words bounced and echoed, but after a moment, John found Simon Slade hunkered in the center of a dismal cell. A heavy chain shackled his ankle and, from its foul smell, had been eating away at the prisoner's skin.

"You know Bianca?" asked John.

"I did know. Now I do not." The man relished this newfound attention. "But I says nothing of what I knew—for nothing."

"If you are a master locksmith, why haven't you lost your shackle?"

The man took exception and howled loud and long enough to rattle John's teeth. "I cannot lose a lock without a pick," said the prisoner. He turned to speak to the thin air beside him. "This world is filled with asses. Look well on this latest."

John peered into the dark, not seeing anyone or anything.

Slade faced John and leered at him. "Pox on you, fool. You lost me faith."

Chagrined, John dug into his jacket for something of worth and withdrew several items. He picked through piddly coin, a key to Boisvert's shop, an auger bit, and a nail.

"You say you are a locksmith. What say you to a pick?" He held up the nail.

Slade's eyes grew wide, and his hand flew to his mouth, trying to contain his happiness. He moderated his enthusiasm and grew cagey. "I might reconsider." He took a step toward the bars, then winced. "Bollocks," he spat. "I needs more than that to spring this friend." He lifted the cumbersome chain and dropped it.

"Then a bit with which to bite?" John held the auger bit between his thumb and finger for Slade to see.

"Aw now, if you give me both, I tells you all I know." Slade's voice turned hopeful, almost giddy.

"I shall gladly hand them over. But you must first tell me what you know of Bianca."

"How do I know you won't dupe me?"

"Sir, it is a case of mutual need. For you, the price of freedom has never come so cheap."

"Do not tease me, lad. It would kill me as sure as murder if you denied me now."

"Tell me where Bianca is, and I shall not deny you."

Simon Slade didn't take long to decide. He leaned forward as far as his ball and chain allowed. "She is no longer here."

John's blood drained from his face, and he thought the worst. "What is your meaning, Slade?"

"I simply mean she has been taken away. By one much older than you, and sporting a fine doublet and sheathed sword."

"Who was it?"

"That . . . I know not." Slade's face twitched in the dim light.

"Did she know him? Did she recognize him?"

Slade guffawed as if that was the best jest he'd heard in a long time. He shook his head, then coyly looked on John. "She did not say. But then she couldn't very well." His eyes rolled up and away.

"Say what you mean, man!"

Slade's eyes traveled down to meet John's. "She was strung up to near senseless. The pain left her speechless." He scratched his flea-bitten chest. "I'd say she was glad to go with him, come whatever may." He winked. "Come whatever may . . ." His voice trailed off.

"Was it the constable who took her?"

"Nay. He was well dressed."

"Not a guard or ward?"

"Nay, not such."

"Then who? What office?"

"Hmm," said Slade, considering. John could see him thinking through a catalog of middlemen until he found what he thought appropriate. "Mayhaps a lawyer type. Or mayhaps a merchant."

It was all John needed to hear. He stretched his arm through the bars and tossed the nail and then the auger bit at Slade. The two pieces rolled to a stop near Slade's feet, and the locksmith stared as if they were manna from heaven. He dove on the treasures and snatched them up as if someone might steal them away.

# CHAPTER 37

If Bianca weren't in such agony, she might have whooped for joy at the sight of the Southwark sky overhead. Being beaten, then shackled to a wall had left her woozy, barely able to keep up with Robert Wynders. Her arms burned in pain, and his yanking and pulling her along didn't help. She had not expected to see the streets of her neighborhood again, and since the opportunity now presented itself, she struggled to overlook her misery and instead think of how she might escape.

She assumed Wynders had bribed the gaoler for her release. The gaoler had pretended to look the other way as Wynders marched her past and out the massive front door. While she didn't welcome Wynders's brutish handling, she didn't object because she knew this was her chance, maybe her last, and she'd better be ready for it.

Wynders said nothing as they trudged toward her room of Medicinals and Physickes. With darkness came the rotten rain of chamber pots emptied out windows onto the lanes below. So far, they'd been lucky to avoid a bath. While Wynders was averse to stepping in suspicious puddles, he didn't mind dragging Bianca through them.

At last they stood opposite her front door, and after Wynders found it locked, he threw her against it, demanding entry.

"I haven't the key," she said. "Someone else must have locked it after Patch arrested me."

Wynders brushed her aside and reared back to land a solid kick. He was a brick of a man, and with his first try the wood planks snapped and splintered. He reached through the hole and worked the bolt to a chorus of barking dogs and someone hollering out a window to pipe down.

The door fell open crookedly, and he shoved her inside.

"Where's a light?" he asked, looking about.

Bianca moved along a wall and stopped under a sconce, unable to lift her arm to point. Perhaps in time she would regain some strength. She couldn't bear to imagine it if she couldn't.

Wynders snatched the tallow and withdrew a flint, and soon a yellow orb illuminated the room.

"You will get me my ring."

How had he known with such certainty that the ring was in her possession? Meddybemps and John would never have told. Then she remembered Banes. She and John had avoided admitting they had it. Even if he knew they had it, she was disappointed he would snitch. "You'll never find it without my help. It could be anywhere." She ran her eyes about the room, a jumbled mess. Jars and crockery lined her shelves. Dirty bowls were stacked in teetering towers. Coils of copper and discarded flasks littered the tables and floor. Dissected rats lined the table, waiting to be disposed of. "I will not cooperate until you answer my question. Did you poison Jolyn?"

Wynders stared at the interior of her room and knew it would take him hours to search it. Threatening this girl with more violence only proved to strengthen her resolve. He spoke through clenched teeth. "It was not I."

"Do you know who did?"

Wynders said nothing, so Bianca tried another tack. "Why must you have this ring?"

"We're not here to discuss the matter. I simply want what belongs to me. I've waited a long time for its return." The blade of his rapier sang from its sheath, and he pointed it between her eyes. "You will get it for me."

Bianca edged along the wall as Wynders followed her with the sword's tip, their eyes holding each other in mutual suspicion. She slowly stepped away from the wall, first looking that she might do so, then backing toward the table where the monstrous distillation apparatus towered. The last few steps she slipped behind it, feeling a small margin of safety.

Its long stretch of metal felt cool beneath her fingers as she lightly traced the metal down to a juncture of coils splitting in different directions. Her shoulder protested at even such a simple exertion, but her eyes never left Wynders's. Nor did the end of his rapier wander from her face.

The red cat jumped to the table and leaned against Bianca for attention. She brushed him off, fearing Wynders might dispense with him more permanently. The distraction only ratcheted the tension, and she wondered if she might venture a question since she felt some measure of protection with the metal apparatus now between them.

"I've seen your warehouse," she said.

"Its location is not a secret."

"No, but its contents might best be kept that way."

Wynders lifted his chin slightly. He waited.

"I sold you rat poison. Enough to handle a problem on a ship . . . but not enough to handle the vermin in your warehouse." Bianca moved her hand down the final length of tubes to an end spout. She had dropped the ring into the earthen receptacle beneath it for safekeeping. She rested her hand on its lip. "Why haven't the bodies been buried?"

He trained the point of the rapier on her mouth, its metal cold against her skin.

She tipped back her chin. "What is your business with Mrs. Beldam? If she had the ring, could she use it to ruin you?"

With the flick of his wrist, Wynders sliced her bottom lip and drew blood. She sucked in but resisted touching the wound. Blood coursed down her chin.

He took a step forward. "You can ill afford any more stalling. The ring!"

Bianca lifted the flask and waved it. "Here," she said, holding it up. She held out the flask, offering it to Wynders.

He refused to take it. "I'll not pour acid in my palm," he said. "You are the daughter of an alchemist. You invert it."

Wynders had no idea how she resented being referred to as an alchemist's daughter. Bianca turned the flagon upside down over her hand. Nothing. Not even a dribble of liquid fell out.

Wynders smiled sardonically. He returned his rapier to its sheath, then reached across the table, gripping her by the collar and pulling her across, upsetting her apparatus, so that their noses touched. "You dare to lead me thus? You'll get the ring, and you'll be quick about it."

"By my honor, this is where I put it."

"Do not play daft, or I shall send you back to the Clink so you can hang for murder." He shook her, and Bianca's exhaustion was so consuming not even nerves or fear of death could summon her strength to resist.

Wynders released her, and she fell on the table, then slid to the floor.

"I swear to you, that is where I hid it."

Wynders snatched the empty flagon and shook it. He smashed it against the stonework of her stove, sending shards of pottery raining down. Then, with a roar of frustration, he overturned the table. He stared at the wreckage, panting, as rivers of perspiration streamed down his face.

Bianca sat against the underside of the table, listening. She looked about for something to defend herself. A thick shard of pottery lay beyond her reach. She crept toward it, still mindful of

Wynders's fury. She had just laid her hand on top of it when his boot came down and drove her palm painfully into the shard.

Wynders shifted his weight, driving the sharp pottery deep into her flesh. "Since you have an interest in my warehouse," he said, stepping off her hand and hauling her to her feet, "I think we should visit it." He forced her out on the street, pulling her by the arm toward the bridge. "Perhaps it will stir your memory."

Her hand dripped with blood as the shard protruded. Bianca mustered every ounce of strength and screamed, which only proved to further infuriate Wynders. "Silence." He reminded her of his rapier's sharp edge by jabbing it in her ribs and nudged her forward.

Perhaps a night watch might have heard her cry. If not, she'd try again as they crossed the bridge, where reputable merchants lived above their shops. She'd save her strength for that.

Bianca stumbled along, took a breath, and quickly yanked out the shard, sucking in her cheeks to keep from crying. A sorry sight she was, her hand and lip bleeding, her arms nearly useless. And now she was on her way to Wynders's warehouse of horror. Her sluggish brain began to come round, even if her body didn't. Ahead lay the bridge with its grim display of beheaded criminals. She could see the outline of pikes appear and disappear in the mist.

What had become of John and Meddybemps? She wished she had not been so brusque with John. He had put up a valiant effort to defend her from arrest. She vowed she'd never take him for granted again—if she should ever live that long.

The heavy air kept the acrid combination of smoke and low tide from escaping into the night sky. The mudflats stretched beside them, stinking in sullen silence. No muckrakers wandered the banks at this hour. Only stray dogs searched the soup for scraps of worth.

It was after curfew, and the bridge gate was closed.

Wynders scanned the river for a ferryman. No wherry plied the Thames at this late hour. He grabbed Bianca's wrist and pulled her farther along the shore, stopping opposite an empty skiff lashed to a piling.

"My luck isn't so black after all." He ordered her through the muck and into the boat, then cut it free. If he hadn't so abused her, he might have made her drag it to the water's edge. But as it was, she sat in the bow and he pushed the boat through the sucking mud and shoved it into the river.

"I'll not have my back to you," he said, stepping in. The skiff tipped as he made Bianca move so he could watch her as he rowed. Her hand throbbed as she held the gunwale to steady herself as she moved to sit in the stern.

Once they had pushed off, water seeped through gaps in the hull, pooling at her feet. "It's leaking," said Bianca. "Perhaps we should find another skiff."

Wynders ignored her comment and pulled on the oars, the veins in his neck and forehead bulging with every stroke. Perhaps if he rowed fast enough they might make it to the other side before capsizing. Bianca gathered her skirt into her lap. She didn't fancy the thought of a swim.

She gazed over Wynders's shoulders at Romeland and its warehouses and cranes dotting the waterfront. London Bridge towered over the river beside them, like a sleeping serpent, silent yet powerfully present.

The thought of mortality weighed heavy on her mind. She might have died in those manacles if Wynders had not intervened. Strange to think he had saved her. She sniffed at the futility of his rescue. Now he was rowing her across the river to possibly kill her on the other side, if they even made it that far.

But as they passed the timber starlings jutting into the slack current, neither Bianca nor Wynders noticed a figure lurking in its shadows. A figure watching them with interest.

# CHAPTER 38

The skiff floated alongside Wool's Key. Wynders threw the rope over a bollard to tie it off. The two climbed out, and Wynders bound Bianca's wrists behind her back before they mounted the steps to the landing along the river. Bianca wished they might encounter a watchman or even a drunk—someone she could implore for help. But her luck was as nonexistent as the number of Londoners out this time of night. She trudged dejectedly beside Wynders. If she could have engaged the many rats that skulked past, she might have had an army to save her.

A number of questions still bothered Bianca, one of which was what did he know of Pandy's murder? She thought with nothing to lose she might as well ask. Could the pain of another cut or thrashing be any worse than what she now endured? She thought not. She took a breath and asked the ship's agent if he had killed Pandy.

"Nay," said Wynders. "But her death is no loss."

His indifference sent a chill through Bianca. If he truly was not guilty, he would want others to know who was. "Why do you say that?"

"She was a meddlesome girl. Of no use."

"Harsh words from a man who used her for his pleasure."

Wynders took no exception. As Bianca suspected, an innocent man with information had no cause to remain silent. "The night of the storm I was walking home, and I saw two women ahead of me. One was as drunk as a mouse in a barrel of rum. She weaved and doubled back as she made her way up the lane. Following her was a figure staying close in the shadows. She darted out from overhangs and hid in dark alcoves. I quickened my step to shorten the distance—out of curiosity mostly. I'd probably have to come to the poor sot's aid. Then I realized who they were."

"Pandy?" offered Bianca. "Who else?"

"Beldam."

"Were they near your home?"

"Aye."

The sound of shutters slammed nearby. A stray dog caught up and trotted alongside Wynders. It gazed hopefully up at the man, staying just ahead of the two of them.

"Get on, you ugly cur," said Wynders, booting it away.

"Was Pandy going to your house?"

Wynders had a distant look in his eye, as if he was thinking out loud instead of telling Bianca everything he knew. "Probably. Certainly Beldam believed it so."

"So Mrs. Beldam was stalking her?"

"Beldam called to Pandy, and she turned around." Wynders stopped walking and stared ahead as if he were visualizing the scene. "Pandy asked why she was following her. She was furious."

"What did Mrs. Beldam say?"

"'I'll not have ye ruin this,' she says.'" Wynders's eyes grew hard. "I could have blinked and missed it. Beldam stepped into her, and I saw Pandy double over, then stagger back . . . I could see the whites of her eyes wide with surprise. . . ."

Bianca waited. She let him continue.

"Pandy collapsed in the lane. I was stunned. I never imagined the depth of malice in that woman. When Beldam turned, she saw me. 'Ye owe me,' she said."

"You had relations with Pandy," said Bianca.

Wynders said nothing.

"Why didn't you tell the constable what Mrs. Beldam had done?" As soon as the words escaped her mouth, Bianca knew the answer. Wynders would never chance speculation about his sullied past. It proved convenient for him to be rid of Pandy. Mrs. Beldam had indeed done him a favor.

Wynders glimpsed at Bianca, and his face clouded as if he had stirred from his recollection. "Enough. You'll have plenty of time to ponder the whereabouts of that ring where I am taking you."

He gripped her arm and led her through the narrow gaps between buildings, avoiding the open lanes until they were opposite the chained door of Chudderly's warehouse. He reached into his doublet and withdrew a key.

The rusty mechanism jammed, and finding it impossible to work the lock with one hand, Wynders let go of Bianca's arm.

Here was her opportunity.

Bianca broke into a run, sprinting down the lane. She knew if he caught up to her she'd be in sorry straits, but the desire for freedom gave her strength she didn't know she had. She headed for Boisvert's. John or Boisvert would be there.

She ignored her aching legs and pumped with all her might, concentrating on the slap of mud beneath her feet. But they grew heavier with every step. If she could only be clear of Romeland and its commercial indifference. Once in a residential area, she could scream and raise a commotion. Someone might hear her. Someone might come.

If her hands hadn't been bound behind her back, she might have gotten farther. She could hear him gaining on her, his pants growing louder. She willed herself to keep running. Her heartbeat was as loud as his breath, and she dashed at an angle like she'd seen rabbits do to lose their enemy. But Wynders's shadow descended like a raven swooping overhead. With a shove she was airborne, pitching forward, unable to check her fall. Her face scraped along the lane as she skidded to a stop.

She scrambled to her knees, and just as she sat back, Wynders struck her across the face. She toppled and lay in the road, blinking up at the murky fog, wondering if this would be the last thing she would ever see.

"If you should think to do that again, I'll not hesitate to slice your cheek in two." Wynders hoisted her up by the arm and threw her over his shoulder. "You continue to waste my time."

He stalked up the road, handling her like a sack of grain. She was nearly senseless from blood rushing to her head. Blood dripped from her lip, leaving a trail in the dirt behind them. Wynders's shoulder dug into her ribs, making it difficult to breathe. When they got to the warehouse, he dumped her on the ground beside him.

Every joint in her body ached. Every beat of her heart sent a throbbing, pulsing pain through her head.

Wynders finished working the lock, then caught her up under her arms and dragged her through the door. "I'm going to ask one last time," he said, with barely contained fury. "Where is the ring?"

Bianca's head swam, and she could not speak.

"Very well," he said. He hauled her farther into the warehouse.

She passed stack after stack of crates towering like trees in a forest. But she knew that in this hellish wood lived evil denizens, and she could hear their rasping grow louder.

Panic built like water starting to boil. "If you leave me, you'll never know where the ring is," she said, thrashing and digging her heels into the dirt floor. "I'll tell you. I know who has the ring."

"So *now* you know. When before you didn't." Wynders continued to pull her through the warehouse.

"Don't be a fool. If I should die, you'll never know where the ring is. You'll never be free of Mrs. Beldam. She'll hold you captive to your past."

As certain as he'd divulged the details of Pandy's murder, he now refused to answer or even listen. He ignored her shrieks.

They reached the room where bodies lay rotting beneath a crawl-ing mountain of rats. The smell made her gag. Wynders dropped her and turned to leave.

"Think well on it," he said, over his shoulder. "If I can't con-vince you, then maybe they can." He lifted his chin toward the feeding mass of vermin. "I believe they are running out of food."

Bianca watched Wynders disappear, leaving her with hun-dreds of pairs of interested watching eyes. She stared back at them and growled, baring her teeth as if she should have them for a meal instead of the other way around.

A rat scampered across her chest.

Bianca screamed and rolled to her side, tangling her skirt be-tween her legs. She frantically wrestled the twisted material, but her struggle only bound her further. She cursed her kirtle, wish-ing for a way to rip it off. Exhausted, she lay still. She knew she must calm herself and think her way out of this. If only she had a knife, if only someone had heard her scream . . . Her head filled with useless, wishful thoughts.

She looked around, forcing herself to think what she could use to untangle herself. There was nothing but walls of wooden crates and dark, and as the hissing grew louder, it drowned any sensible thoughts she had and she panicked again, thrashing more vio-lently than before.

But this time her undoing became her salvation. She'd spilled so many experimental solutions on her old skirt that the wool had worn thin in places, and now, with her thrashing, it ripped enough so that she was able to kick a leg free. She swung it over and rolled onto her knees, wiggling to give herself room, and with effort staggered to her feet. The rats had moved closer, and she cursed and screamed, scaring them back. It worked, but only for a moment.

She began moving as fast as her weary legs allowed. Soon she could make out a faint light in the direction of the entrance. Fighting her exhaustion, she stumbled forward, bumping into crates and sending them crashing down behind her. She had created an inadvertent barrier. Soon she began driving her aching shoulders into more crates, creating even more obstacles between her and the rats.

Hindered by her tied wrists, she found a splintered crate with a sharp edge and worked to saw apart the rope. Her back was to the edge so she couldn't tell if it was cutting through the thick jute, but as the horrible hiss of rats closed in, she furiously pumped her arms up and down against its edge.

One by one, the fibers split. The rope began to fray. She felt the taut grip on her wrists begin to relax. She forced her wrists apart, tightening the jute against the sharp edge, and with a final stroke, her hands sprang free.

Bianca swung her arms about, regaining their feeling and yowling at the pain that shot through her shoulder joints, still stretched and sore from her stay at the Clink. She didn't know how she would escape the warehouse, but if she had to climb to the top of a tower of crates, so be it. It would be easier to fend off the rats from there.

Bianca had barely turned before a rat landed on her back. She threw it off and looked up. Above her, a wall of rats peered down from the tops of crates. Their claws were dug into the rough wood planking as they started down the sides. Some dropped off and landed at her feet.

She stumbled forward, pushing over more crates and sending them crashing to the floor. Containers broke apart, wood splintered, and silken cloth and Oriental spices spilled onto the warehouse floor. Desperately, she kept pulling down boxes in spite of the pain in her shoulders.

Her plan might have worked. She might have been able to buy valuable time to smash through the door to the outside. But as she paused, gasping for breath beside the strewn remnants, one lone container creaked with a sickening moan. Precariously balanced, its weight shifted, and Bianca looked up to see it totter—then fall straight for her.

# CHAPTER 39

Constable Patch should have slept like a babe. He should have slept with the peaceful conscience of the righteous. After all, he had performed his duty and delivered that murderess Bianca Goddard to her rightful destination: the Clink. But as he lay staring up at the mouse scampering along the rafter over his bed, he couldn't stop thinking of her story and the warehouse in Romeland.

What if it was true? What if this Robert Wynders was planning to unleash a torrent of sniveling, dirty rodents on London's fair citizenry? Patch rolled over, pulling the blanket off his snoring wife.

As far as he knew, he was the only one who could do anything about it. As it was, he would be commended for bringing a murderer to justice and he expected to win the notice of the ward alderman. And if he had forgotten, Patch would make certain he remembered the connection between Bianca and her suspect father—a man accused of trying to poison the king. Nothing good could come of an alchemist and his "chemiste" spawn. But preventing a possible pestilence on the town of London and nabbing the architect behind it? He couldn't have engineered a more propitious scenario. And here it was being given to him. He'd be a fool not to act.

Exposed to the room's chill, Constable Patch's wife roused from a warm and comfortable slumber, peevishly yanked the covers off her restless husband, and told him to sod off. Patch obliged. Within a few minutes he was dressed and wending his way through the sinister back alleys to the Clink.

Since he didn't know where the ignoble warehouse was exactly, he'd have to enlist the help of the young transgressor. He wondered if he'd have to entice her cooperation with promises of mercy, but decided it was best to try to avoid negotiations of that sort if possible. He wasn't sure what he'd say to her. He would think of something when the time came.

Instead, Patch preferred to think on his new appointment as deputy of a London parish. With the extra money and prestige, a new uniform might be in order. One made of fine peacock-blue velvet with multipleated sleeves. A bounce worked its way into Constable Patch's step. He didn't even mind the drunk sprawled across his path, but trod on his chest without altering his gait.

Of course his wife would be pleased. A move across the river might gentle her surly disposition, and who knows? She might even become more amenable to performing her wifely duty.

With heady dreams of a new and improved future, Constable Patch ignored the grim murmurings issuing from the Clink and rapped on its door. Even several minutes of waiting and continued knocks did not diminish his sunny mood.

The turnkey peered out at Patch with a spiritless expression. "Late for you, isn't it, Patch?"

"Aye, that," answered the constable, undeterred. "I have a matter of utmost importance—elst I wouldn'ts be here."

The turnkey's dull eyes ranged over Patch, uninterested. He appeared to have been woken and was none too thrilled. "Mayhaps ye tell me your business at this hour. I see ye have no criminal."

Constable Patch confirmed the obvious. "True, my good man. I have come on a missile which will save the good folk of London from a scourge of epic proportion. A bane of such dour consequence that, if left unchecked, could spell the end of our fair city and, in particular, its citizenry."

"That's been said of the ale at the Cockeyed Gull."

Patch pressed on. "If ye should aid me in this noble cause, I shall reward ye well."

"With what?" The turnkey tittered. "You'll never amount to more than what you already is: the lowly public servant of this cur-ridden coop of a borough. No moneys in that, never wills be. Still, a man's gotta eat—I can't deny you that." He scratched his belly through his rough wool tunic. "For a scab, you have lofty expectations, Patch."

"I see no need for ye to be flappin' ye jaw about it. There is something in it for ye, if ye see me by. Are ye in or outs?"

The turnkey took another precious minute to consider Patch's offer. He saw no need to rush into additional work, especially at this hour. Then again, since he was up and an opportunity was presenting itself, he might as well hear the knave out. "So's what do you need?"

Constable Patch cheered to hear the brute ask. "I needs ye to release Bianca Goddard to me."

"What's for? You just brought her here."

"It has something to do with whats I just told ye." Patch didn't want to go through another explanation trying to convince the sourpuss. "This has direct import to the king," he added, hoping that might carry some weight.

"Says who?" challenged the turnkey. "You?"

"Enough! Bring me Bianca Goddard, and be quick about it."

"Can't do that."

"Do not try to waylay me, man. I have no patience for it."

"Patience or not, I cannot bring her abouts."

This is not what Patch wanted to hear. "What? I brought her in, and I can bring her out. If ye don't do as I ask, I'll inform

every alderman from here to Shoreditch that ye are a lazy, obsti-
nate turnkey. No more capable of tending our criminals than a
house full of hens. Now get her before I lose my temper."

"I tolds you. She is not here."

Constable Patch cocked his head. "She is not here? She is not
here?" He paused, as if letting it seep in, then jabbed his finger
into the guard's face. "Ye will not toy with me, knave."

"An official sort came and gots her, Patch."

"An official sort of what?

"An official sort of . . . man came and removed her."

"Removed her herewith?"

"Aye. Herewith," he mumbled.

"And did this official sort of man wield a coin for such cooperation?"

The turnkey balked. Bribes were neither unusual nor unexpected. How was he to know this prisoner, Bianca Goddard, was
anything more than the murderer of a trifling young woman?
"Don't be so self-righteous, Patch. Coin speaks louder than
virtue here. A beggar makes more money than a turnkey in this
rotting borough."

Constable Patch knew all too well the corruption got from low
wage. Hadn't he accepted coin concerning this very case? Yet
when it worked against him, he became indignant. But being the
double-dealing public servant that he was, he was not above pre-
tending to be uncompromisingly moral, and this he slung about
as if it were a five-pointed mace.

"I'll have ye charged for bribery before the day is done."

"Thunder on, Patch, but you can't change the world. You will
get nowhere threatening me such."

"We shall see," sniffed Patch, turning on his heel. But if Patch
were honest with himself, he knew, regrettably, that the turnkey
was right.

# CHAPTER 40

The pain Bianca had suffered dangling from manacles in the Clink was minor by comparison. She thought the crate must be filled with sand it was so heavy and immobile. She lay helplessly beneath it, pinned against the cold, damp floor.

She had tried to avoid the falling crate, but its mammoth size had prevented her from completely clearing it. She landed facedown—her legs trapped beneath, her back exposed. If the crate had hit her head, her skull would have cracked like a walnut. She pressed her forearms and palms into the floor and tried to pull herself free, but it was useless. She no longer felt her legs. They had gone numb.

She lifted her forehead, feeling a sharp pain course down her neck, and looked around.

Destroyed crates and their contents lay scattered about. Spices streamed from battered containers like sand from an hourglass. Bolts of cloth had unrolled, forming long banners of silk that draped down the sides of her makeshift wall. She had hoped to buy time and create a barrier by pushing over the crates. She feared she had succeeded at neither.

As she peered up at the iridescent fabrics, she realized that day must be dawning. From whatever cracks or openings there might be in the warehouse, she could see muted hues of color, not just the gray and blue shadows of night. And with day came the chance that someone might hear her cries for help.

She screamed. Surely someone would be passing by. She screamed loud enough to rattle the chains at Newgate, then fell silent and listened.

No one called back. No one pounded the warehouse door in answer. Silence—nothing but the maddening quiet of the most hushed moments before day.

Then a low, unearthly squabble insinuated the calm. It grew in intensity. Rasping. Hissing.

Bianca slowly turned her head. Lining the top of the crates was a legion of rats. Bianca gasped. Their teeth glinted in the faint light, and their hungry eyes stared down at her. If they jumped, they would land on her head.

She pushed against the heavy crate and screamed with every ounce of breath she had. A public hanging was preferable to being eaten alive by rats. Bianca had wanted to prove her innocence in Jolyn's murder and find some measure of justice for her dead friend. How could such good intentions end so badly?

She squirmed helplessly beneath the crate. The thought of being torn apart by hundreds of rats kept her struggling, even though she knew it was useless. Soon they would fight over her flesh. And there was nothing she could do.

A thud sounded beside her.

She held her breath.

A second thud. She dared not turn her head to look.

Panic screamed up her spine, and she waved her arms wildly, hoping to scare the vermin. For a moment, it seemed to work.

They retreated.

If she could just keep shouting until someone heard her. She kept screaming and flailing, willing herself to keep moving. But if no one came to her aid, eventually the rats would overwhelm her. Eventually, she would suffer the same fate as the corpses in the back.

She regretted having taken John for granted. If she had not been so confident and had listened to his suggestions, she might not have found herself lying on a warehouse floor, fending off a torrent of rats. If she had let him help her instead of erecting a wall of resistance, had kept him close instead of dismissing him, she might be sitting in Boisvert's shop enjoying a glass of French wine right now.

Despite her arms trembling with fatigue, Bianca willed herself to keep waving them. She managed well enough at first. Then, each wave grew increasingly difficult, as if she were lifting bricks instead of her arms. Finally, no amount of self-imposed will or desire could keep them going. They simply would not cooperate. Her arms collapsed, limp and completely spent.

And the rats came.

They dropped onto her back and landed beside her.

One.

Then, another.

They skittered down her spine, pulled her hair, and nosed under it. They nipped the back of her neck, tugged her ear . . . She dragged her arms to cover her head, but not before glimpsing a dozen more rappelling down bolts of fabric and falling like rain.

Exhaustion dulled her senses. She drifted in and out of consciousness, and thankfully, her mind wandered to a more peaceful place.

She didn't notice the squabble in front of her.

Translucent bubbles appeared in her mind, marbled with the colors of the rainbow. They rose from the bottoms of flasks, growing, then bursting at the surface.

Solutions.

Her solutions. Her tonics, her medicinals. They bubbled and churned, popped softly as she looked down a row of flasks lined atop tripods, stretching to infinity.

Then, from an opaque distance, grew the sound of human voices. Shouting voices.

Was she dead? She no longer felt the rats' horrible teeth. She no longer heard their hiss. She must be dead. So is this what it felt like? No more pain, no more torment? Her mind went a hundred directions all at once. Then, a sudden clash of metal on metal roused her and she opened her eyes. Bold colored silks still hung about. She raised her head and looked around.

No rats. But she saw their eyes glowing red from behind broken bits of crate and refuse, waiting.

Bianca craned her head and saw Wynders standing atop the crates with his rapier drawn. His blade slashed the air as he parried forward and back. Boards loosened and tumbled down, clattering and just missing her.

Then she heard a familiar voice.

John.

Wynders skidded down the wall and landed beside her, sending down a shower of planks. His arm blocked some of the boards, but his rapier was ill suited for the falling debris.

Bianca covered her head and cried out.

"Bianca?" John's voice echoed off the walls. "Are you there?"

"John!"

Wynders eyed Bianca pinned beneath the crate. "Your lady is in a bit of a position, lad. Mind you, not a good one. You might want to help her. She appears somewhat heavily burdened." He paused, waiting for effect. "The only thing standing between the two of you . . . is me." Wynders withdrew a kerchief from his pocket and mopped his brow. He tucked it back into his doublet with a gentlemanly flourish. "I will gladly move, but you must give me my ring. If you refuse, I see no use in prolonging this girl's agony. Whether she perishes beneath a crate, is eaten or hanged, it matters not to me."

Bianca recognized Meddybemps's voice but could not decipher it. She arched her back and rested on her forearms, listening.

The rats' eyes glinted in the dim light.

"Do not dawdle, lad. I'm not the only one losing patience," called Wynders, seeing the rats poke their sharp noses forward

"John," yelled Bianca, exasperated.

"I shall give you leave, Wynders, if you throw me your sword."

"Give me the ring and I will throw you my sword," said Wynders. "We will both get what we want."

"John, do it!"

But all that transpired was a confounding silence. The rats began a low, ominous hiss, and Bianca's hope turned to despair. They inched forward, no longer threatened by clattering wood and scuffle.

Bianca took a breath to scream, but stopped at the sound of someone scaling the mound of broken crates. She craned her head to see John appear at the top of the heap, his face soaked with sweat. He stepped to the edge and peered down. He held no weapon, no plank or bludgeon. His arms hung at his sides, strong from years of hauling buckets of molten metal.

His eyes met Bianca's, and she knew he would not fail her.

They had practically grown up together. And from the familiarity that comes with knowing someone for that long, through awkward stages of life and foolish behavior, she knew he would not forsake her. In spite of all their differences, they had remained each other's single strongest influence, a steadfast presence.

Bianca looked on John with renewed hope and a smatter of humility. He would save her—a not so small undertaking.

"Such a lot of fuss for something so small," said John, reaching into his trouser pocket. He withdrew the ring and held it up, the gold glinting in the weak morning light. "How could this lump of metal move a person to murder? Is its value worth more than a life?"

"Toss me the ring and you shall have leave of your lady."

But John went on. "The design carved in its face is your family crest, isn't it, Wynders? And in that crest lies your reputation. Am I right?"

"I haven't the patience to listen to you pontificate. And neither does your lady."

"But this ring holds secrets. Secrets someone uses against you."

"It does not serve you to speculate."

"So who is keeping your secrets? Mrs. Beldam?"

"Lad, look on your lady." Wynders gestured to Bianca lying under the crate. "I imagine her legs have lost their feeling by now."

"So, tell me," John continued, much to Bianca's annoyance, "who deserves this ring? The man who keeps secrets to preserve his honor and family's reputation or the woman whose daughter's ruin is her most lucrative secret?"

"I haven't time for philosophic discussion. Nor does your lady."

Bianca didn't care if she was playing into Wynders's plan. She screamed at John to help her.

"Throw me your sword, Wynders, and the ring is yours."

"My sword and free passage."

John thought. "Aye, that."

"And what proof do I have that your word is true?" Wynders cocked his head.

"By my honor," said John, "as mine is unvarnished."

Wynders smirked. "You are young, lad. Even silver tarnishes with time." He gave over his sword, throwing it to the top of the heap, where it landed at John's feet.

John bent to grab the weapon and tested its weight in his hand. "As I promised, Wynders," he said. "Your ring." He brought the gold ring to his lips and kissed it. "A more cursed bauble I have never seen." John tossed it to Wynders, and it fell in an arc of glimmering gold.

Wynders leapt to snatch it out of the air, but it sailed beyond his reach. The band landed behind Bianca, and he scuttled after it, scrambling over debris as it hit the ground and rolled beneath a crate. Wynders dropped to his knees and reached under the container.

John slid down the pile and landed in front of Bianca. Meddybemps followed more gingerly, picking his way down the unstable boards.

"I'll lift the container, and you pull her out," said John when Meddybemps reached the bottom.

John studied the crate from different angles; then, just as he braced himself against it, Wynders unleashed a torrent of expletives. John and Meddybemps paid him no mind as they concentrated on freeing Bianca. As John leaned his shoulder into the crate and tipped it backward, the streetseller grabbed under her arms and dragged her clear. Freed at last, Bianca sat back against Meddybemps's shins and examined her wounds, pulling her torn kirtle above her ankles. Her stockings were torn and soaked with blood, but despite the gash and scrapes, thankfully, no bones protruded.

"Let's try to stand you," said John.

"I can barely feel my legs."

Meddybemps and John grasped her waist and carefully brought her to her feet. Her legs trembled like twigs ready to snap. She had no strength and very little control.

"You'll get your strength back. For now, though, you'll have to let me carry you."

Bianca welcomed John gathering her in his arms and, for the first time in days, felt as if she would be fine.

Then, they heard Wynders.

The ship's agent had caught his sleeve beneath the crate and was tugging and cursing in frustration, clutching his ring. He hated ripping his new velvet doublet. It had cost him two quid and two months of waiting to have it tailored with pleats to accentuate his muscular forearms. His curses rang through the warehouse.

John noted how light Bianca was. The week had taken its toll on her—she felt no heavier than a child. He began to scale the pile of debris and was pleased when she wrapped her arms about his neck and rested her head against his chest.

Meddybemps scampered up the mound and found the sturdiest footholds, pointing them out to John. "We're nearly there. I'll be glad to be rid of this place." He scrambled to the top and waited for John and Bianca to join him. "The Thames will never smell so sweet," he said, noting the rats' curious eyes, watching.

Just as John and Bianca reached Meddybemps, a terrible scream filled the cavernous warehouse, echoing off its walls.

Wynders had freed his sleeve, but not before the rats had moved in. He kicked and stumbled, screeching for help while vermin attacked his legs and bit into his meaty thighs. Within seconds, the rats swarmed Wynders and covered him like angry bees. His face disappeared beneath a mass of fur and biting teeth. He was drowning in a sea of vermin.

Meddybemps turned away and started down the other side.

John felt somewhat remiss ignoring Wynders's pleas for help, but he was not about to abandon Bianca—not now, not after all she'd been through—and so he clasped her closer and grimly followed the streetseller.

Once they reached the ground, they hurried to the front of the warehouse, weaving through the walls of crates in their haste to be done with Wynders and the Chudderly Shipping warehouse.

Meddybemps threw himself against the door before flinging it open. "I'll be spending the rest of the day at the Dim Dragon Inn, drowning meself in a few pottle pots of their best swill," he said, over his shoulder. "Methinks that's the only way to forget the smell of this awful place."

But when he took a step into the lane, he was denied his breath of open air.

# CHAPTER 41

"We meet again," said Constable Patch.

Meddybemps drew up, surprised to be standing face-to-face with the ineffectual plod.

Still carrying Bianca, John squeezed past the two of them.

"Well, this is promising," said Patch, tugging his chin hairs. "Seems to me I've found a murdereress escaped from the Clink *and* the warehouse supposedly harboring unspeakable, ghastly horrors. What did that playwright say? 'Persistence begets fortune'? Indeed. It does seem that way, does it not? And I am nothing if not persistent."

Meddybemps and John exchanged looks. They could run, but John wouldn't get far toting Bianca.

"This is the warehouse I spoke of," said Bianca, releasing her hold from John's neck and attempting to stand. Her legs shook, and she clutched John's arm for support. "Robert Wynders is inside. Perhaps you might wish to speak with him."

"Ah! Most certainly. But first, I must deal with the likes of ye. I would be remiss to let a criminal walk the streets before due process."

"That is hardly a concern. Bianca can hardly stand, much less walk the streets," said Meddybemps.

Constable Patch observed Bianca standing as if her legs were made of splinters. He'd seen criminals fake all sorts of maladies to avoid arrest. He eyed her suspiciously.

Bianca continued. "You didn't believe me when I told you this warehouse is teeming with rats. Now that you are here, I should think you would want to see."

"Mayhaps. But first, methinks I should deliver ye back to the Clink." Patch reached for her arm.

John was not about to let Constable Patch haul her away again. This time, Patch was alone. He could easily dispense with the pigeon-hearted constable and make their escape. He handed Bianca over to Meddybemps, then shoved Patch backward and rounded his hands into fists.

Patch snickered. "Look there, I'm only doing me duty. No needs to go off half-cocked." He smiled congenially, but when John's expression remained unmoved, the smile slid from his face. He eyed the three of them, then without warning lunged for Bianca.

John struck him in the chin and sent him sprawling. "You'll not take her again, Constable."

Patch sat up and tested his jaw to find it still working. "That did little to help your cause. I can arrest ye for assault of a public official."

"You must fight me first." John hovered over Patch, wheeling his fists, ready to pound him at the least provocation.

Threats and jaw punching might have ensued if they had not been interrupted by a scream so unnerving, so desperate, so blood-numbingly awful, that all of them stopped and turned to look at the warehouse.

"It is Wynders, as I said."

Constable Patch was skeptical. For all he knew, she could have bound the man within or enlisted him in a scheme to draw him in. "What did ye do to the man?" he asked, watching Bianca's face.

"I did nothing but try to escape. He brought this on himself."

Another scream beckoned, and Constable Patch got to his feet. The scream was too genuine to be faked. "A man is in trouble, and we must help him." He looked round at the three and saw their lack of enthusiasm. "I'll not have ye trick me. While I am inside, ye will make your escapes."

"Then we will go with you," offered Bianca.

"Speak for yourself, Bianca," said Meddybemps, aghast. "I'll not willingly go back inside. I can stand guard out here."

"We all go in," said Constable Patch, drawing his blade. "Exceptions ye," he said, grandiosely pointing the tip at Meddybemps, "since I have no quarrels with ye—for now."

Bianca saw her chance for redemption and was not about to let the moment pass. She attempted to lead the way, but barely staggered a few steps before her knees began to buckle.

"You cannot walk," said John, lifting her in his arms and ignoring her protests. The two headed back in the warehouse.

When Constable Patch stepped through the door, he was overcome by the smell, but he masked his revulsion and followed behind the pair.

John wound a path through walls of broken crates and fallen debris. He stepped on piles of splintered wood, testing his foothold before placing his full weight and moving on. A glimpse over his shoulder revealed the constable's face screwed in disgust and one hand pinching his nose closed.

"Shall we keep going?" John asked, turning round to face him.

"Of course," said Patch, quickly assuming a fearless pose. But as John turned back to continue their course, Patch covered his mouth and stifled an involuntary retch.

Perhaps the girl was telling the truth. A fouler smell he'd never known. He'd have rather sat in the bottom of a privy hole than this. But he must know if what she said was true, and in spite of his hesitancy he would see this through.

John stopped at the top of a heap and set Bianca beside him. She leaned against John, and Constable Patch observed him turn away and gag while she looked on, as if mesmerized.

He drew up beside them and followed her gaze to what lay below. He could barely look on it.

Below was a heaving mass of fur and teeth, ripping and tearing Robert Wynders's flesh. With clothing and doublet shredded, his bare arm reached out, imploringly, but was then covered in more rats. He writhed beneath the throng; his legs kicked, his boots the last protection against their determined chewing. One gnawed through the leather, tugged it off, exposing his meaty calf. Wynders screamed as his muscle was stripped from the bone.

Constable Patch turned away to steel himself. The man was in trouble, but he could not muster the nerve to save him.

Wynders's pleas grew muffled, and his cries became less frequent, fading into nothing but the sound of fighting, feeding rats.

"He's lost too much blood," said Bianca. "There's nothing to do for him."

Constable Patch readily agreed, relieved not to intervene. He started back down the pile of rubble, more concerned that the rats might still be hungry than that he was leaving a man to suffer a painful and ignoble death. John and Bianca followed. They reached the warehouse entrance and silently exited, closing the door and securing it. London still had not fully woken; a lone rooster crowed in the distance. The gray-blue shadows had not yet given way to the fullness of day.

Meddybemps did not ask what happened. He could see their bewildered expressions and color as pale as birch.

# CHAPTER 42

The four stood motionless, each sorting through what they'd just seen and privately wondering why Wynders had allowed the warehouse to become home to a legion of rats. Their backs warmed in the morning sun, and eventually they shook off their reverie. Carts creaked down the quay, and horse-drawn drays arrived to cart away goods arriving to port. A muckraker strolled past, carrying a bucket and shovel. London was awake, and she called them back and deposited them on the steps of the normal and expected.

John draped his arm protectively around Bianca's shoulder and glanced furtively at Patch. The constable had not shed his expression of shock and dismay. John wondered if he and Bianca might escape without his notice. It was worth a try to gain time to convince Bianca to leave London. John took hold of her hand.

Meddybemps hadn't noticed John and Bianca silently backing away. He roused from his stupor and spoke of the one thing that could comfort him. "I could do with a decent pottle pot of ale."

John and Bianca froze. They glared at him.

"Aye, that," agreed Constable Patch. "But it'll take more than

one for me to feel right again. I've seen enough to last me a whiles."
He glanced at Meddybemps, then looked around for John and
Bianca. Spying them, his brows knit together. "Bianca Goddard,
I'm not finished with the likes of ye."

John started to speak, but Bianca shot him a look and he kept
quiet.

"I've gots to hash this one over," said Patch, chagrined he
was alone with no support to effectively arrest her. He was out-
numbered, and he knew his threats were useless. At least for now.
"I'll join ye back to Southwark." He sounded almost chummy.

No one dared object. Bianca's fate was still in the officious
public servant's hands. It would do her little good to flee. With
her legs still weak, she wouldn't get far.

Meddybemps regretted ruining his friends' chance to sneak
away. He followed behind, mouthing silent words of apology as
they traipsed back across London Bridge, passing through the
gate in glum silence into Southwark.

Finally, the constable spoke. "Ye knows, Goddard," he said, "I
have been thinking 'bouts what ye told me. Seems it played out
the way ye said. Wynders had a warehouse of vermin, and no
telling what he was thinkin' to do with them. Suppose the rats
escape and overrun London? They be a dirty scourge for sure."
Patch shook his head.

"Perhaps it was easier to store the bodies in the back of a warehouse than give them a proper burial," said John. "Certainly less
expensive."

"Perhaps he was hiding them until he got the *Cristofur* out of
quarantine," said Bianca.

Constable Patch considered this. "Possibly. Chudderly Shipping has been under scrutiny of late. They are in tax arrears and
stand to have their license revoked. Their goods and warehouse
are due to be seized. Perhaps Wynders expected the rats would
deter its seizure."

However, it was Meddybemps who put forth the best theory.
"Given what I have learned from my inquiries," said the randy
streetseller, his one eye whirling with sentimental remembrance,

"I believe the man might have had a contentious relationship with his father-in-law's company. He did have a bastard child after he was married."

"But to bring down the family business?" said John.

"Perhaps it was the weighted dice," said Meddybemps, well schooled in winning at hazards. "A threat. Or, if not a threat, a distraction from his own scandal."

No one commented until Constable Patch spoke. "I'll have to inform the tax collector and a few others of his despise. In fact, the aldermen of London should know of his intents. It might fare me well."

"You'll have to enlist the city officials to rid the warehouse of the rats," said Bianca.

Patch grimaced, thinking of the unpleasant task before him. "I've only time for one restorative tankard; then I must see to it the aldermen know what has happened." His gaze settled on Bianca. "I haven't time to dally with the likes of trivial murderes-sae—like youse," he said, pointedly.

"So, she may go her way?" ventured Meddybemps.

Constable Patch studied the three of them. It did seem to Patch that Bianca, while still the easiest to convict in the murder of Jolyn Carmichael, was probably not the most likely culprit. The whole matter seemed inconsequential now, compared to what he had just seen. The debacle of Wynders and Chudderly Shipping would garner the attention of more than just the aldermen of London. The import to the king's most precious coffers could catapult him to a coveted position in a London ward. And if he couldn't impress the aldermen that he'd just saved London from pestilence, he could always pursue Jolyn Carmichael's murder at a later date. Bianca would not be difficult to find.

However, it would not do to let a miscreant think she'd gotten off scot-free. Patch never shied from the opportunity to instill a healthy dose of fear in anyone. To neglect doing so would be remiss.

"I'll not bother with ye," he said, then added, "for now. But," he warned, ticking his forehead toward Bianca, "do not try to leave London. I'll have every guard from here to Spitalfields watching."

A weight fell from John's shoulders. He saw the opportunity, and would start convincing Bianca of the importance of thinking on her future straightaway.

As they neared the Dim Dragon Inn, an acrid smell permeated the air, and the sky over Southwark grew dark.

"I smell smoke," said John.

Meddybemps noted the formation of the billowing cloud. "It's coming from Bermondsey Street."

People began to come out of their rents and gather in the streets, sniffing the air and scanning the sky. The smell of smoke was a death knell in this warren of rents. Fires could spread from one thrush roof to another in seconds, consuming entire rows of buildings and burning them to the ground.

The four hurried toward Bermondsey and arrived as curious spectators lined the road, gawking at the conflagration. Flames licked the sky and a haze of gray smoke began to settle. Bianca pushed through the crowd to better see.

Barke House was in flames.

The recent fog had not dampened the dry tender of thatch, and the entire roof roiled in flame. Skeletal crossbeams and roof timbers burned with abandon, and heavy buttresses snapped— booming as they cracked and fell upon the second floor, unleashing even more fury.

A few men with buckets sloshing with water from Morgan's Lane stream waited for a ladder to be leaned against the adjoining residence. One brave soul attempted to climb, but the heat and smoke proved too much and he retreated, knowing the effort was like trying to put out the flames of hell with a thimble of water.

Constable Patch ran forward, trying to organize a second effort to contain the flames, but when that proved futile, he contented himself with shouting at people to stay back.

John found Bianca standing too close and grabbed her arm,

pulling her back to a safe distance. "Is anyone inside?" he shouted, over the roar of fire.

"God help them," answered Meddybemps.

"But Banes and Mrs. Beldam . . ." Bianca looked about at the faces in the crowd. "Did they get out?"

Meddybemps glanced around, and after a moment he shook his head. "I don't see them."

"They may be inside. And who knows how many women there might be in there."

"Hopefully, none," said Meddybemps. "There's no sense in running in to find out. The building is going to collapse any second."

"But we can't stand here and do nothing." Bianca looked desperate, as if she might be considering dashing toward the house.

John held Bianca's arm, preventing her from bolting forward. "Bianca, surely you know as well as I that it is useless. It would be mad to run inside and search for anyone. Besides, your legs are still weak." He had no sooner spoken when the door flew open, and out stumbled a figure, clothes and skin black from smoke. He managed a few steps, then collapsed, choking and clutching his throat, gulping for air.

# CHAPTER 43

"Banes!" gasped Bianca.

She broke free of John's grip and pushed past the gathering onlookers. Her legs ached, but she ignored the pain along with the heat and menacing blaze. She dropped to her knees and lifted Banes's head into her lap.

John and Meddybemps ran after her just as an inner wall gave a loud, ominous crack. They each grabbed an arm and dragged Banes toward the crowd, and Bianca followed, avoiding a spray of smoldering debris as more timbers snapped and the structure began to fracture.

"Is anyone else inside?" asked Bianca.

Banes's chest heaved for breath, and he managed to answer with a simple nod.

Bianca looked over her shoulder. Rents up and down the row had been vacated, and people looked on, some staring in shock, others weeping, some praying and some cursing an unmerciful god. Fate would have her way, and they were helpless to stop her.

"It's useless," warned John.

Barke House was the first to fall. The joists gave with a sickening, fractious moan and the trusses—no longer supported—swung loose and fell. The entire structure buckled, as if the building was dropping to its knees. Unable to further support its weight, Barke House collapsed to the ground with a deafening violence. A percussion of smoke and debris spewed forth, catching some spectators in a shower of flying cinders and burning rubble. Barke House would not surrender without a last word, it seemed.

John draped himself over Bianca, protecting her, and when the fallout subsided, he looked around at the house, a bonfire of its remains.

Meddybemps crossed himself. "God have mercy. They'll not survive."

Most realized they could do no more than wait until the fire had run its course. Even Constable Patch fell silent and retreated to the throng of bystanders held spellbound by the wild conflagration. Beyond a few whimpers and shrieks of outrage, a heavy pall settled over the onlookers. The fire raged on, consuming three more homes before finally subsiding and dwindling to a smoldering heap of ruin.

John and Bianca helped Banes sit up, and Meddybemps offered him a drink from his wineskin. Banes stared at the wreckage of Barke House, his face taut with emotion. "She was my grandmother," he said. "All these years of her treating me as a burden and a cripple. Never once acknowledging that I was of her blood." His voice faltered with anguish. "I was the embarrassment, the mistake she used to bleed money from Wynders. I am the grotesque creation of that man's indiscretion and sordid love affair. Shunned and dispassionately used by my own grandmother." Banes struggled to his feet, his incredulity giving him strength.

"But, Banes, your last name?" asked Bianca.

"Perkins," he answered. "She made it up." Banes smiled cynically, then continued.

"As long as she possessed the Chudderly family ring, she could manipulate him. She always kept it on her body in a purse attached to a rope around her waist. Her constant fretting, the incessant patting and checking of the pouch, wore the wool thin and the ring was lost. But she kept the threat alive with her lies to Wynders, knowing full well that without the ring she had no proof that I was his son. She kept the missing ring a secret for as long as she could.

"Then Jolyn, with an eye for valuables, found the ring in the mud of Southwark. And my grandmother in the course of her dealings saw it hanging about her neck. So she schemed to get it back," said Banes. He motioned to Meddybemps for another swig of wine, then, staring round at each of them, continued. "She offered Jolyn a home at Barke House." He smiled cynically. "How could a muckraker refuse a pallet on which to sleep?"

John shook his head. "The poor girl," he said. "She believed the ring had brought her luck."

Banes snorted. "And then Wynders met Jolyn and saw the ring dangling from her neck. He saw his chance to gain it back, along with his freedom."

"The two vied to secure it," said Bianca. "But it wasn't around her neck when she died."

"No, it wasn't," said Banes.

"Because I found it in her glove." Bianca looked round at the four of them. "Apparently someone had put a good measure of rat poison in her gloves. Jolyn didn't have to ingest the poison for it to kill her." Bianca looked pointedly at John. "Remember how her hands were red and chapped from chores? Mrs. Beldam had her scrubbing floors and doing laundry in the cool spring water. She made sure Jolyn's hands became cracked and raw, then sprinkled rat poison in the gloves Jolyn got from Wynders. Jolyn would not notice a fine powder being absorbed into her skin. A smell of terebinth would not trouble her since she had never known the feel or smell of fine leather."

"She wagered that Jolyn would die at Barke House," said Banes. "Then she could retrieve the ring and continue her extortion."

"But Jolyn didn't die at Barke House," said Bianca, thinking of the visit from Mrs. Beldam soon after Jolyn's death. "Mrs. Beldam came to my room of Medicinals and Physickes with the pretense of grieving for Jolyn. I remember her acting queer. Distracted. Now I know why."

"She was looking for the ring," said Meddybemps.

Banes grew uncomfortable keeping silent about his complicity on the night of the storm. He felt compelled to admit his involvement—as trivial in the overall scheme though it seemed. Banes forced the words from his mouth. "The night of the storm we came to your room, Bianca. We broke in, and before I knew why, she had clubbed you over the head. We searched for the ring. She would have beaten you to death if I had not stopped her."

"I didn't know I had the ring. John found Jolyn's glove buried under the rush just yesterday. I hid the ring in an empty flask for safekeeping."

"And I retrieved it," said John. "No one would think that I had it."

"I would have been spared a trip to Wynders's warehouse if you had left it there."

"Aws, now," said Meddybemps. "Don't begrudge John his help. His finding the ring served a purpose. And a fortunate one at that. The streets of London might be swarming with rats if Wynders hadn't dragged you to his warehouse and we hadn't found you there. Wynders died by his own doing."

"But the rats . . ." said John. "At least they are locked inside the warehouse . . . for now."

Constable Patch listened intently, tugging his scraggly goatee. "Well, as I saids," he said to Bianca, "looks to me ye was sayin' the truths all along." Patch had a satisfied look on his face—perhaps one of relief at not having to further deal with Bianca Goddard, daughter of the ignoble alchemist.

"Wynders dragged me out of Barke House expecting I would take him to the ring," said Banes. "I assumed it was in your possession and told him you were in the Clink."

"Dangling from manacles," said Bianca.

Constable Patch glanced back at the charred remains of Barke House. "So where is Madam Beldam?"

"After Wynders left me battered in the road, the last thing I wanted to do was go back to Barke House. I only just returned," said Banes. "When I got here, smoke was streaming from the windows, and I cannot deny that I stood in the street, savoring the thought of watching Barke House burn to the ground. But as I stood watching it wheeze and spew, I knew I was not the soulless wretch of my kin. I rushed in. The smoke made it impossible to see, so I felt along the wall and called out. There was no answer. Beds were burning, blankets blazed. I ran down the stairs, a falling timber just missing me." Banes fell morosely silent.

"Ye didn't answer me question," said Patch. "Is Mrs. Beldam still inside?"

"Aye," said Banes, softly.

Bianca and the others exchanged looks, but Constable Patch, being naturally curious and interfering, persisted. "Ye left her there?"

Banes roused. "Wynders had struck her. I started for the kitchen . . ."

"Ye left ye own grandmother to burn?" Patch indignantly puffed out his chest as if he'd just gotten Banes to confess murder.

"I may be bred of treachery, but I am not of it. I dropped to the floor and crawled toward the kitchen. I was blinded by smoke and choking, but I made my way there." Banes glanced at the constable. "I found her. She did not respond when I tried to rouse her." A defiant look came over Banes's face. "I did not abandon her as she had willingly done to me. I dragged her body toward the door." Banes held up his foreshortened limb. "A not so easy task. We had cleared the door when a floor joist let go from above. . . ." Banes's voice trailed off, and his expression appeared pained. "The joist fell across her legs."

Meddybemps offered Banes another drink from his wineskin, and Banes greedily drank. He handed the skin back. "I could not free her."

Sympathy had never been fully cultivated in Constable Patch, and while the latest incidents in the warehouse had left him subdued, he still could not suppress a certain urge to challenge Banes. "So ye lefts her to burn," he said.

"Should I have burned with her?"

Bianca turned on Patch. "Surely you do not suggest that he stay and die along with her?"

John riled at Constable Patch's presumption. "How long does one try to free a dead woman from a burning house before it is acceptable to leave her? Is one's own death the only proof of innocence?"

"She may not have been dead," said Patch.

"And are you to make that determination?" said Bianca.

Constable Patch read the outrage on their faces and so withdrew his argument. But his stare lingered on Banes. "I have matters I must attend. Ye may not be bound to answer my question," he said to Banes, "but I woulds not think ye should never have to. For now I shall stay my inquiry." He glanced round at them and gave a curt nod, never one to leave on friendly terms.

# CHAPTER 44

The sun warmed Bianca's face as she headed across London Bridge for the first time in nearly a month. Spring had arrived and laid to rest the quibbling days of late winter. Dangling catkins caught the breeze on a hazel bush, and the iridescent yellow of ranunculus peeked from softening patches of earth. She was glad for the approach of the vernal equinox, and with it the promise of longer days.

She'd spent her time healing in her room of Medicinals and Physickes, sleeping long and dreaming up new combinations of herbs to try. She drank fennel tea and let John bring her cheese and bread from market. He'd showered her with attention and care and proven himself indispensable to her recuperation. Now she was feeling strong and confident and had grown bored cooped up in her rent with stills and jars of concoctions her only company.

She'd not seen Banes since Barke House burned. John and Boisvert had given him a place to stay until he knew what to do. It hadn't been long before he'd left Southwark for lands east of London. Bianca wondered how he would survive highways overrun with padders and runagates, but she imagined Banes would never fall fool to anyone ever again. Still, she hoped he fared well.

"He's gone to find his mother," Meddybemps had said. "Mrs. Beldam sent her to live with nuns in France. A purported nattering simpleton she was, says Maude. Mrs. Beldam did herself a favor sending her away."

"Does Banes know she is of light wit?"

"Does it matter?" said Meddybemps. "I'm sure he seeks the truth whatever comes with it. Wouldn't you?"

Bianca knew she would have done the same.

Now, as she crossed into London and passed the leering fortress of the White Tower, she turned her thoughts to a time when she had spent her mornings scouring the banks of the river outside its walls, searching for plants to study and stash in her pocket. It was along these banks she had first met Jolyn. Bianca paused to sweep her eyes along the river and recalled her friend's laugh. She could remember it clear as a bell. And, like the tinkle of a bell, it cheered her.

"I shall always remember your laugh," she whispered. Then, as if Jolyn had heard, Bianca saw her friend look up from raking mud and smile. Bianca stared, daring not to look away. She was so pleased that she did not wonder whether this was her imagination or an apparition. But it was impossible not to blink, and when she did, Jolyn was gone.

Bianca tried to conjure again the vision of her friend but could not. And so, tucking away the memory, she continued on and turned up Lambeth Hill.

Not much had changed. The same timber-frame rents lined the street, their daub an earthy sorrel, with gray and brown oak crossbeams adding a bit of decorative strength. The upper stories leaned precariously over the lane, with their thatch roofs smelling somewhat musty, though they'd experienced several sun-drenched days, as witnessed by the chalky film of dirt riding her shoe.

Goodwife Templeton shooed a goose out her door and stopped

long enough to stare suspiciously at Bianca walking up the lane.
When Bianca neared, the old woman cleared her throat and spat
the phlegm over her shoulder. "'Aven't seen ye 'bouts since the
twelfth of never," she said.

"I live in Southwark now."

"Phaa, I'd ask ye whys, but then, knowin' ye queer family, I
cans just as rightly guess."

"Are my parents well?" Bianca asked. She might as well prepare herself by asking a neighbor's opinion.

"As well as right, I suppose," she answered. "I don't hear
clamoring or smell peculiar odors emanatin' from withins. So I
hazard they is behavin' their persons."

"Well, I am glad you approve of my parents' performance."

The irritable woman pinched her mouth and squinted with
distrust as Bianca passed.

As she neared the old rent, Bianca squelched her rising guilt.
She'd asked her mother to live with her in Southwark and leave
behind the machinations of her father, but she had declined.
Bianca had never understood her mother's loyalty to a man who
cared not a fig in return. Perhaps she would never understand.

Bianca supposed her own practical nature, although some
might call it cold, was learned from her father, who never put anyone above his dogged pursuit of the philosopher's stone. Couldn't
the same be said of her? She grimaced at the notion of it.

And so she resolved to balance her attention between those
she loved and her obsession with dabbling in medicinals. She
would start by visiting her mother, whether her father was home
or not.

She stopped outside the door of her parents' rent and found it
more weathered than the last time she'd visited. The wood had
grayed, and moss clung near its bottom, forming a soft green mat.
She lifted her hand to knock. Would she tell her mother about
what she'd been through? She didn't think so. Sometimes love is
about knowing when to stay silent. But would she tell her mother
about John and her marrying?

A mother deserves to know.

# Chapter 45

The *Cristofur* departed as she had come, without fanfare. The ship avoided a long quarantine thanks to the venal inclinations of a certain customs officer. There could be no avoiding some time spent in quarantine once it had been enacted. But witnessing the bonfire of bodies alongside the ship's hull had waylaid his worst fears. He wrote an amendment to the customhouse docket certifying payment in full of duty owed by Chudderly Shipping in regards to the *Cristofur* (which it was). Compliance of said party to dispose of undesirable contents in the ship's hull (meaning bodies and rats), he did attest. However, the customs agent knew nothing of Wynders's other murky secrets lurking in the Chudderly warehouse. Nor did he trouble to find out. The stores of so many shipping companies in the warren of warehouses lining the Thames were not his concern. Let the tax inspectors deal with that.

And when the customs officer later heard of the demise of Wynders, agent for Chudderly Shipping, he breathed a sigh of relief. For if only one man is left standing, a bribe cannot bite.

The crew did have to wait before disembarking. This was to

please the medical authority of His Majesty's council. The crew obliged without fractious grumbling so long as they could look over the sides and see the wood of a pier on one side of them. And the captain's allowance of a few bawds in the dark of night effectively quelled their mutinous dispositions.

If authorities had needed further proof of the *Cristofur*'s clean bill of health, the Rat Man could have given it. After Wynders's demise, the Rat Man diligently kept watch over the ship for further infestation of furry elements until she prepared to sail and pulled anchor.

Ravenous vermin had infiltrated the streets, causing some outbreak of illness, which the Rat Man, in his infinite wisdom, knew was related. The Black Death was ever present in small numbers, but depending on the season and circumstances, it often resolved without panic and widespread infection. And so what could have raged . . . did not.

Bills of mortality were not posted, street fires to purge the air of pestilent stink were infrequent, and the incessant bell ringing of plague carts to collect corpses was not heard. The wraith of the Thames could continue his vigilance comfortable that this time the scourge had been averted.

He watched the *Cristofur* drift away from the pier, entrusting her fate to the river's ebbing tide. Who knew what the great force of the sea would impart on her uncertain future? Perhaps a tempest or scurvy might challenge her crew? Fate and nature were undoubtedly fickle. The Rat Man chuckled.

*Non est ad astra mollis e terris via.* There is no easy way from the earth to the stars.

Possessing the collective wisdom of thousands of souls, the specter knew one thing for certain as he watched the *Cristofur* fade out of sight: London would forever struggle, but she would forever endure.

# ACKNOWLEDGMENTS

It is my pleasure to thank the many people who helped bring this book to life and who have supported my writing over the years.

My eternal thanks to:

Claire McNeely, friend and reader who never fails to lift my spirits and offer sage advice. Linda Stevens, Marjorie Gilbert, and Anne Brudevold for slogging through numerous writing projects.

Andrea Jones, for her friendship, hand holding, and wonderful eye for story and editing.

Ali Bothwell Mancini, who wasn't afraid to tell me to cut or add.

The amazing crew at Kensington.

Mary Beth Constant, for both exasperating and impressing me with her attention to detail. She succeeded in making me appear smarter than I am.

Alison Picard, whose persistence inspired me to keep writing. Despite years of rejections, she still believed.

My family and friends who politely refrained from telling me that maybe I should find another dream.

The felines in my life who kept me company. Am I so weird that I thank my cats? Indeed, I am!

David, for never doubting and never complaining.

Fred Tribuzzo and John Scognamiglio for saying, Yes!

# Author's Note

The Bianca Goddard Mysteries take place in London during the 1540s in the final years of Henry VIII's reign. His legacy as king can be characterized as extraordinary not only in the religious changes that shaped future England, but also in the political intrigues that defined his tenure.

In 1543, Henry was fifty-two years old, obese, and in failing health. At the time of Book 1, *The Alchemist's Daughter*, he is courting Katherine Parr, his sixth and final wife. That summer, Henry made plans for an invasion of France scheduled for the following year.

The citizens of Tudor England dealt with poverty, war, greed, and the whims of a petulant monarch. It is in this world that Bianca must survive. And while Bianca rarely involves herself in matters of political intrigue, its effects are felt every day in the lives of the general population.

The Bianca Goddard Series focuses on the commoners of Tudor London and how they navigated Henry's strange and brutal policies. In many ways, their existence echoes our own—the focus is on a government controlled by the elite few, but the more interesting story, in my opinion, is about the common man.

I tried to capture the feeling of the time, and I apologize if my attempts at merging period words and syntax fall short of smooth readability. If when the reader sees "ye" and pronounces it more like the "ye" in "yellow," it will flow easier. It is an ongoing dilemma deciding how to approach dialogue from this time period. I could ignore the obvious or sprinkle it in; either way, I am sure to offend someone.

Several words were taken from a glossary of Thomas Dekker's works, and some, I simply made up.